Dear Stranger
Paper Cuts #3

Winter Renshaw

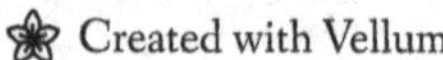 Created with Vellum

Also By Winter Renshaw

<u>THE NEVER SERIES</u>

Never Kiss a Stranger

Never is a Promise

Never Say Never

Bitter Rivals

<u>THE ARROGANT SERIES</u>

Arrogant Bastard

Arrogant Master

Arrogant Playboy

<u>THE RIXTON FALLS SERIES</u>

Royal

Bachelor

Filthy

Priceless (Amato Brothers crossover)

<u>THE AMATO BROTHERS SERIES</u>

Heartless

Reckless

Priceless

<u>THE P.S. SERIES</u>

P.S. I Hate You

P.S. I Miss You

P.S. I Dare You

THE MONTGOMERY BROTHERS DUET

Dark Paradise

Dark Promises

PAPER CUTS

Hate Mail

Yours Cruelly

Dear Stranger

BOX SETS

The Best of Winter Renshaw

His & Hers

STANDALONES

Single Dad Next Door

Cold Hearted

The Perfect Illusion

Country Nights

Absinthe

The Rebound

Love and Other Lies

The Executive

Pricked

For Lila, Forever

The Marriage Pact

Hate the Game

The Cruelest Stranger

The Best Man

Trillion

Enemy Dearest

The Match

Whiskey Moon

Stone Cold

The Dirty Truth

Love and Kerosene

You or Someone Like You

Fake-ish (December 2023)

All Books Available here!

Free Content Available here!

Description

Online lovers… offline rivals.

Ambitious and career-driven, I have zero time for dating until Blind Love—an app designed for those seeking genuine romantic connections without the hassle of awkward first dates—hooks me in. The only catch? Ninety days of anonymous messaging are required before identities are revealed.

I connect with Stranger88 immediately, and before long our flirty banter becomes a welcome escape from my demanding schedule.

Soon I'm desperate to know his true identity, so I go digging —only to discover that Stranger88… is no stranger at all.

In a cruel twist of fate, it turns out the mystery man consuming my every thought is fellow attorney Brooks Abbott—a sharp-tongued devil in a three-piece suit, my biggest office rival, and the one obstacle standing between me and the promotion of my dreams: a job Brooks has every intention of landing.

Behind the screens, there's no denying our electric chemistry, but at work, our rivalry grows stronger than ever.

But when passion meets profession, will we redefine the Law of Attraction... or will our hearts face a ruthless cross-examination with no chance of appeal?

1

Tenley

I've spent almost two-thirds of my life in hell—kind of.

My mother used to tell me goals were a necessary ingredient of life, but equally important was celebrating—and enjoying—the little achievements along the way. She said failing to recognize those wins would be doing myself a disservice; that it'd be the equivalent of glazing over the journey and living solely in pursuit of the destination, thereby missing all of the good stuff. In my youthful naivety, I staunchly disagreed with her. When "ambition" is your middle name, the destination is the *only* thing that matters. Screw the journey. It's a means to an end. I brushed her advice aside back then, razzing her about her obsession with self-help books and motivational posters.

Now that I'm a little older, I've learned the hard way that the she was right.

But breaking up with my ambition would be akin to

severing a limb. It's a necessary and vital part of me and has been for as long as I can remember—beginning with one particular Christmas morning. I sprinted downstairs, expecting to burst at the sight of colorfully wrapped gifts under our sparse little Charlie Brown tree. Only there was nothing. I quickly learned my mother's boyfriend at the time had lost his job the day before and my mother had to return all the gifts so we could pay our rent. Later that day, over a meager dinner of toast and eggs, I heard the two of them discussing how to fight his wrongful termination—except they couldn't afford a lawyer.

I made up my mind then and there that I was going to be a lawyer someday. And not just any lawyer. One with power and influence and a big, fat bank account. I'd see to it that my family would have to worry about money again. We would be happy.

At twenty-eight, I'm so close to achieving that goal I can almost taste it.

And while I'm proud of myself, I have to admit it doesn't feel the way I thought it would. Every A, every debate team win, every trophy, and every hood, stole, and cord I've worn as I've walked graduation stages—have all felt like ticking a box before moving on to the next thing.

Now that I'm on the verge of a life-changing promotion, the prospect of not having any more boxes left to tick has been weighing on my mind lately along with a single glaring question: *what comes next?*

I'm standing at the front door of my apartment, where my dry-cleaning has been delivered and is waiting on the hook on my door. Every week, it's like clockwork.

Same gray, black, and navy suits, same white blouses, same old routine.

I grab the plastic-wrapped bundle and step inside the abyss of my dark apartment, dropping the clothes, bag, and keys on the floor and fumbling for the light switch on the wall. When I finally flip it on, my gaze lands on the pyramid of cardboard boxes in the corner. If a person didn't know me, they'd think I only recently moved in, but the fact is I've lived here for over a year already, ever since finishing law school at the University of Maine and starting as a junior associate at Foster and Foster, one of Maine's most prestigious law firms.

It's nearly midnight and I'm dead on my feet after another twelve-hour shift. But that's what a girl has to do if she's going to make partner at Foster and Foster and start cashing the big paychecks. Once I'm promoted, I'll start getting bonuses. Big bonuses—not the laughable ones they give out to juniors and associates and paralegals at Christmas time. Bonuses that will allow me to pay off my mom's house so she can finally retire. Bonuses that will allow me to donate to all of my favorite causes and not think twice. Bonuses that will allow me to finally book that girls' trip to Paris with my best friends and not have to worry about checking my bank account as we live like queens. Bonuses that will allow me to pick and choose my clientele so that I can help people going through the same hardship my mother went through a lifetime ago.

Trudging to my fridge, I come face-to-face with Bevin, my roommate from USM, in the form of a wedding invitation tacked to my fridge. In the image, she's gazing adoringly into the eyes of a tall man with a trimmed beard and quirky bowtie, both of them looking deliriously in love. While I'm thrilled for her, it'll be yet another wedding I'll be attending... alone.

And it's not even that I mind going to these things alone. I can talk to anyone about anything. It's the fielding questions part that sucks. Everyone wants to know why I'm single, as if it's some medical condition or I'm trying to make some statement. Inevitably, when I explain that I'm married to my job and don't have time to date, I'm always met with the same reaction—pity. Even if the person asking doesn't say anything, it's still written all over their face.

The response card is tucked underneath the invite because I was foolishly waiting in case I happened to find a plus-one. But who am I kidding? I've had one boyfriend my entire life, who took my virginity at prom and never spoke to me again. After that, I decided focusing on things I could control, things that could move me forward in life and not hold me back, was the way to go.

I yank it down and fill it out. *Ms. Tenley Bayliss. No guest. Chicken Bruschetta.*

For a second, I fantasize about declining, but I can't do that to Bevin. We might have drifted apart, or at least, *I* drifted, ignoring all her girls'-night-out invitations in favor of legal briefings and cold Thai food consumed right from the carton, but I can't miss the most important day of Bevin's life.

She deserves all the happiness in the world.

And I deserve... well, all *this*.

I open the fridge and find nothing but a bottle of mustard and a half empty quart of expired milk. Grabbing the milk anyway, praying it's not too sour, I pour myself a bowl of Cheerios from my equally empty pantry and prepare to inhale them. When I take the cap off the milk though, the stench hits like a bomb. My eyes water as I inspect the curdling mass.

Dumping the jug in the sink, I trek to the couch and

collapse on it, eating handfuls of dry, cereal. Predictably, it's stale. I haven't had a proper meal at home in a month. When I'm not swerving through Starbucks drive-thrus or entertaining clients at swanky Portland restaurants like Fore Street and Periwinkle, I've been known to make a meal or two. But those nights have been few and far between as I work towards this promotion.

I grab my phone and scroll through it, lazily thinking about what I'll wear to Bev's wedding. I'm not sure I even have anything other than dull gray and charcoal suits. I can't even remember the last time I went shopping. And my schedule from now until May is packed. I don't have time.

As my mind wanders, I entertain myself with a scenario where I meet some handsome stranger at Bevin's wedding.

Another delusion.

If I show up in one of my no-nonsense, buttoned-up business suits, I'll bleed into the background. And it's probably too much to think there'll even *be* single guys there. Everyone my age is attached. I've gone to five weddings this year alone. It won't be long before people start spawning too, and then I'll have to attend more baby showers than I can shake a stick at.

I grit my teeth at the thought of what my friends will say when I show up solo to Bevin's wedding: *There's Tenley. Alone again. Married to her work. Poor girl.*

Poor girl...

Those words have haunted me since childhood, though not for the same reasons.

Maybe I'm not poor, money-wise, now, but I am lacking in other ways.

The thing about finding your special someone though, is that it's not something you can work towards like good grades or a college degree.

It just has to... happen.

I've never been good at leaving things to chance, though.

In the final hours of my evening, I scroll through social media, soaking in my friends' first-year anniversaries, growing families, and whirlwind trips to the Maldives. And then there's me, number one, with a bullet to make partner at Foster and Foster before I'm thirty.

None of them can say that.

But they can say so much more.

The thought alone stirs something in me, but before I have a chance to explore what exactly that is, I decide I've done enough scrolling for the day.

As I'm about to close out though, my finger accidentally hits a button for an ad, and the next thing I know, an app called Blind Love appears on my phone screen.

Another dating app—just what the world needs.

Before clicking away, I stare at the photograph of an adoring couple on a turquoise beach. The man is giving the woman a piggyback ride in the warm sun, and they're both laughing like they're on happy pills.

Even if they are, jealousy spikes in me.

I read the goofy headline: *DIVE INTO THE DATING POOL! THE WATER'S FINE!*

I cringe, though that doesn't stop me from reading the smaller caption below. *Since you can only share photographs and personal information after 90 days of chatting, you'll make real emotional connections with other singles like you.*

It's a good idea in theory, but knowing my luck, I'll probably wind up making a 'real emotional connection' with a serial killer.

Still, what if he's a serial killer with a heart of gold?

Chuckling to myself, I download the app and set up my

profile because I have absolutely nothing to lose (but my dignity) and chatting for someone anonymously for ninety days sounds a lot better than suffering through some awkward swipe date.

A minute later, I'm officially **Stranger7721**, a username the system automatically generated for me.

Apparently, we're all strangers on here.

Since no pictures are required, I provide my basic stats and a bio.

28/F. *Love my job but not much else.*

It's not the most inventive bio, but it works for now.

I spend the next few moments scrolling through the profiles of available men. Because of the ninety-day requirement, there doesn't seem to be many guys fishing for one-night stands. As impressive as that is, it doesn't really improve the pool. Most of them have glaringly obvious egos. They're way too wordy, trying too hard, talking about all their quirks and accomplishments and quoting Stoic philosophers. As someone who takes herself too seriously, the last thing I need is someone who does the same.

But then I find a guy called **Stranger88** whose bio simply states: *Just here to get laid.*

I laugh out loud.

If he wants to do that, this isn't the app to do it on.

A little green light under his profile says he's online, which means I can't *not* respond.

Stranger7721: *Hey dumbass. Nice bio. You know you have to chat with someone for 90 days before you can even see their picture? There are better apps for your purpose.*

Shoving a handful of Cheerios in my mouth, I decide to see what's on Netflix. By the time I grab the remote, he's already responded.

Stranger88: *Hang on. Updating my bio.*

I snort. A second later, I refresh his profile and read his new bio which states, *Just here to find a meaningful connection that ultimately leads to intercourse.*

Stranger7721: *Much better.*

Stranger88: *I believe in honesty. That said, there's absolutely no way I can get laid at this present moment, so I'll settle for talking to women on the internet. You're not a bot, right? Please tell me you're not a bot.*

Stranger7721: *Not a bot. Why can't you get laid?*

Stranger88: *In the name of brutal honesty, I'm... married.*

Stranger7721: *Omg! Fuck off.*

I'm seconds from blocking him when another message comes through.

Stranger88: *You didn't let me finish! I'm married... to my JOB.*

On one hand, I can relate. On the other? An app like this would be the perfect place for a married person to have an anonymous affair, even if it's only messaging.

Stranger7721: *Convenient.*

Stranger88: *It's the truth. If I could prove that to you, I would. Ask me something only a non-married person would know.*

Maybe it's the boredom and the fatigue washing over me, but I'm intrigued. And also stumped. It's an impossible question for someone to answer, let alone for someone to ask. I change the subject.

Stranger7721: *You still live in your parents' basement?*

Stranger88: *Something like that.*

I can't help picturing a soft-bodied slob who spends all

his time doing remote IT work in his parents' house. Even so, communicating with this dude beats sitting here alone. And at least he's not putting on airs, trying to be someone he's not, like all the other people on this lame site. He could easily claim to be some Fortune500 CEO and quote Proust and Poe, and yet he's not. Have to say it's refreshing.

Stranger88: *How was your day?*

I can't recall the last time anyone asked me that who wasn't my mom.

Stranger7721: *LONG. If we're being honest here, I'm also married to my job.*

Stranger88: *Ah. You just want to get laid, too.*

Stranger7721: *Maybe... ;-) Actually, I just got an invite to a friend's wedding, and it made me realize I'm the only one of my friends who is still unattached. This ad popped up and the next thing I know, I'm downloading this stupid app and talking to you.*

Stranger88: *So you're looking for a wedding date... here?*

Stranger7721: *I have no idea what I'm looking for. I don't think you can find anything meaningful on an app.*

Stranger88: *Sure you can.*

Stranger7721: *So you've convinced other women with your "just want to get laid" schtick before?*

Stranger88: *No, never. I was talking about Door Dash. I'm eating some damn good Pad Thai right now and I think that's pretty meaningful.*

I laugh out loud and look over at my bowl of dry, stale Cheerios.

Stranger88: *Why? Is it working on you? Do you find me charming?*

Stranger7721: *Too soon to say, sorry. Let me ask you*

*a question. I just signed up today, and I'm 7721. You're 88.
Does that mean you've been here a while?*

Stranger88: *Yes. And I still have no takers.*

Stranger7721: *Tragic.*

Stranger88: *I cry about it every night. Right into my
pillow.*

Stranger7721: *Feeling sorry for yourself isn't sexy
though.*

Stranger88: *Who said anything about feeling sorry for
myself? I'm feeling bad for all the women who're missing out
on me. Now that's a damn tragedy.*

I sniff a laugh, rolling my eyes. I like his sense of humor.
But this world is full of people who are funny and charis-
matic online and awkward as hell in person. I can't get my
hopes up.

Stranger88: *For the record, I've had more than one
woman tell me I've rocked her world.*

Stranger7721: *Did you rock their worlds in your
parents' basement?*

Stranger88: *Not exclusively, no. I've also rocked
worlds in bathrooms, dressing rooms, and libraries. I was
with a girl at the office once. That was hot.*

I blush. So maybe he doesn't work from home.

Stranger7721: *Was it?*

Stranger88: *Yeah. I was all stressed, wanting to blow
off steam. And then she was there and... damn. It felt good.
Gave me the energy to power through the rest of the day.
Little afternoon pick-me-up.*

I open my mouth. I know the feeling of being stressed. I
live it. But I never once thought of relieving it *that* way. It's
bold. Genius. Risky. I could never. But the idea of it excites
me anyway.

Stranger7721: *So you did it right on the desk in your cubicle then?*

Stranger88: *In an unused cubicle. My office is too private. That's no fun.*

I gnaw on my lip, intrigued. He has an office. Interesting. That image of the IT slob is slowly disintegrating in my head, being replaced by someone else...

Stranger7721: *Was she your admin?*

Stranger88: *No. I don't dip my pen in the company ink. She was from a delivery service.*

I let out a ragged breath. All I can think is that he must be *very* good at convincing people, just like he said. We have clerks come up to our office from the copy place all the time, and they're there and gone so fast, trying to keep up with their delivery schedule. How on earth did he manage to...?

Two possibilities stand out in my mind—either he's bullshitting me or he truly is as charming as he claims to be.

Because his bio is as no-bullshit as they come and because I'm getting a little flustered just typing with him... I have to think it's the latter.

But if that's the case, why's he on this app talking to me?

I find myself growing hot. I'm speechless, ready to close out the conversation when he sends another message. Clearly, I've waited too long.

Stranger88: *I take it you don't do things like that?*

Stranger7721: *One-night stands? No, I think they're gross.*

Stranger88: *Fair enough. And you've never done public?*

I guess I have no reason not to be honest.

Stranger7721: *No, I never have.*

Stranger88: *You don't know what you're missing.*

Probably. I have the feeling I've been missing a lot, but public sex is the least of it. Still, it's been a long time since I've gotten quite so hot under the collar. I undo the top button on my blouse and imagine what it would be like, all stressed out, getting it on in a corner of Foster and Foster while other people are working and meeting and taking calls all within earshot. It sends a little zing of excitement through me, one I'm not sure I want—especially from some random stranger on an app.

I shift in my seat and sit up straighter.

Stranger7721: *And I suppose you think you can show me.*

Stranger88: *I don't think I could. I know I could.*

Why am I so intrigued by this guy? Odds are he's an IT slob bullshitting me for fun. Or maybe a group of teenage boys killing boredom by trolling people. I've always been a healthy skeptic, but yet I'm flushed and breathing hard at his invitation.

Stranger7721: *But in 90 days, right? Those are the rules.*

Stranger88: *I don't ever play by the rules.*

Despite my heart beating faster, I shake my head, then close out of the app without saying goodbye. I *do* play by the rules. Law is my vocation, after all. A lack of it tends to bring out the worst in people. Plus, I don't do one-night stands, and I never have. Odds are that in ninety days, I'll have forgotten all about this BLIND LOVE app anyway.

Odds are, I'll still be alone too.

Heading upstairs, I change into pajamas, brush my teeth, and climb into bed. Usually, I spend this time in the dark before I drift off, going through a mental list of things I need to accomplish at work the following day.

Only tonight I think of a nameless, faceless man, bending me over the desk in one of the unused cubicles at Foster and Foster, providing a much-needed relief from all that built-up tension.

And it's all Stranger88's fault.

2

Brooks

"You know you've got it in the bag," Mike Wilson, my fellow associate, says to me as we sit at the head of the conference table.

The meeting doesn't start for ten more minutes, but that's how I operate. Early bird gets the worm. You have to show you want to be here and show you care enough to be here early—or at least that you care more than everyone else.

I grin as the other associates begin to file in after a few minutes, then say in a low voice, "I wouldn't say that. Not yet."

"Why not? Like anyone else could hold a candle to you?" I smirk. Mike is the Le Fou to my Gaston, and I love him for it.

I know I have a damn good shot at the new junior partner position opening up. I had a long talk with Ed Foster, senior partner, last night, where he'd shared some of his private label scotch which he usually only breaks out when a big case is won. He'd clapped me on the back, laughed with me, and even invited me to his hunting cabin upstate for the weekend.

So yeah... it *is* in the bag.

But I'm trying to be humble.

Mike's right. I've been here the longest. I have a more favorable track record of case outcomes than any other associate here. And though I don't like to throw my Ivy League pedigree around, but I *did* graduate from Harvard and then Yale Law at the top of my class. I'm a shoo-in.

Except there's one thing stopping me from saying it aloud.

As if on cue, that *one thing* appears in the doorway in her sedate gray suit and blouse.

Holding her legal pad tight to her chest, she meets my eyes for a split second before scanning the room. She frowns when she realizes the only open spot is the seat next to me.

Sighing as if being this close to me is a sentence in front of the firing squad, she marches over. Ordinarily, I'd pull it out for any other associate because the chairs are heavy and unwieldy.

But I won't do it for Tenley Bayliss.

Knowing her, if I did, she'd give me eye-daggers and snap at me that she's perfectly capable of pulling out her own chair. She's one of those women's lib-types who would rather have a door slammed in her face than be forced to thank a man for holding it open for her. Fiercely independent and unapologetic about it.

Not to mention, she hates me.

All the men here, really, but me, especially.

And the feeling is mutual.

Talk about an ass-kissing, brown-nosing, perfect little

snot. She started at Foster and Foster six months after I did, and since then, there's been a fire under her perfect heart-shaped ass to prove herself.

She's in her office when I get here in the morning, and she's still there when I leave at night. I think she has less of a life than I do, which is saying something. And either she's oblivious to the fact that no one in the office likes her, or making friends isn't something she wants to do. She's always pointing out flaws in our arguments, contradicting us, trying to look like the smart one by throwing us under the bus so she can win brownie points with the Fosters.

The worst part? She's almost always right.

The woman is a shark.

The Foster brothers love her because she's a legal robot, living and breathing the law as if it's the only thing on her mind. No denying she does everything right, without breaking a sweat, and has had some really good wins lately.

Tenley struggles to pull out the chair, then sits and walks the chair under the table until she's right up next to it, pen at the ready to take her nerdy little notes.

Teacher's pet.

Takes one to know one, if I'm being fair.

She stares almost with reverence at Ed Foster as he walks through the door and sits at the other head of the table. Meanwhile, everyone glares at her, unable to hide their disgust over her fawning. She doesn't notice. For all her smarts, the girl cannot read the room at all. That or she simply doesn't care.

I'm inclined to believe the latter.

Ed starts the meeting as he usually does, making idle small talk, and we all laugh and tease one another, which is great for team building and relieving stress.

Not Tenley, though. She's quiet, and by the time I look over at her notebook, she already has half a page of notes.

On what? What the hell is she taking notes for?

"Enough of that," Ed says, tenting his hands fingers in front of him. "What we need to talk about is the Stokes child custody case. Mr. Stokes isn't coming to town, correct? Do we have his statement?"

Mike nods. "We have it on tape."

"Did you transcribe it?" Ed asks.

"It's a little hard," Mike admits. "It's not the best quality, sounded like there was some machinery in the background. But I've pieced it together as best I could."

"I don't think that'll hold up," Tenley points out. "Not against the 'mirror the tape' rule."

Everyone stares her way.

Mike gives her a smug look. "Well, you haven't heard the tape. I've done due diligence to make sure—"

"Actually, I *did* hear the tape," she says, sitting up straighter and directing her response to Ed. "And the transcript that gets distributed to the jury should not be an amalgam of the recording and the hearsay testimony of persons present at the conversation. And that's what your transcript is. It won't hold up in court. If I were the judge, I'd throw the whole thing out on account of that alone."

Mike begins to argue, but Ed cuts him off. "Is that true? I need to have a listen. I don't need to tell you Michael—that can damn your entire case. I'll make the determination."

Mike shrinks back in his chair, wounded, because we all know Tenley is right.

Maddeningly, she's *always* right.

A stony silence settles in. I decide to break it.

"What, your caseload too light, Bayliss?" I ask. "You

have to go sticking your nose in other people's business? Listening to their tapes?"

Around the room, a couple of people smile slyly at me, indicating they were thinking the same thing. I kind of feel bad for it, but that's what she gets for chiming in on other people's caseloads without being asked.

She shoots me a stiff look, and for a second, I see a bit of red creeping out of her ruffled, high, puritan collar.

"I care about the *kid*. I don't want him to suffer from the scars of an absent father because of something his idiot attorney did." Tenley leans back, arms crossed, ignoring the laser-beam glare Mike's giving her.

Shots fired...

But that's fine. The more unlikeable she is to fellow associates, the more I can taste that partnership.

That taste disappears from my tongue the instant I glance at Ed, who's beaming at her with the kind of the adoration an owner would show their beloved golden retriever.

Shit.

I don't let it rattle me though. She might be hard-nosed and gritty, a true shark, but she's damned unlikable. That could cost us clients. She is not an asset to the firm. Not the way I am. Everyone loves me, and I mean everyone. Plus, I know her type. Ambitious to a fault. I'm the same. But I also know that people use their ambition as a mask to hide what's going on underneath.

Despite it all, I've often wondered what I'd find if I peeled back her layers.

The meeting wraps a short while later. I head out and find Kenzie hanging at my office door.

"Hey, Kenz." I aim to be friendly, but not overly so. The girl's looking like she wants to make a meal out of me, but I don't mix business and pleasure. Not in real life. And especially not when a promotion's on the line.

"Hey, Brooks! Just wanted to see if you'd like me to order you lunch? I have the menu for that place on the corner that has those paninis you like." She waves it in front of me.

Kenzie is an intern, three weeks now. She'll be in her last year at U of M this year. Interns do things like make copies and compile briefs. One thing that's *not* on their list of duties is ordering associates their lunch.

I guess I'm special.

"You're the best. I'll take the bacon club. And one of those strawberry smoothies you got me last time." I reach into my wallet and hand her two twenties. "Get yourself something, too."

She giggles and goes on her merry way.

As she leaves, I see Tenley thundering by, shooting me another one of her hellfire looks.

Whatever she's thinking, she's got it wrong.

I would never hook up with an intern—though I can't lie, I've been tempted before and the only one seeing the inside of my bedroom on a regular basis these days is my housekeeper—every other Wednesday. Kenzie smiling at me is probably the most action I've gotten in months. Even if it sparks my dirty mind, I'd never make a move. I'm always careful not to be *too* nice, to stick within the boundaries of propriety.

Tenley could learn a thing or two from me.

But will she? Hell no.

She'll go on sticking her head everywhere it doesn't belong and I won't see her for the rest of the day, until I walk past her office at quitting time and find her hunched over her desk surrounded by thick stacks of files.

The rest of the day flies by because there's too much to do. Just as I expected, I don't see Tenley until closing time, when the only people left on the floor are the cleaning staff. I wave goodbye to Marty, the janitor, as he comes into my office to empty my trash.

"Take care," I say, grabbing my jacket off the hook behind my door.

"Hey, Brooksy, my man, you see the game last night?"

"Oh, yeah, team's looking real good. I think the Sox have it in them to go all the way this year," I say. I've never been that into baseball and I didn't watch the game because I was elbows-deep in a divorce briefing, but I heard enough commentary on the radio on the way into Portland, so I can hold a conversation.

These are exactly the kind of skills that make me an asset around here.

Unlike Tenley Bayliss.

If someone asked her about baseball, she'd probably look at them like they had red horns growing out of their forehead.

Speaking of the devil, Tenley's still sitting there at her desk, on a phone call, barking something about a motion that she's going to make, and how she doesn't give a damn if the other attorney doesn't like it because she came to win.

"I won't accept anything less," she practically snarls, and I wonder how she hasn't sported fangs yet.

I hesitate at her door just long enough that she must sense I'm there, because she looks up. A frown settles on her face as she rises from her desk. She moves toward me, phone cradled between her shoulder and her ear, then grabs the door and slams it so hard, the whole frame shudders.

"Good night to you too," I say under my breath as I head toward the parking garage.

As much as I want to leave my work at the office, I think about Tenley on the ride home. I have to wonder if she even has a life outside of work, or if she's gunning hard for that promotion. My promotion.

She sure as hell isn't going to get it, though.

Not if I can help it.

I'm already on my A-game, but I'll double down if I have to.

My condo is in a swanky newer complex on the North end of Sapphire Shores. It was still under construction when I bought it—I even picked the colors on the shutters. I was so proud of that purchase because I finally thought I'd made it—I was making real money for the first time, as a junior associate at Foster and Foster. From there, the sky was the limit. No longer would I have to worry about money. I was on my own, responsible for only myself.

Or so I thought.

"Brooksy!" The high-pitch scream of my name nearly pierces my eardrum as a tiny tornado comes running into the foyer, grabbing hold of my mid-section.

"Hey, buddy," I say, dropping my things, scooping the kid up under his armpits, and swinging him around. "Were you good while I was gone?"

"Oh yeah," he says, smirking like the little devil I know he is.

I narrow my eyes. "Jace? Level with me."

I take a step until I'm in the doorway of the living room. My sister Ellie is there, on the couch, watching some television show that doesn't look anywhere near appropriate for a six-year-old. She doesn't take her eyes off the screen, but I can see exhaustion in them. "He was a terror."

"What did he do?"

"The more appropriate question is, what *didn't* he do?" She sinks down deeper against the cushions.

My once-sedate, professional living room is a minefield of scattered Matchbox cars, Legos, building bricks, the works. There's a bright red, wet splotch of something on my new, cream-colored rug. My glass coffee table has a half-eaten Uncrustable on it. Among the wreckage is a laptop, which hasn't moved since I sat it down ten hours ago, before I left for work.

Carefully, I ask, "So... how's the job hunt going? Any prospects?"

Ellie fixes me with a pointed stare, as if it's my fault she lost her last job. My fault her apartment complex in South Portland burned to the ground last year, sending everything she owned up in smoke. My fault she just can't seem to spring back, no matter what she does.

"No. Jace wanted to go to the park. I'll do it tomorrow," she says.

I don't tell her she said that yesterday. And last week. And the week before. There's always some excuse.

But she's been through hell. I have to believe she's trying to get her life together and that one day, she will. Not just for herself, but for my nephew, too. Until then, they've got me.

"All right." I sniff the air, not smelling anything but crayon wax and maybe Play-Doh. "What should we have for dinner?"

She gives me a confused look, as if I just asked her to donate a kidney. "We've been snacking all day. Don't worry about us."

I'm about to remind her the kid needs a proper meal,

but I think better of it because she's clearly had some kind of day.

Despite the fact that we had Thai last night and fast food burgers the night before, I pull up my Door Dash app and order a pizza from Ted's—half cheese, half supreme.

After I place the order for delivery, I gently pry Jace's sticky hands from my suit. "Okay, Bud. Let me go and get changed out of this suit. If you go wash up for dinner right now, your mom will let you have a scoop of ice cream after we eat."

I look to my sister, who doesn't appear to have heard a word I said.

His eyes light up. "Okay! But only if it's chocolate."

"Chocolate it is."

He practically bounces off the walls on his way to the bathroom to wash up. A second later, the faucet's running and he's singing to himself.

I love that kid. And I know Ellie does, too. But I also know she can't do this on her own.

It might be hard as hell some days, but I'll always be here to help her, no matter what.

When I'm finally up in my suite, I kick off my dress shoes, pull off my blazer, and quickly change into a hoodie and jogging pants. As I'm about to go downstairs, my phone lights up with a notification from BLIND LOVE: *You have one message!*

I rush to check it. Stranger7721 ghosted me too fast last night, without so much as a goodbye. A shame, since she was the first person on this damned app I actually enjoyed talking to.

But the message isn't from her.

Stranger581: *Are you ghosting me?*

The irony of her question isn't lost on me.

You think? She's sent me fourteen texts, one a day for the past two weeks, and I haven't responded. It's safe to say I'm not interested. I was once. Marginally. Even then, I saw red flags, but it was right after Ellie had lost her third job and I couldn't see a light at the end of the tunnel, so I was desperate. Stranger581 is into healing crystals and metaphysical bullshit. Not my thing. And she kept telling me she could sense my aura. When she asked me what my date and time of birth were so she could do my astrology chart, that was the final nail in the coffin.

If she were truly that intuitive, she'd have sensed that my aura was telling her to give up.

Blocking her seemed harsh, so I thought if I ignored some of her messages, she'd get the hint. Since that hasn't happened, it's time to put her out of her misery.

Stranger88: *Hey! Sorry. Been busy with work and family stuff. Also, I think you seem like a nice person, but I don't think we're a good match. Take care.*

I hit send and immediately open up the conversation I'd had with Stranger7721. She's not online and hasn't responded to my last message.

Stranger88: *I don't ever play by the rules.*

I reread the messages. I must have scared her off. Maybe I came on too strong. She's sounded cute. Innocent. But she also mentioned being a workaholic, just like me. She's probably working right now, and I'm the furthest thing from her mind.

I re-read her bio. *Love my job, but not much else.*

And then I send her a message:

Stranger88: *Okay, fine. I'll play by the rules. Only 89 days to go. I'm willing to wait if you are.*

3

Tenley

I sip my tepid coffee at my desk and attempt to concentrate on the endless stream of unread emails in front of me.

It's only a quarter past nine and I'm yawning already and finding it impossible to focus. I usually come to work, ready and raring to go. Today I can't keep my eyes open to save my life.

I was able to put Stranger88 out of my head at around two AM, when I fell into a deep, dreamless sleep, only to be woken by my alarm three hours later. I pride myself on being the first person into the office every day, turning on the lights and watching everyone step off the elevator exactly at nine. It shows pluck. Drive. Ambition. Motivation. Self-discipline. All the things an up-and-coming attorney should possess.

I'd never dream of sneaking off into a dark corner of the office to have fun with a delivery person. That's not me. I actually have respect for myself, for the law, and for this institution. I'm here to work and only to work.

But apparently not today, which is concerning with that promotion on the table.

In an attempt to keep my eyes open, I decide to get up, stretch, and refill my coffee. Only the second I rise from my chair, the elevator across the hall dings, the doors part, and out steps Brooks Gentry—swagger, arrogant smile, and all.

The sight of him makes most women wet. He has thick, dark hair that tumbles over his forehead in a devil-may-care way, ice-blue eyes, a strong jaw that always has a five o'clock shadow, even early in the morning. I've never seen him in anything other than a suit, though he rarely wears the jacket and always seems to have his sleeves rolled up in a *let's get to work* kind of way.

Not that I've ever seen him do much actual work.

Everything comes so easy to him—especially the women around here.

I'm not sure what bothers me more... the fact that highly intelligent women in this place act like groupies at a concert the second he walks by—or the fact that he's my number one competitor for this promotion.

I pride myself on never showing a ripple, but it's impossible with him. The mere sight of him makes it nearly impossible to control my facial expressions. Then there's the fact that he's an Ivy League snob, from Yale or Harvard or some law school that wouldn't even look at me. Secondly, he's infuriatingly gorgeous, tall and athletic and easy on the eyes—and he knows it. He has the entire office wrapped around his charming little pinky finger. If the man had a single pore on his perfect face, it'd be oozing confidence.

Brooks gets want he wants almost as easily as he breathes. It all comes naturally, effortlessly. The wins, the adoration, the accolades. He's the practice darling, the superhero in an office full of overworked women desperate for male attention.

What makes this entire thing all the more maddening is that because of him, I have to work twice as hard to get noticed.

At the end of the day, Brooks Gentry is the reason I'm here from seven in the morning until ten at night. Whenever I think I might want to pack it in, all I need to do is picture his smug, gorgeous, annoying face.

Good thing I love my job.

Brooks glances at me for a moment before striding toward his office.

"Morning, Ms. Bayliss," he says almost off-handedly as he passes by.

I nod. "Mr. Gentry."

We separate as quickly as possible, like two rockets shooting in opposite directions. A second later, as I'm heading into the break room, I happen to glance over and spot Mr. Popular hanging over one of the pretty interns' desks, his hand on his hip and a schmaltzy grin on his face.

He thinks he's so smooth.

His ploys would never work on me.

I see through them like cheap cellophane.

Rolling my eyes, I go to myself a coffee. When I return, he's still there, remarking on some photo on the blonde intern's desk. She giggles, too loud, and then fusses with her hair.

Shaking my head, I return to my office and shut the door.

A minute later, my inbox dings with a meeting request from Lisa Hamilton, one of the four main partners at the firm. She, Ed Foster, and his younger brother Tom Foster, are the cornerstones of Foster and Foster, along with Bill Lindsey, who's retiring this summer and the sole reason there's an open partnership position and corner office on the horizon.

The meeting subject is: *FUTURE PLANS*.

My breath hitches. Ed handles the day-to-day business of the firm, Tom is the face of the firm, so he's always traveling. But Lisa primarily works from home and when she's here, she handles the HR and staffing concerns. Because of that, I've rarely met with her. The last time I did, it was when I'd been promoted from Junior Associate to Senior Associate a few months ago.

Is this about the promotion? Is it finally happening? Surely I've done nothing that would warrant disciplinary action of any kind. Certainly not a termination.

My fingers tremble as I click on it. It was set up by Shelly, Lisa's executive assistant, as all important meetings are, and there's an exclamation point on it, indicating it's urgent.

Of course it is.

Lisa wants to meet this afternoon.

I can't click the ACCEPT button fast enough.

After several minutes of analyzing this urgent, last minute request, I decide this has to be about the partnership. Bill Lindsey is leaving in less than two months. He made the announcement last year, which was when I kicked my campaign to be his replacement into overdrive. They're going to have to select someone soon so the candidate can get up to speed before we cut the cake at his retirement party.

My excitement reaches a fever pitch—until I glance at the top of the invitation, which names *other* meeting invitees. I expect to see Ed. Tom if he's between trips. Maybe

Bill if he hasn't checked out yet. They'd want to congratulate me.

But it's not the partners' names I see.

Other than Lisa and me, there's only one other name.

Brooks Gentry.

Immediately, my jaw tightens.

I hear a crack and realize I'm gripping the mouse so hard I might have damaged it.

It's 10:05 now. Quite simply, I'm going to die if I have to wait until five in the afternoon to find out what this meeting is about.

My mother always told me action was the antidote to anxiety, which means either I can sit here paralyzed for the next seven hours—or I can go straight to the horse's mouth to find out what this is about. I'll make some pretense about how I want to be prepared. Lisa and I aren't on the closest of terms—we're more like professional acquaintances—but she's no-nonsense, like me.

Springing from my office chair, I head to the hall. As I'm about to march over to Lisa's corner office, I freeze in my tracks when I see Brooks's wayward curls above one of the cubicles.

He's leaning against Lisa's doorway, coffee in hand, shooting the shit like he has all the time in the world. On cue, he lets out a raucous laugh, as if she just said the funniest thing.

What... the... hell?

I've never laughed with, or joked with, or even dreamed about laughing and joking with one of the partners. Especially Lisa. She's always been sour-faced and serious. I didn't know she had a sense of humor.

Apparently, Brooks is already on her good side.

I'm not surprised though. He has a good rapport with all

the partners. Brooks automatically plants himself on the sunny side of everyone he meets. He's like a weed. He thrives everywhere, always.

I shrink back to my seat, trying to listen in on their conversation, but I'm too far away. All I can make out is a few more laughs from Brooks and even some from Lisa.

A full ten-minutes later, he saunters past my office, hands in the pockets of his dress slacks. He casts a glance over at me and raises his eyebrows in a dick-ish way, as if to say, *I know something you don't know.*

I grit my teeth.

I'd rather perform my own appendectomy than ask him directly, so I wait to make sure that he's gone back into his office before getting up and quietly making my way to Lisa's.

By the time I get there, her office door is closed, and she's on the phone.

"Can I help you, Tenley?" Shelly, Lisa's assistant, taps me on the shoulder, causing me to jump. I get the feeling she doesn't like me very much.

Checking to make sure Brooks hasn't popped his head out of his office, I smile and say in a low voice, "Oh, I just wanted to ask Lisa—"

"She's in meetings all day today." Shelly squints, as if to silently scold me for not checking Lisa's calendar before moseying this way.

"Well, if she has a moment, can you ask her to stop by and—"

"—Sure." She gives me a look that says it's highly unlikely.

For the remainder of the day, I'm on pins and needles. No word from Lisa. Not so much as an email between meetings. By the time five o'clock rolls around, my stomach is in knots and I'm so behind on my work I'll for sure be taking it home with me this weekend.

With my heart in my teeth, I knock on her door.

She looks up over her wire-rimmed reading glasses. "Oh, Tenley. Five already?"

I keep my shoulders back and head held high, steadying my nervousness the way I was trained to in law school. "Yes."

"Come in. Have a seat."

Lisa is smart. She's in her mid-forties, beautiful, always impeccably dressed, and has it all—husband, kids, great legal career. Somehow she juggles it all and makes it look like a walk in the park.

I've never had the chance to tell her this, but I admire her and her career has become a beacon for my own.

"Sorry, I got Shelly's message but didn't have time. You had something to discuss with me?" She's not looking up from the papers on her desk.

"Oh, no, it's nothing. I figured it out myself." A good future partner should be resourceful.

"Good," she says, "I like to hear that."

I glance around her office. It's twice the size of my own, with its own bathroom and a panoramic view of the Portland Harbor. Her desk, her chair, everything is bigger, and I can only imagine how it feels to sit on the other side of it. I'm halfway through a daydream when there's a friendly knock on the door, a *bup-bup-bah-bup-bup*. I glance over and see Brooks sauntering in.

"Hey, Lis." He's grinning like an idiot. A hot idiot, but still.

And what's with the nickname?

He takes the seat next to me and though I'm not looking at him, I can tell his gaze has shifted my direction.

"Bayliss," he says as if uttering a particularly nasty legal term.

Arrearage. Temporary Restraining Order. Termination. Cease and desist.

My lips twist, fighting a snarl. I stiffen and cross my legs before matching his tone. "Gentry."

He crosses his legs too and piles his hands on his knee. We both stare expectantly at Lisa. The silence is painful. He's quite a bit more relaxed than I am—the bastard—because I get the feeling he knows exactly what this is about. Maybe he doesn't know everything, but he knows the gist. He's had time to prepare his reaction.

The certainty I had this morning is all but gone.

There's no way Brooks Gentry would be invited to *my* promotion meeting.

Lisa looks up, laces her fingers together in front of her, and says, "Thanks, you two, for making time in your schedules to meet with me. I know how valuable our time is, so I'll cut to the chase. As you may or may not suspect, you're both in the running to be the next partner. We'd like to have our decision made sooner than later, but it's been a little challenging for us... we've been splitting hairs and it's a whole... well, I won't get into the nitty gritty."

Just like that I know where this is going.

The illustrious head of Foster and Foster is going to make us compete head-to-head for this partnership. Like *The Hunger Games.*

As if we haven't been doing that every day already.

Except now it's going to be even more vicious. The gloves are off. Blood will be spilled.

And I'm ready. I've been preparing for this all day. If they want me to plead my case, fine. I've been amassing all my wins. All my assets. Everything I bring to the table. I have running list in my head, and it's impressive.

Brooks can bring it, but I'm going to slaughter him. I'm going to fight, and fight, and fight, beating my opponent until he's just a bloody spot on the ground. There's no way he's beating me.

"I called this meeting because first and foremost, I want to convey our deep appreciation for your ongoing dedication to the success of this firm." Her gaze lands on Brooks, and she smiles. "Brooks, your skills in the courtroom are second to none. You have a way of swinging everyone present to your way of thinking, almost effortlessly. I've never seen anything like it. You're a natural."

He nods his thanks, but this is nothing he doesn't already know. Vomit gurgles in the back of my throat, but I swallow it back as her gaze shifts to me. She doesn't offer me the same warmth.

"Tenley, your skills at researching and picking apart the opposing counsel's arguments have helped our clients win many cases, especially in the last year," she says.

I wait for more. I, too, am skilled in the courtroom. I make things happen. I persuade. I'm a bulldog. I play hard ball. What about the number of times I've gotten a client's child support payouts doubled, even tripled? What about the many ex-husbands I've sent home from divorce proceedings cursing my name? One of them even *cried*, which I have to say, was the highlight of my career thus far because he was one of the worst kinds of people. It was beautiful—he'd come into the courtroom all swagger, not unlike Brooks—and left a shell of a man.

But she seems to be waiting for me.

"Thank you," I respond.

"Anyway," she says, opening a folder. "A complicated

case just landed on my desk. You've heard of James and Courtney Perry, right?"

I nod. But Brooks speaks first. "Yeah, the Perrys own Periwinkle's, don't they?"

"That's right. The concept restaurant that's impossible to get into. And they have over 1.3 million followers on their social media feed. At least, they *did*. They're in the midst of a divorce, a very public, nasty, high-profile divorce, and Courtney Perry has hired us to be their counsel."

I blink. This is news. But I suppose it makes sense. While the Perrys had painted themselves as the All-American perfect family on social media, the husband was caught red-handed having sex with his head chef in the alley behind the restaurant. After that, they'd gone suspiciously radio silent. I don't follow them religiously, but the last time I checked, they hadn't posted since the bomb dropped. Couldn't blame them. No one likes to fall from grace and there's not really a way to do it elegantly when the circumstances are so devastating.

"Good for her," I say, under my breath. I'm already itching to tear James Perry a new one. And that's just what I need—a case I can really get behind—to show my stuff. "I'll take that case."

They both look at me.

"Not so fast," Lisa says. "That's why I brought you both here. I want you two to tackle it, *together*."

That vomit that was gurgling in the back of my throat before nearly spews out my mouth. I have to swallow it back first. "What?"

Brooks says nothing. He just sits there, a smug smile on his face, clearly enjoying that I've been caught unaware.

Unlike him. He *knew* this. Lisa already told him.

I imagine the partners sitting around a table in a closed-door meeting, Lisa advocating for Brooks. Disappointment floods through me as the unswerving role model I once idolized is reduced to just-another-attention-starved-woman-in-the-office falling under Brooks's spell.

"Well, don't you see?" Lisa says brightly, her eyes volleying between us. "You two complement each other so well. Brooks is so likable; he always wins over the judge. And you..."

She pauses just long enough to let me fill in the blanks. *No one really likes you, but you're great at being behind the scenes. You'll make him look good, which makes our firm look good, so it's win-win for everyone.*

Like hell.

"I'm sorry," I say, "but is it really necessary to put your two best attorneys on a single case? I can certainly handle this case on my own. And—"

"—The Fosters and I have agreed that a case this complicated and high-profile would be best managed by a team," Lisa says, speaking over me and putting up her hands to indicate this isn't up for debate.

I stare at her, then at Brooks, wondering how he could be okay with this. He must like the idea of torturing me... because that's exactly what this case is going to be.

Pure, utter torture.

Months, maybe even years of it potentially.

A divorce this high-profile could drag out for ages.

"But... what does this have to do with future plans for the firm?" I ask, the idea of becoming partner suddenly feeling so far away when just this morning I was so sure it was in the bag.

"Yes. Thank you, Tenley. As I was saying before, we haven't been able to make a final determination as to which one of you would make the best partner moving forward, so we've decided that whoever wows us on this case will get the partnership," she states simply.

All those long hours. All that sacrifice. All those cases I opened a vein and bled my heart and soul out to win. They've all been for nothing.

It's down to this case.

I look over at my competition, envisioning spending endless hours in his presence, and my gut lurches.

Lisa hands us each a file. "Go ahead, you two. Don't be afraid to dazzle me."

Dazzle her? Gentry here can dazzle anyone by merely strolling into a room.

Me? It's not so simple.

I know I'm going to be sick as I take my folder and rise from my seat. Even so, I remember who I'm dealing with.

"Thank you, Lisa," I tell her before turning to Brooks. "I look forward to the challenge."

I head for the door, trying to ignore the fact that he's still lingering there, sitting all relaxed like he's not in a hurry to go anywhere anytime soon. Knowing him, he's going to attempt to charm her some more after I leave.

"Brooks, you have any questions?" Lisa asks before eyeing the door.

Miraculously Brooks takes the hint, grabbing his folder and standing to leave.

"After you," he says, still smiling smugly when he meets me at the door.

"Thanks." I remain stoic and professional. It's best not to give him a reaction—positive, negative, or otherwise.

I power-walk in my heels to my office, trying to ignore that he's right behind me. As soon as I get there, I'm going to open this folder right away so I can get a leg up. I'm planning for another three hours, butt-in-chair, getting familiar with the case.

Alone.

As I turn to close the door, though, he's looking at me.

"So we'll get started, tomorrow?" he asks, his voice thick with confidence.

"Sure." By then, I'll be so far ahead of him, he'll wish he never locked horns with me.

"Great." He gives me a thumbs up and starts to walk off, but a second later, he stops. "Hey. I know, this is a little awkward, working together to decide which of us gets the promotion. But you know, I think we're both worthy of it. You're a hell of an attorney, Bayliss. So whatever happens, happens, right?"

I freeze as he extends his hand out to shake mine.

And then I snap out of it.

"You might be able to bullshit everyone else in this office, Gentry," I say. "But you can't bullshit me."

"Good luck," he sniffs, turning to head back to his office. But as soon as I duck back into mine, I could swear I hear him add, "You're going to need it."

4

Brooks

Dinner tonight is fried chicken from a place in Falmouth.

I swear, if the only thing I give Jace is high cholesterol, I'll never forgive myself. But what can I do? I have work to think about—specifically a case that'll decide whether I become partner at Foster and Foster. Career-wise, this is going to be the most important two months of my life.

But I'll think about it tomorrow.

Tonight, though, after I shower and change into pajama pants, I sit in bed and open my phone to BLIND LOVE.

I only have one message. I'm expecting it to be the daily missive from my crystal loving Stranger581. But I'm wrong. It's from Stranger7721, responding to my, "*Okay. Only 89 days. I'm willing to wait if you are.*"

Stranger7721: *How do I know you're worth that kind of time investment? I'm a busy girl.*

I chuff. So that's how it's going to be?

Stranger88: *I promise you... it'll be worth the wait.*

Stranger7721: *Really? Just what do you have planned for me?*

Stranger88: *You'll like it.*

Stranger7721: *Don't be so sure. I can be hard to impress.*

I smirk, imagining her there, just like me, lying in bed after a long day at work. In my mind's eye, she's pulled her hair from her professional ponytail, letting it spill over her shoulders. She's wearing a lace camisole, silk stockings. Not much else.

For some absolutely insane reason, I think of Tenley from the office, probably because she's the last person I saw today before I left. She's easily the most buttoned-up girl, tightly wound person I've ever known, and much like Stranger 7721, she's immune to my charms.

Stranger88: *You want to know what I would do to you if you were here right now?*

Stranger7721: *Please enlighten me. And for the record, I don't do sex in public places. Not looking to be on the sex offender registry.*

Stranger88: *Well, now I feel like a pervert... which I'm not. For the record.*

Stranger7721: *So was the delivery girl story a lie?*

I smile. She doesn't forget a thing I said. I wonder if she read over our transcripts the way I have, picking them apart to see if there was anything to read between the lines. Then again, there's not much to read... yet.

Stranger88: *I plead the fifth.*

Stranger7721: *Ah. So it never really happened. So what would you do to me, if I were your fantasy delivery girl?*

There was a delivery girl. Once. Not at Foster and Foster because I'm not that stupid. I was just a nineteen-year-old college freshman working part-time at the university copy center and she delivered our weekly paper order. I liked that she was older, more experienced than me at the time, and that it took me months of flirting to finally get her to take me seriously.

I guess you could say I love a good challenge.

Stranger88: *I'd start by offering you a tour of the office, stealing looks at you every time you turn away. Of course, I'd be flirting and dropping hints left and right the whole time, but you'll be ignoring them because I feel like that's the kind of woman you are. It's not a bad thing. I'm just picking up on that from you. You want me to work for you. And I will. By the time we get to the unused cubicles, I'll be so worked up that I'll have no choice but to spin around, press you up against the wall, tell you how hot you make me, and kiss you. You'll melt against me, giving in, knowing you're about to have the hottest sex of your life with someone who wants nothing more than to fuck you so hard that you forget your own name.*

Next, I'd unbutton your blouse as I kissed you, pulling down the cups of your bra and gently running my teeth along your nipples. You'll moan, but I'll tell you to be quiet because there are people right in the next row over. And then I'll turn you around, lift up your skirt, pull your panties to your knees, and lick you.

While you're pinned against an empty desk, I'm burying my face between your thighs, tasting you until you're squirming underneath me. I'll have to give you my hand to bite because you'll be so close to coming, it'll be impossible not to make a sound. When it happens, you'll bite me so hard that I'll have scars on my hand. A badge of honor to remind me that I found something Stranger7721 likes more than her job.

I have to admit, I got carried away, so when she doesn't respond for a couple minutes afterwards, I think I've lost her again.

But then I get the message:

Stranger7721: *That's... quite the fantasy.*

Stranger88: *I told you I'll be worth the wait.*

Stranger7721: *I'm actually pretty turned on right now.*

Stranger88: *See, I think there are other things you'd like. You just haven't experienced them yet.*

Stranger7721: *Don't get your hopes up. We still have 88 days and I'm not convinced yet.*

I chuff, hardly surprised by her response.

The harder the hunt, the more satisfying the reward.

Stranger88: *Challenge accepted.*

"Brooksy?"

I look up to find Jace staring at me from my bedroom doorway. Without warning, he sprints across the room and launches himself onto the bed and into my arms. I quickly close out of the app and set my phone down.

"Hey, Bud. What's up?"

"You said you'd read me a bedtime story forever ago!"

I blink and stare at the clock at my bedside. I guess it has been that long, in kid-hours.

"So I did." I sit up. "Let's go. You brush your teeth yet? Let me see."

He grins wide then sticks his tongue out.

"Not good enough. I still see chocolate in there," I say.

I lift him onto my shoulder and deposit him on the stool in front of the bathroom mirror, where I oversee a more thorough brushing. I've been doing a lot of that overseeing whenever I'm home. It's not that Ellie's slacking so much.

It's more that whenever I'm home, Jace attaches to me like Velcro. I barely get a breath when I get through the door because Jace finds me. The kid is like a heat-seeking missile.

I don't blame him though. Jace never met his dad, and my father—a stereotypical absentee alcoholic—passed away when Jace was just a baby. I'm the closest thing he has to a father, a role I take seriously.

A role that also means that as much as I want to get laid, it's probably not happening. Not anytime soon. At least not in my own home. For now, the best I can do is come up with hot fantasies, like the one I told Stranger7721.

I know she was blushing. I wish I could've been there to see it. To touch her. To do exactly what I said I would and then some. Instead, I'm here, playing dad. And what I didn't tell her was that I don't see that changing, even after 88 days.

After Jace does a passable job at cleaning his pearly whites, I carry him to his bed, pretending to be an airplane, and toss him in. "What story are we reading, tonight?"

"*The Old Lady Who Swallowed a Porcupine.*"

I catch sight of it on his nightstand.

"Ouch." Grabbing it, I sit beside him and crack it open. "Okay. Let's do this."

Leaning back against the headboard, I start to read, but in the back of my mind, I can't help thinking about Stranger7721.

5

Tenley

Stranger88: *Challenge accepted.*

A minute ago, I was lying on my bed, one hand in my panties, stroking myself, wanting more of this silly little fantasy when the messages just... stopped.

Half of me felt a little foolish. The other half wanted to continue more than anything, to see what other kinds of fantasies he'd conjure up. In a world where porn is a click away 24/7, sometimes it's nice to not to browse for ages, to let someone else do all of the work for a change.

I needed it after the day I've had. I'd plummeted from the highest of highs—thinking I was about to be awarded the promotion of a lifetime—to the lowest of lows, having to work with Brooks freaking Gentry. Even though I wanted to stay and get up to speed on the file, I'd had to call it a day early after that devastating blow. All I wanted to do was come home and eat a gallon of ice cream and mope.

I'm not myself, and I'm not quite sure what to make of it.

The day wasn't all bad though.

My internet stranger may not have been a promotion, but he'd at least made me feel *wanted*.

And then he was gone. Just like that. No goodbye. No nothing.

Given my profession, my mind wanders to a worst-case-scenario where he's a married man and his wife came home from work early so he had to put his phone away.

Ugh.

I shove my phone away and pick up a book. Maybe some light reading before bed will do me good and get me out of my own head for a bit.

Except a few pages in, I'm finding it impossible to concentrate. My mind's wandering all over the place. It's a good book, but a sad substitute for the words my stranger wrote to me. And it doesn't stop the ache I feel down below. My clit is engorged, throbbing. Begging for another release —again, this isn't like me.

So I reach into my night table and pull out 'Old Reliable' —my nickname for my pink vibrator with all the bells and whistles.

I switch it on, tug the waistband of my panties down, and slip it in, spreading my legs wide.

Closing my eyes, I start with the same, familiar fantasy that has done the trick, all through college and law school and my many lonely nights in this room. Roses, candlelight, a big king bed, and sensual sex with a man who looks an awful lot like Ryan Gosling.

But tonight that doesn't quite do it for me. It is a bit vanilla, I'll admit. After my chat with my stranger, I need more.

So instead, I summon a different fantasy.

The second I picture a tall, faceless man, nudging me into a cubicle, kissing me, the ache between my legs intensifies. I can't even feel shame at this point... I'm too aroused. Within minutes, I've found the spot, jolts of electricity spasming through my body that I tamp down because I'm not ready for this to be over so soon.

I squeeze my eyes tighter. In my mind, my faceless stranger sidles up behind me, his strong hands molding my breasts as he dips his head to bite my nipples. Then, he turns me around with an ease that commands my entire body, sending me into a state of liquid mercury. He nudges me back upon the cold surface of the desk, lifting my skirt, inch by teasing inch, delving his warm, rough fingers under my panties. Throwing my back against the headboard, I steady myself.

"Harder," I whisper as the need gets fiercer, creating a friction so euphoric I never want it to end. Without warning, it changes, becoming something more.

"Come for me," my fantasy man commands, and I shake my head, because we're in public, and I know I'll be too loud. "Yes you will. I'm good at convincing people."

I buck up on the bed, moaning wildly. It's just when this new world is opening up to me that the man leans forward slightly to steady my thrashing body. It's then that his face emerges from the shadows.

Brooks Gentry...

Everything falls apart after that, the fantasy in my mind's eye disintegrating. Contrary to what I'd expected, his face is twisted into a sultry expression as he appears to be genuinely enjoying this.

My hand stops moving in my panties as the shock courses through me, along with the fluttering waves of an incomplete orgasm. I yank Old Reliable from my waistband. What did I just do? What does this mean?

I sit there, coming down from all of this, waiting to catch my breath as I wrap my head around the fact that I just imagined myself having sex with Brooks Gentry, someone I wouldn't screw if he were the last man on Earth.

Good god, it's official.

I'm losing my mind.

6

Brooks

I don't have the energy for this and I know it the second I stroll into the conference room where we'd planned to meet.

Without looking up from her legal pad, Tenley says, "Oh, wow. You're actually on time."

Throwing my things down on the table, I notice she's well into whatever research she's been doing for the case. I've barely cracked it. But that's okay. I do my best work on the fly and under pressure. It's kind of my thing. Plus, she's supposed to be the research arm of this operation. I'm the face of it. The closer.

"Is that supposed to be an insult?" I ask.

She glances at the clock, which says nine on the dot. She still hasn't looked at me. "I'm not insulting you. I'm describing you."

I sit down on the other end of the table, and considering the size of the it, we might as well be in different zip codes. I don't think I can stand to be any closer to this negativity. Not right now.

"Are you insinuating I'm not usually on time?"

"You're not the most punctual person on earth." She motions to the papers in front of her.

"I'm punctual when it matters." I've never been late to a court hearing in my life.

"Like when a promotion's on the line?"

I shrug. She said it, not me.

"Being on time means being early," she adds. "Have you even looked at the case file yet?"

I'm about to tell her I have a life outside the office—unlike her, but before I get the chance she snorts.

"Thought so," she says, still not looking at me.

Jaw clenched, I crack the file open, trying to stop my pulse from spiking. From the moment she started working here, she's made no bones about her disdain for me. Any attempts at friendly conversation would always get shot down, so eventually I stopped trying, stopped giving a damn. It was easy to ignore her, given that she was always holed up in her office and never hung out around the proverbial water cooler, but now that we're going to be working closely together for the foreseeable future, I no longer have that option.

I woke up thinking today would be a good day. I was ready to tackle the challenge, to prove that I'm the one for this job. I got in my five AM run feeling like a million bucks, ready to take on anything this day was going to throw at me. Only the second I got home and trekked to the basement laundry room to grab a towel for my shower, I discovered Ellie apparently had some friends over last night. They were all trashed, sleeping in the downstairs family room, pizza boxes and beer bottles and cigarette butts scattered everywhere. I have a white noise machine in my bedroom, so after I put Jace in bed and went to my room, I was dead to the world.

Ellie was still drunk, so I'd had to throw everyone out, get her into her bed, and spend the morning picking up the mess. After that, I was late getting Jace up for school, so he missed the bus and I had to drive him. Now I have to worry about whether Ellie will have it together enough to remember to pick him up this afternoon.

Grabbing my phone, I send her a text under the table, to confirm.

When I glance up, Tenley is glaring at me with mild disgust. She quickly averts her eyes and goes back to her work.

Placing my phone down, I pick up my case file and start reading. I already know what I've seen in the news. James Perry, chef extraordinaire, making waves in culinary circles with his quirky, fun, healthy dishes. He and his wife Courtney started Periwinkle a decade ago in an old factory overlooking the Portland Harbor. Since then, it had risen in popularity, as had the Perrys' star status. The family, and their two kids, were everywhere on social media, projecting a wholesome-yet-glamorous kind of lifestyle, one people could aspire to via the fake confines of social media.

Everything came crashing down when a fan had to snap a ten-second video in the back alley of Periwinkle. James Perry, on his knees, giving head to *his* head. Chef, that is. Raul San Pedro, Brazilian wonder-chef, who is as almost as famous as James is.

After the resulting media shitstorm, Courtney Perry promptly kicked him out of their McMansion. This should be cut and dry; she should be holding all the cards, except for one thing—the file says that Courtney Perry is a recovering addict. Ten years ago, before she met James, she had a serious battle with heroin, resulting in her losing the custody of her older children—children their 1.3 million followers likely don't know exist because their biological father refuses to let them serve as what he calls 'props.' James, of course, is wasting no time using Courtney's past to his advantage, suddenly claiming he doesn't think the younger kids are safe with her.

That strike against her might be hard to overcome—depending on the judge we get for the trial.

My phone buzzes beside me. I check the message, hoping it's from Ellie, but it's nothing.

Again, when I look up, Tenley's eyes are just shifting back to her work. The disgusted look on her face is still there. She sighs.

I cross my arms. "Well?"

"Well what?"

"Is there something you're not saying? You clearly have an issue with me."

"Hmm," she says, still not looking up at me. She taps the legal pad with her pen. "I just find there to be more important things in life than my phone. That's all."

Okay. Not only is my new 'partner' not deigning to look at me, she's insulting—no, *describing* me—in the most unflattering way possible. Contrary to what she thinks, I'm not some dumbass who gets by solely on my charm and good looks.

"I'm up to speed on the case," I tell her.

"Then what angle do you think we should use? James Perry is charging extreme cruelty and gross neglect of duties due to substance abuse."

"Our client's been clean ten years."

"She had a DUI last year. *And* the kids were in the car."

I glance down at the folder. Okay, so I missed that. Small point. "Look. The partners put us together because we should complement each other. You heard Lisa. You do the research. I'll provide the win in the courtroom. Just give me the facts and I'll take it from there."

Her eyes narrow. "I'll do the research, yes. But I can *also* win in the courtroom. I don't need your help at all. In fact, you—with all your little dings and buzzes from your phone over there—are only distracting me."

I snort. "Winston Churchill once said that tact is the ability to tell someone to go to hell in such a way that they look forward to the trip. You don't have it. When you tell people to go to hell—and I know you do—they hate you for it."

She scowls, still not looking my way. "Good thing I care more about winning than being liked. And winning's what I'm going to do with or without your help."

We're starting off on a terrible foot.

If this continues, neither of us will get that promotion.

I soften my voice. "Look, I—"

"*Shhh.*"

I stop. Okay, that didn't work the way I'd hoped. "Listen, I just want to—"

"*Shhh,*" she says, louder.

Annoyed, I push away from the table and stand up, heading for the door.

She finally looks up at me. "What are you doing?"

"What does it look like? You don't want me here. So I'll let you do your research, and when you're ready to get down to business and win this case, you let me know."

She raises an eyebrow. "So that's it? You're just going to let me do everything myself?"

"Isn't that what you want?"

She sits back, and I see her chest rise and fall beneath that silky, covered-up blouse of hers that leaves way too much room for my imagination to run wild, which is exactly what it's doing for some crazy reason.

"What I want doesn't matter," she says, interrupting my errant fantasy. "We were told to work together."

"But you're not making that easy."

She releases a huffy little breath. "Neither are you. How am I supposed to get things done with you distracting me every two seconds with all your fidgeting and sound effects?"

"I don't fidget." I sit straight, resenting her comment. I'd have my phone on DND mode for complete silence if I didn't have Jace to worry about.

"Agree to disagree." She returns her attention to the pile of papers in front of her, crossing things off and making marks with her pen like a teacher on a mission with a red marker. It's kind of sexy how serious she is, how unconcerned she is with whether or not I like her. I'm used to women hurling themselves at me, but not Tenley.

I think about how I'd pictured her the other night, while I was talking to my workaholic stranger. Silk stockings, lacy camisole. The hair from that severe ponytail, loose around her shoulders.

Suddenly, I'm imagining her as the girl from that fantasy I told to my sweet stranger.

Shit. I need to stop that.

Squelching that thought, I take my phone, lift it, making a show of turning it off before pocketing it so it's out of the way. If there's a true emergency, Ellie or the school knows the number to the office and someone can track me down.

"Better?" I ask.

She nods, though she's unimpressed. "Much. Now, let's get to work."

7

Tenley

It's nearly two-thirty when I finally come up for air and realize I'm late.

Well, not really. On-time. But in my book, on time *is* late. My walk to the shelter on Congress Street usually takes twenty minutes, and I like to get there well ahead of my three o'clock time slot so that I can answer emails and be prepared for my meeting with my mentee, Rhonda. Just like in my regular job, the early bird gets the worm.

Standing and buttoning my blazer, smoothing my hair, I grab my briefcase and start throwing my research in. I have twenty pages full of information about the case, and there's still so much more to do.

But some things are more important—the Portland Women's Center being one of them.

I owe my entire existence to the place. If it weren't for the caring women within those walls, I'd never be here today.

Twenty years ago, my mother was a struggling, single mom, trying to raise me. I never knew my father, who walked out when I was a toddler and never came back. She worked every shift she could at a local seafood diner, trying to make enough for us to stop living paycheck-to-paycheck. But that was hard, considering her tips were never guaranteed, and often we'd go hungry. Once, we had to spend a night in my mother's car, during the coldest night of the winter. She didn't have money for gas, so she would have to turn on the ignition, just long enough for us to not freeze to death, then turn it off to save what little gas was left.

It was a woman named Ruth who first took her under her wing, offering her a helping hand to get her on her feet. While we were staying at the shelter, Ruth, an attorney, had put my mom through paralegal school, which had allowed her to finally get a good job, and a nice apartment. But my mother didn't stop there. She went to college during nights, and then law school, eventually becoming an attorney herself.

Because I saw my mother working hard to realize her dreams, I knew I wanted to do the same. I've always dreamed of starting my own center for women, helping them the way Ruth helped my mom with training, scholarships, and anything else she needed to be able to stand on her own two feet.

Unfortunately, that takes money. A lot of it.

And as a senior associate at a small-time law firm, I don't exactly make the big bucks.

The promotion, though, should help.

Months ago, when Bill Lindsey said he was going to retire, Lisa sent out an email saying they'd begin the process to fill his shoes soon. She'd included an information sheet with salary ranges, benefits, et cetera. In addition to earning a salary that's nearly twice what I'm currently making, the partner position has various other perks—profit sharing, a flexible schedule, the opportunity to pick and choose which cases I want to handle. All of that will help me to pour my extra earnings and time into giving back.

Even though I live to work, I've always set aside something—whether it be time, money, donations— for the Portland Women's Center. It's never felt like a sacrifice.

Snapping my briefcase closed, I head for the door. I'm just about to jab the button on the elevator when Brooks wanders out from his office. He spots me, and a curious look spreads over his perfectly symmetrical face. He's been looking at me strangely ever since this morning, and I haven't quite been able to figure out why that is.

It was hard enough sharing a conference room with him this morning. I could hardly bring myself to make eye contact because every time I tried, I thought of my fantasy, of him hovering over me, his hands molding my body.

Even now, those thoughts threaten to invade. I shove them away as he saunters closer.

"Half day, Bayliss?" He makes a show of checking his watch.

I frown. "Considering I always get here at seven, Thursdays are my early day. Not that it's any of your business."

I step aside as he stands beside me. "So you actually have a life outside this place? Who'd have thought?"

I shouldn't entertain him, but I can't help it. "Well, not you, apparently. Then again, you're usually too busy schmoozing to notice anything."

Schmoozing isn't a word in my everyday vocabulary but it's nicer than what I really want to say.

The elevator dings, and the doors open. I side-step around him and go in, leaving him staring after me. Grabbing my phone, I check the messages I last received from Rhonda. She's doing so much better these days—she has a full-time job from an interview I set up for her, and her three kids are thriving in school. There's no better feeling than helping someone succeed, especially when they deserve it. It puts a smile on my face.

When I look up, just before the doors close, I realize he's still staring after me.

8

Brooks

The weekend blows up before it even starts.

Friday afternoon, I'm feeling at the top of my game because I just came in from the courthouse where I managed to negotiate far more favorable terms for my client than she'd expected. She was so delighted, she hugged me, and promptly invited me over to dinner this weekend. The stars in her eyes told me it was a little more than a simple dinner invite. I turned her down. Not that I could accept anyway. Firstly, I don't date clients or colleagues... and secondly, because, well... Jace and Ellie.

I was hoping to at least start on building the air hockey table I gave Jace for his sixth birthday. Three weeks, and it's still sitting in the box. I know he must be dying to play, but he's such a good kid—he hasn't begged me once. I figure we can put it in the empty dining room, since we always eat at the kitchen island and I'm probably not going to need a formal dining set anytime soon.

The other associates give me high-fives and cheer me on as I walk in, giving them thumbs up. Good news travels fast, as they say.

"So you tore him a new one, huh?" Mike asks in passing.

"Total bloodbath," I say.

Kenzie chuckles. "As if we could expect anything else?"

I wink at her. More interns pop from their cubicles, and soon, they're all applauding me. It's like my own ticker-tape parade. I milk it, bowing, hoping it'll continue so that some of the partners will see and realize that this farce of a competition between me and Tenley Bayliss shouldn't even be happening, and I'm the one they want.

At the thought of Tenley, I glance toward her office. The door is open, the light on. I don't know what she's doing in there, but I can guarantee it's not applauding for me.

"Thanks, guys," I say, checking the clock before heading into my office. Work calls. Hopefully not much of it. I'm hoping I can finish up with whatever emails I have, clock out at a normal hour, and be home so I can make burgers and dogs on the grill for dinner. Jace loves cookouts.

But the second I sit down, I see it.

One meeting request.

I grab my mouse and click on it. I get these all day long. It's probably for next week.

Except that it isn't...

It's for today. For *now*.

What the hell? Only a masochist would make a meeting request for five pm. on a Friday evening.

As soon as my eyes land on the meeting organizer, it all makes sense.

Tenley Bayliss. Who, despite all her ruses to make it seem like she actually does have a life outside of Foster & Foster, clearly doesn't.

Taking great satisfaction out of hitting the DECLINE button, I type into the box for a reason: *Because it's Friday night and I want to live.*

A moment later, I hear purposeful footsteps coming my way before Tenley appears in my doorway, that typical frown on her face. "I just had a call with James Perry's attorney, and he told me he wants full custody and he's not going to spare a single penny. This is going to get ugly."

The chances of Jace playing with that air hockey table before he hits puberty are officially slim to none.

I stare at her. I knew this case was contentious and bitter, but now it appears the situation is quite a bit more dire than I'd expected. Full custody battles are lengthy, expensive, and exhausting. Part of me can't help thinking it might be because of my partner. I remember her on the phone earlier saying: *I won't accept anything less.*

Did her lack of tact get us here? There's a time and place to be a shark and there's a time and place to be a friendly, affable golden retriever.

"Why were you on the phone with Perry's attorney?" I ask. "As your partner on this case, you should have conferenced me in."

She gives me a confused look. "I had a quick question. I wanted to ask if—"

"Do me a favor and leave the communication to me from now on," I snap, annoyed. Grabbing my pen and paper and heading toward the conference room she reserved, my movements tight and clipped. This is definitely her doing— her and her goddamn stubborn streak of hers. "Come on. Let's go."

She doesn't follow me. "What do you mean?"

I turn back to her to find her staring at me accusingly,

hands on her hips. "I mean that you're no Winston Churchill."

"What?" Her brows knit.

"There's such a thing as tact, and you don't have it. And you're now the reason why I can't go home and enjoy my weekend."

"I did no such thing. How about you do *me* a favor and save the theatrics for the courtroom?"

"Right." I draw the word out so she can hear all the doubt in it.

"What, did you have a hot date tonight or something?" Her question comes out of left field, but I'm too worked up to care.

"Something like that."

"Guess your intern of the week will just have to reschedule."

I almost laugh. Is that what she thinks of me? The office manwhore?

"It's called being nice to people Maybe you should try it sometime," I say.

"I'm sure you're more than just *nice.*" She stampedes past me, as other people on the floor pack up and say their weekend goodbyes. A few of them stop and watch us. This entire exchange reeks of a divorcing couple locking horns, a scene far too common around here some weeks.

Tenley ducks into the conference room, slamming the door hard behind her. If she's mad at me or embarrassed about having an audience, it's anyone's guess. Probably both.

Opening the door, I wave goodbye to a few of the other staff members and follow her in. Then I close the door and lean against it, assessing her. Her face is red, and she's practically panting. I think she knows she ran her mouth a little too loosely back there and she's regretting it. This isn't going to bode well for her promotion.

So of course, I have to call her on it.

"I don't hook up with co-workers," I say. "And I'd never touch an intern."

She's busy shuffling through papers and doesn't say anything.

"I told you not to bullshit me, Gentry," Tenley says with a sigh.

"Did someone say I slept with them?" I can't let this go. Not when my reputation's on the line.

"Can we skip this conversation that we both know isn't going to go anywhere and just get to work?"

"Fine." But only because she has a point. The sooner we work, the sooner we can get out of here, and that's the only thing I want to do.

The second I grab my phone from my pocket to text Ellie that I'll be home late, Tenley fixes me with her signature death glare.

I hold it up. "I'm going to silence it, but if we're going to be stuck in this hell on a Friday night, can't we at least order food?"

She gives me a barely noticeable shrug. "Fine. Thai."

"Thai it is. What do you want?"

"Pad Thai."

I order two cartons of Pad Thai, text Ellie that I'm going to miss dinner but will bring them back something, and deposit my phone back into my pocket.

About five minutes later, when I'm deep in the transcript of Courtney Perry's testimony, Tenley says, quietly and out of nowhere, "I'm sorry if I was uncouth before.

James Perry is such an asshole, and I just really want to win this case. If we could keep to being professionals..."

I'm stunned for a moment, surprised by her admission.

Is she softening? Is she going to let her guard down for once?

"Understand and agree," I say, though as a skilled attorney, she could very well be manipulating me into a more docile state. I can be cordial, but I can't let my guard down around her. Not yet. Not when this promotion's still on the line. "Can I just state again, for the record, I don't sleep with colleagues or interns. Ever."

"If you say so," she says.

"They chase me."

"Sure."

"You sound like you don't believe me." I know better than to let this bother me, but I can't help it. I'm a stickler for the truth—and for justice—especially when it involves a career I've worked my ass off to have.

"Because I don't."

"And why not?"

She places her pen down. "Fine. You want to know why I don't believe you? Because it's the same reason you can go into a courtroom and automatically win before you say a word. You smile, you wink. You use your body language. And that's enough. You may not think you're trying, you might not think you're doing anything... but you are. Trust me. People fawn over you like you're some kind of celebrity. You'd have to be a psychopath not to take advantage of that."

"Really? Because I think a psychopath *would* take advantage of that." She's not completely wrong. My entire life there's been something about me that instantly puts people on my side. Aside from living off the grid or intentionally disfiguring myself, I don't know what she expects me to do.

"Can we please focus on this." She taps the paperwork in front of her and cracks open her laptop.

"Sure," I say, "after we finish this conversation."

Tenley rolls her eyes.

"So according to your logic, women take one look at me... with my magic, mysterious, indefinable magnetism... and they just want to drop their panties? And I go along with it because I'm just an average, red-blooded guy who lacks self-control?"

She types her password into her computer, answering me with silence.

"Why do you hate me so much?" I ask a question I've always wanted to ask but have never had the chance.

"I don't hate you. I don't hate anyone."

"Could've fooled me."

"Does it bother you that I'm not fawning over you like everyone else?"

"Not at all," I lie. It bothers me. A little. "I'm curious though. If I've ever done something to offend you, I'd like to know."

"You're just... not my cup of tea."

I sniff. "That's such a cop-out answer."

"Fine," she says. "I don't respect you. Is that a better answer?"

Ouch.

"Why?" I ask.

"For starters, you went to Yale on an athletic scholarship and you look like you just walked off a Versace billboard in Times Square. Everyone loves you for literally no reason at all. Like I said, you're not my cup of tea. I don't know why that bothers you so much. Let it go."

"I went to Harvard," I correct her. "And who said it bothered me?"

"You asked. Clearly it bothers you."

It's in this moment I realize I know absolutely nothing about her.

"So what's your story anyway?" I ask. If we're going to get through this case, we need to find some common ground.

"My story is neither here nor there." She squints at her screen.

"Your story is what got you to where you are today, so it's technically here."

Tenley blows a strand of hair from her forehead, annoyed. "Single mom. Bouts of homelessness. Put myself through college. Just your average, everyday Cinderella story."

"It's a shame."

Her eyes flick to mine. "What is?"

"How hard you've worked to get to where you are," I say, "and you can't stop to enjoy it."

"What makes you think that?"

"Because you're always here. Working. You can't enjoy life and work at the same time."

"Speak for yourself," she snips.

"What do you do for fun?"

"I'm going to pretend like you didn't ask me that. I'm going to pretend like you just asked me a relevant question that pertains to the Perry case."

The little section of creamy skin above her Puritanical blouse flushes red. I'm getting under her skin. But to be fair, she's getting under mine too.

No one has ever spoken to me the way she does.

And it's kind of... hot.

My cock pulses at the thought of silencing her smart

little mouth with a punishing kiss, tearing off that starched white top and that tight pencil skirt and having scorching hot hate sex right here on this conference table.

Flipping through my folder, I pull out my copy of the brief, which is the closest thing I have to a cold shower at the moment.

Out in the hallway, the elevator dings. Our food. Pushing away from the desk and making sure my pants are not tenting, I grab some cash from my wallet for a tip, head for the lobby and collect the food. When I return, I realize we're alone in the office. It's cleared out as it probably always does on Friday nights, not that I'm ever here to see it.

Tenley's still in the same place I left her, though she's on another page of notes. I set the bag and a couple of sodas on the table. "Dinner time."

Surprisingly, she pushes away from her work and reaches for it.

I've watched her work through lunch more times than I can count, so I imagine she's starving.

We each dig in, and as I'm winding the noodles around my chopsticks, she says, "This is going to get nasty. I can feel it."

"Between you and me?"

She snorts.

"Oh, you're talking about the case." I nod. "Well, they got a lot of damning stuff on our client, but what do we have on James? That guy he was with. Is it serious? Do we know?"

"Yes." Of course she does. She's ten steps ahead of me, always. "Apparently, they're together now. Rumor is he's claiming she withheld sex from him the last two years, and during that time, he developed the relationship with Raul, the chef. You know, because withholding sex from a man turns him gay…"

It wouldn't be the first time I've heard that line of thinking and it won't be the last.

"Okay…" I'm trying to connect the dots as to where we can go with that. It's irrelevant to the case as that argument won't hold up in court to excuse his cheating, but it shows he's willing to say whatever it takes to get sympathy.

"What we need to do is look into this Raul. Find out how long he was employed there, how long they knew each other. Maybe ask around the restaurant and see how serious it was."

"Agree." This might be the first time we've ever agreed on anything.

"I called the police to pull the report on this DUI our client had that they're so hot on. Obviously, it doesn't look good for Courtney, but I want to know the circumstances behind it. We should get it soon."

I nod. "Okay, and do you think—"

"Apparently, they were *both* heroin addicts. They actually met in rehab. He got clean before she did, though. Still, James can't be damning his wife for something he's also guilty of." She digs her chopsticks into her carton. "What's interesting though is she isn't using that against him. What does he have on her? There's got to be more to this."

Jesus. She's all over the place, but those gears in her head have been turning in directions I haven't even thought of going in yet. I stare at her, not wanting to interrupt until I know she's finished.

"Are you done?" I ask.

She nods and lifts a roll of shiny noodles to her lips, still staring at the brief in front of her, but it falls from the sticks and snakes its way down her ivory blouse, leaving an obvious stain. She doesn't seem to realize until the noodles have disappeared under the table, probably into her lap.

Looking down, she mumbles, "Damn it."

I look around for napkins. Unfortunately, the delivery service forgot those. I head for the break room. "Hold on. Let me get you some paper—"

"—Forget it," she says, jumping to her feet, taking the wayward noodles from her lap, and throwing them in the garbage. She pulls off her blazer, and I realize her blouse is sleeveless.

I've never actually seen this much skin on her.

I find myself staring as she starts to unbutton the blouse, hypnotized like a goddamned school boy.

This isn't a dream, right? I'm still here, still awake, right? I cross my arms and stealthily pinch myself.

Nope. This is real. Tenley Bayliss is actually stripping in front of me.

But then she shrugs off her blouse, revealing a sedate, modest silk camisole. Well, modest for other girls. For Tenley, she looks practically naked. Her skin is flawless, and her subtle, feminine curves are perfection. I can practically see the outline of her nipples as they cut through the paper-thin fabric of her remaining top.

Not to mention that I'm pretty sure that's the camisole from my fantasies.

My cock throbs, coming to life all over again.

She doesn't notice me staring. She simply power-walks to the door. "Hold on. I just need to run this under the sink so it doesn't stain."

Her footsteps fade off in the hallway, allowing my heart rate to return to normal.

Meanwhile, I'm still hard as a fucking rock.

What the hell am I doing? So what if the woman could

fulfill every naughty librarian fantasy I've ever had? So what if she's packing a smoking hot body? None of that matters. She'll never let me touch it.

She hates me.

And that, I think, might be the hottest thing of all.

9

Tenley

I get home shortly after eleven PM.

Everyone else my age is probably living it up. It's Friday night. I bet even Brooks is sitting at some trendy bar right now having a drink to kick off his weekend. That's what normal people in their twenties do.

But me?

I trudge into my bedroom, kick off my heels, then look down at my blouse. The greasy Thai stain is fainter, but still there. Great. It's ruined. First world problems of course, but growing up knowing poverty, I've always been grateful to have nice clothes and I've always taken meticulous care of them so they'll last forever.

I work on the stain for a solid twenty minutes before accepting it's a hopeless cause, and then I have a little funeral service for the blouse before tossing it into the garbage.

A moment later, I grab it back and set it to soak in my sink with some more stain remover.

I can't give up that easily.

Like my mom says, there's always hope. I can almost hear her cheering me on from her home in DownEast Maine four hours away from here.

I collapse in front of the couch, attempting to unwind. I need to sleep, because we arranged a meeting with Courtney Perry for Saturday morning, since it's the only time she could get a babysitter. But if I pass out now, I know I'll dream about legal motions until it turns into a nightmare.

Grabbing my phone, I casually browse the minefield that is social media, and I'm right—it's full of friends out at clubs, parties, exotic vacation destinations. And the ones that aren't living out the dwindling years of their twenties in high-style are married, really adulting, with families of their own.

Looking around *my* place though, I sigh. All I see is everything that's wrong—the boxes piled up around me, the run in my brand new nylons, the dirty dishes piling up in the sink. Not to mention...

There's such a thing as tact, and you don't have it.

The words run through my head like a freight train. If a man has an opinion, he's applauded. If a woman has one? She's tactless. Still, I have no plan on changing my ways all because some pretty boy who's never known adversity a day in his life thinks his opinion matters to me.

I swallow as a sickening realization washes through me.

Something tells me Brooks is going to be partner.

Everyone loves him.

And he's going to be the face of this case, the part the people see. Even if I work my fingers to the bone in the background, when we win, everyone will notice him first. And I will be left behind.

Because as much as I hate to admit it, Brooks is right.

He's a people-person.

I'm not.

It doesn't matter how good I am at my job or how hard I work to win this case if he's the one everyone notices.

Sighing, I navigate to BLIND LOVE. I've been so busy lately, I haven't checked it. I only had that one connection, with Stranger88, and I was kind of embarrassed by the fact that I'd responded to his sex fantasy with an enthusiastic, *Sounds interesting,* only to receive nothing but crickets in return. Apparently, I lack tact even with a sex-starved stranger.

But then I realize he's responded to my message.

Stranger88: *I thought about what I want to do with you after I have my way with you in the cubicle.*

A little shiver of excitement skitters down my spine at the thought.

There's a blinking, bold message in the corner of our chat box that says: *You are in danger of losing your streak! Respond now!*

There's a little countdown clock, slowly ticking down.

Five minutes to go or today won't count.

I stare at it for a moment before realizing that not only had Stranger88 responded, but he's online now. He isn't out, partying it up on a Friday night, like everyone else. I quickly type in a reply, effectively stopping the countdown clock.

Stranger7721: *Not out living it up on a Friday night?*

Stranger88: *Same could be said for you. Just got home.*

Stranger7721: *Hot date?*

Stranger88: *I wish. Worked late. You?*

There's a little voice in the back of my mind, once again telling me he's probably some married loser and tonight he had to wait until his wife went to bed so he could get online. I have no proof of any of this, of course, but you never know with internet strangers.

Stranger7721: *Same.*

Stranger88: *How was your day? Good? Bad? Little of both?*

His question gives me pause, but in a good way. I can't remember the last time anyone but him asked me about my day.

Stranger7721: *You really want to discuss work right now?*

Stranger88: *No actually. I'd rather talk about you. Tell me what you you're wearing. ;-)*

I look down. For a second I consider lying and saying I'm wearing pink lingerie. Isn't that what you're supposed to do in these situations?

Stranger7721: *Why do you want to know?*

Stranger88: *I want a mental image to go along with my fantasies.*

I sigh. What the hell. Might as well. It's not like I have anything to lose. It's all just a game of make believe anyway, something to entertain and pass the time.

Stranger7721: *I just got home and took my hair down. It's chestnut brown, straight and several inches past my shoulders. I'm wearing a skirt, a camisole. Nylons.*

I press send and gnaw on my lip. I'm terrible at this. I'm much better with facts over fiction.

Stranger88: *Nylons? I'm sorry, are you 88?*

Stranger7721: *Might as well be. What's wrong with nylons anyway? Kate Middleton wears them. They're back in style, you know.*

Stranger88: *I have nothing against nylons other than the fact that they're an unnecessary obstacle in these kinds of situations. Ripping them off you with my bare hands could be hot though...*

I hate the idea of ruining perfectly good clothing items, but in this case, I might be willing to sacrifice a pair of L'eggs in the name of good sex—in my mind, of course.

Stranger7721: *Says the guy who fantasizes about cubicle sex.*

Rising, I shimmy out of my ruined pantyhose and toss them in the trash, but only because there's no saving them. I still have hope for my blouse though. By the time I grab myself a handful of stale Cheerios and go back to my phone, I've gotten a barrage of IMs from him.

Stranger88: *Anything can be sexy if you just believe.*

Stranger88: *What are your turn ons anyway?*

Stranger88: *Or you can tell me about the hottest sex you've ever had.*

Stranger88: *I won't judge.*

Stranger88: *Still there...?*

Stranger7721: *Sorry. I was throwing away those unsexy nylons.*

Stranger88: *Smart move. Thank you. Now we can finally move forward with this conversation. You know, now that it's past midnight this counts towards tomorrow's streak too. We're on a roll here.*

I gnaw on my lip as I look around my apartment, fantasizing about what it would be like to have someone on speed dial to call in my 'times of need.' I'm getting ahead of myself though. I've never even brought a lover home. Not to this place. Too busy working to even think about it.

Stranger7721: *Sorry, was just saying a little prayer service from my nylons. They were brand new. And I've never been rich, so it hurts.*

Stranger88: *I feel you. I was born on that side of the tracks too.*

Stranger7721: *Really?*

Stranger88: *Yeah. It's probably why I'm so driven.*

Stranger7721: *Same, hence working on a Friday night.*

Stranger88: *Right. But there are always people who don't get it. Who don't see all the work you put in and think things come easy to you.*

Stranger7721: *Exactly! I'm going for a promotion at work, and I don't think any of my bosses have seen the good things I've been doing. I feel like I'm screaming in a crowded room and no one's even looking at me.*

Stranger88: *I hate that—when people make assumptions about you good or bad. Everyone thinks I have it easy. They don't know I battled dyslexia and worked my ass off to get a college scholarship. Got into a great school, but I never fully felt like I belonged there... which was hard for me because I'm such a people person.*

The man has faced adversity and he has grit and social awareness to boot. I love it.

Stranger7721: *Really? How did you deal?*

Stranger88: *Head down, eyes on the prize. Is there any other way?*

Stranger7721: *Of course not. Where'd you go to school?*

Stranger88: *I'll tell you as long as you promise not to make assumptions about it.*

Stranger7721: *Pinky swear.*

Stranger88: *Harvard.*

My jaw hangs open. Not because that's damn impressive, but because he's so matter of fact about it. Earlier today Brooks told me he went to Harvard. Small world.

Stranger7721: *So that's why you felt out of place there? Because you were a scholarship kid in a sea of kids whose parents were footing the bill?*

Stranger88: *Mostly, yeah. I was a poor kid, child of a single mother. My father was a drunk, died when I was young. Like I said, I wasn't one of 'them.'*

Stranger7721: *I love that. Cheers to the underdogs of the world.*

Stranger88: *Where did you go to college? Or did you? I don't mean to assume. When you said you wear nylons, I immediately pictured a CEO or something.*

I sniff a laugh.

Stranger7721: *I went to a public university here in Maine.*

Stranger88: *Respectable.*

Stranger7721: *We have a lot in common, you know. When my father left, my mom had nothing. We were homeless for a time. But she was determined to get us out of that situation. She was able to get her paralegal license, put herself through law school... everything. She's my hero.*

As we head into the small, quiet hours of the night, we continue our conversation, telling each other everything. I tell him things I've never told anyone before. Before long, there are birds singing outside the window and the sky is turning from the deepest darkest navy to a dreamy shade of cerulean blue.

It's morning. And I haven't slept a single wink.

Thank goodness it's Saturday.

After my meeting with Courtney, I'll rush home and catch some sleep.

And yet, I can't help grinning as I stare at the message that pops up from my stranger. Forget the meeting. I feel like I can talk to him forever.

Stranger88: *I should sign off... loved talking with you tonight. Even if you're actually 88 in real life.*

Stranger7721: *Thanks, cubicle pervert. That really means a lot.*

I can't wait until next time. But when I look up from the screen, my eyes bleary and unfocused, the real world starts to intercede, and I remember that our online interaction, as sweet and wonderful as it was, really means very little.

I don't know what he looks like.

I don't know if everything he told me was true.

I don't even know his name.

Even though we just spent hours pouring out our hearts to each other, it's nothing more than a fantasy, a frivolous escape. I can't get too wrapped up in this, even if it feels amazing in the moment.

10

Brooks

Saturday morning I feel like I've been hit by a truck.

At five, just as the sun is starting to make its appearance, I burrow under the covers, hoping to catch a little shut eye before I have to get ready for the meeting with the soon-to-be ex Mrs. Perry.

I'm almost asleep a few minutes later, when Jace bursts in with his toy airplane, making zooming noises. He launches himself on my bed and burrows in with me, wiggling like a worm.

"Little dude, let me sleep," I mumble into my pillow.

After about ten minutes of trying and failing to ignore him, I finally pull the covers off us. He's so cute. I really do need to assemble that air hockey table for him.

"I'm hungry and Mom is still sleeping," he says.

I can't fault Ellie—it's five AM. Everyone should be sleeping.

"Let me guess. You want pancakes."

"Duh! It's Saturday!" He's nodding, his freckled face full of excitement. Pancakes on Saturday is a tradition around here.

"I have to go into work, but okay..."

"Work? Ew!" He makes a face that makes me feel like the world's worst uncle.

"After I make pancakes of course." I pick him up in a football-hold and carry him downstairs. "You get the syrup and butter and I'll do the rest."

We spend the next thirty minutes in relative harmony, making and eating breakfast. Jace helps, to the best of his ability, and then we sit down and talk, man-to-man. He tells me about a stained-glass project he's doing in art class and how he's thinking about asking the blonde who sits next to him to be his girlfriend.

"You have time," I tell him. "Play it cool. Don't come on too strong. Girls don't like that."

"She's nice though. She might like it," he says, raking his fork through the syrup.

"It's almost summer break. Did you ask her what her plans are? You think she'll be in first grade with you?"

His brow knits. "I haven't really talked to her yet."

"That could be a problem," I acknowledge, as Ellie scuffs in, wearing her robe and pink fuzzy slippers. She looks like hell. When I got home shortly after eleven last night, she was dressed and ready to go out. I could tell she was pissed, just waiting for her babysitter—that would be me— to come home so she could start her night.

Such is the life of a twenty-four-year-old.

But after I got Jace to bed, I was so wrapped up with my conversation with Stranger7721 that I never heard her come in. Sad to say, I think she wound up getting more sleep than I did.

I can*not* do a repeat of last night. I love sleep like a fat kid loves cake.

And yet when I think about staying up and talking to my stranger, I'm raring and ready to pull another all-nighter. Those early morning hours flew by. It's like I blinked and suddenly the sun was coming up. We still have so much to talk about, and I can't wait for the next time. I just need to catch up on some zzz's first.

Ellie pours herself coffee and leans against the counter, ignoring us as she brings the mug to her nose and inhales the brew. She's completely oblivious to Jace, who is saying, "Mom! Mom! Mom!" over and over again.

"Hey, bud. What do you want to tell her?" I interject, because I have to admit, it's a little grating. "She's standing right there."

"I just want to show her this cool pancake you made. It's shaped like a plane!"

"Uh-huh," Ellie nods, not looking. "Neat."

That's even more grating. She's not even trying right now. She *does*, usually, when she's not hungover. For someone who's twenty-four and saddled with all the responsibility of taking care of this little firecracker, she does a hell of a lot. She's a good mom when she's not dealing with the weight of the world on her shoulders, which is why I'm trying to cut her more slack lately. She doesn't have it easy. And I know she loves Jace more than anything. But going out like a carefree teenager is not doing her any favors. I'm going to have to talk to her about this sooner than later because it's not any kind of path she needs to go down. It's a slippery slope from here.

"Let your mom get some coffee in her first, all right?" I take a napkin and wipe his mouth, but he's sticky everywhere. "Why don't you go up and wash your face? Get that sticky junk off."

"But—"

"No buts."

He runs off, leaving me alone with Ellie. I wipe my mouth with a napkin. "Can you wash the dishes? I have to go into work in a few minu—"

"What?" Her eyes bulge. I've finally woken her up. "I literally just woke up. Can you give me a minute?"

"Yeah, I have a meeting with a—"

"But you can't go," she says, looking at the clock. "I need you to stay here with Jace. I have somewhere to be."

Ellie's heart might be in the right place, but by being vague with the *somewhere to be,* I automatically suspect the worst. She's going out with a guy. She's partying. Living it up. And I'm the one playing clean-up for her mistakes.

"Listen. The other night was, frankly, bullshit. It's fine if you want to have friends over, but you need to have a little respect. I had to clean up for you and get Jace off to school, and I was late to work. You know I'm going for that promotion, El. It's important. I'm here for you, but we need to get some things straight."

"I *know*. But what I'm doing is important now too," she says, pulling her robe over herself, taking a defensive stance. "I have a job interview."

I cross my arms, surprised. "You do?"

She nods.

This is good news. After she lost the last job, I started to worry she was slacking. She's had a couple of job leads since then, but nothing that resulted in an interview. Up until now, I was starting to think she wasn't really trying.

"Where?" I ask.

"Ted's Pizza. You know, that place we get our takeout from, on Main."

Of course, everyone knows Ted's Pizza. The place has been around forever and serves the most godawful pieces of cardboard coated in tomato sauce, passing it off as pizza. "What will you doing there?"

"Waiting tables."

That's a step in the right direction, but I'm wary. If she's waiting tables during the dinner rush, that means I need to be home to take care of Jace. "What are the hours like?"

"I don't know. That's what the interview is for. To find out."

I'm putting the cart before the horse. She hasn't even gotten the job yet. She might come home and tell me she's decided she doesn't like the uniform or Ted might decide she's unemployable. I'll cross that bridge if she gets the job.

The bridge I need to cross right now is what we're going to do about Jace.

"What about Kelly?" I ask. She's our back-up sitter, but she has her own family to take care of and usually needs an advanced notice. "You think she's available?"

Ellie shrugs and looks at her phone. "I don't know. But I have to get to the pizza place by nine."

"Nine?" I grit my teeth as I check the clock. Our meeting with Courtney is at nine-thirty and right now it's twenty after eight.

"That's what they said," she says. "I wouldn't have said yes if you'd have told me about this meeting."

Fair enough, but I wasn't expecting her to have a job interview on a Saturday morning either.

"I'll reach out to Kelly," I say with a sigh, pinching the bridge of my nose. "You need to get going."

I scoop my phone out of the pocket of my pajama pants

and call Kelly. Thankfully, she's available for the morning. I make plans to drop Jace off there by nine and pick him up before noon. That should be enough time.

With those plans in place, I jog upstairs to get ready for the day. As I'm passing the guest bedroom, I find Jace, lying on his stomach on the carpet, playing with his toy cars.

"Hey, kid. Your mom's got a job interview and I—"

"—I know, I know," he says sullenly, not looking up at me. "I'm going to Kelly's."

"Yeah, it'll be fun. You love Kelly."

"Not as much as I love you guys."

Break my heart, why don't you...

I take a seat on the edge of the futon, which doubles as his bed. Since my condo's a three-bedroom, Ellie's taken up the guest bedroom, and I let this little monster have what used to be my office. It's not ideal for a Pokémon-and-Lego obsessed kid—it's sterile white, and it still has my desk, my chair, my bookcase from college in it. His toys and things are stuffed in the closet, not that he has much left from the fire.

"Listen to me. I'm not going to be long. I'll pick you up at noon, and we can go have smoothies. Or ice cream. Whatever you want."

He nods, but I guess I haven't sweetened the deal enough because he's not nearly as happy as he was this morning, before I mentioned I had to go in to work.

"Come on, Bud. Get ready for me, okay? Teeth, clothes, and shoes. Let's go." I motion for him to get off the floor, which he does begrudgingly.

Once he's moving, I rush for the shower. Even though I cut my usual morning routine in half, we wind up getting out the door by nine. I drop Jace at Kelly's at nine-fifteen, and then it's on to Foster & Foster in Portland, which is a twenty-minute drive. By the time I park in the garage and walk up Market Street to the office... I'm late.

Not even just a few minutes. Big-time late.

And this might not be a partner, but it's *important*. Being late for a client is a big, glaring no-no, the first rule in my playbook.

The second I rush into the darkened office, I see the light coming from the large conference room. I can imagine Tenley in there, wondering where the hell I am. It's probably the reason my phone has been blowing up—I bet she's been calling and texting me, but I haven't had time to look.

I run for the door, practically throwing myself through it as if it could possibly make up for my tardiness.

Two sets of eyes, on the other side of the conference room, swing toward me. Tenley's expression is just as I expected—it radiates pure hatred. Does she practice looking that hateful in a mirror? Because she's a pro. But our client simply looks confused.

I only know Courtney Perry from her social media accounts. She's pretty and young-looking, despite being a full decade older than me. She's in all black athleisure, her long dark hair pulled into a low ponytail. The puffiness around her eyes leads me to believe she's been crying recently.

Sensing the tension in the room, I snap out of it and flash a smile.

"Hi!" I say, ignoring Tenley's eye-daggers as I sidle over to Courtney's side of the table and shake her hand. "Courtney Perry? It's so great to finally meet you. I'm Brooks Gentry, the other half of your dream-team. Sorry I'm late, I'll spare you my excuses so we can get to work."

Her confusion gives way to a smile. "Oh, gosh, no worries at all..."

Just like that, I'm forgiven. But as I sit down and look over at the other side of the table, I realize that applies to only half of the room.

"So, Courtney—" I start, looking between them. "May I call you Courtney?"

"Yes, of course." She smooths a hand along her hair.

"I don't mean to interrupt what you two have been discussing, but how are you doing?" I ask, giving her concern. I try to remember that every woman who comes into my office is going through a traumatic experience, so I try to treat every female client the way I'd want my mother to be treated.

"I'm hanging in there," she says. "Thank you so much for asking."

Sometimes it's the little things that mean the most to people in these situations. Simply asking someone how they're doing almost always puts them at ease. I hope Tenley's taking notes.

I continue. "Can I get you anything? Coffee? Tea? Water?"

"I offered that," Tenley says flatly. "She said she's—"

"—Actually, I'll take a coffee if you don't mind," Courtney says, folding her hands and watching me intently.

I don't have to look at Tenley to sense her annoyance at the situation. Courtney didn't want coffee when it was first offered to her but now that I'm here...

"One coffee, coming up. Actually, I'll make that two." I look over at Tenley as I head for the kitchen. "Three?"

"No, thank you." Her voice is neutral. Groggy almost. Given the fact that we worked until almost eleven last night, I imagine she's tired. Makes me wonder if she's turning down the coffee out of spite.

Three minutes later, I return with two paper cups of

coffee. The room was eerily quiet before I stepped in—I get the feeling Tenley was struggling with the small talk. I set a cup in front of Courtney, along with a stirrer, some tubs of creamer and sugar packets. "Forgot to ask how you took it so I brought a little of everything."

She smiles. "That's perfect. Thank you."

As I sit down again, Tenley gives me a hardened squint and says, "As I was saying to Ms. Perry before you arrived, Brooks, matters are slightly more complicated now that James has decided to file for full custody, but—"

"—He's such a bastard," she says under her breath. "I did everything for those kids. He wouldn't even know how to wipe their asses. It's infuriating."

Courtney looks at me for affirmation.

"We agree," I say, sure to include Tenley in this since we're a team and should appear as a united front regardless of our opinions of one another. "Which is why we're not going to let him get away with it."

Courtney smiles at me, and only me. "That's why I know you're the man for the job."

It's as if Tenley doesn't exist.

For the first time ever, I actually feel bad for her.

11

Tenley

I woke from my Saturday nap around eight o'clock, immediately checking my phone to see if it's 8 AM or PM because I slept so hard I wasn't sure at first. After coming home from our meeting with Courtney Perry, where I was rendered practically invisible, I crashed hard, not even bothering to change out of my suit.

Now I'm wide-awake, lying in bed, waiting for Stranger88's response to respond to my latest message. I see the dots dancing, indicating he's responding, and my breath hitches.

Stranger88: *I don't know. Probably a giraffe. I always wondered what it would be like to be that tall.*

I laugh, and it hits me.

Stranger7721: *So you're short.*

Stranger88: *Nope. But it must be great to be that tall. Why? You like tall men?*

Stranger7721: *Yes. Not giraffe tall. But yes.*

Stranger88: *I hope you are not disappointed when you see me. I'm only six three.*

Stranger7721: *Ah, shoot.*

Stranger88: *What's wrong?*

Stranger7721: *Unfortunately you're not tall enough to ride...*

Stranger88: *Height doesn't matter when you're horizontal.*

I fixate on the fact that he said *when you see me*. This is really happening. We've casually mentioned making plans to see each other when these ninety days are up, but I haven't expected either of us to follow through with it. It's just one of those things you say because they feel good in the moment.

Stranger7721: *I really don't even care what you look like.*

The rules of the app state you're not supposed to talk about looks in any specific kind of way, but I'm not sure how they would police that? Surely there are ways around it. A person could easily say, "I have BLU3 3Y3$" and avoid any bots patrolling for rule-breakers.

Stranger88: *You say that now...*

Stranger7721: *No, it's true! I've always been more attracted to someone's brain than anything. Intelligence is the sexiest thing in the world.*

Stranger88: *Agree. Also, one more question. I know you would love to be a dolphin, and I'd love to be a giraffe. But what animal would people say you most resemble?*

Stranger7721: *Hmmm. That's a tough one.*

Stranger88: *Not really.*

Stranger7721: *Okay, so you go first.*

Stranger88: *A teacup poodle.*

I snort.

Stranger7721: *So you're… little?*

Stranger88: *No, I'm just lovable and strangers want to hug me all the time. And I don't shed so I'm hypoallergenic.*

Stranger7721: *Oh good because I'm terribly allergic to anything with fur.*

Stranger88: *Noted. I won't wear my mink boxers when we meet.*

I blush.

Stranger88: *Anyway, you haven't answered the question. What animal represents you best?*

Stranger7721: *A porcupine.*

Stranger88: *Interesting. So you're prickly?*

Stranger7721: *People at work—well, one person in particular—seems to think I am.*

Stranger88: *What happened?*

Stranger7721: *We were meeting with an important client and he made a fool out of me.*

Stranger88: *I don't think that makes you a porcupine. It makes him a dick.*

Stranger7721: *Thank you for saying that!! This guy's a piece of work. The bane of my existence in the office.*

Stranger88: *Maybe one of these days I'll come to your office and you can point him out to me. I've got some good one-liners I can use to put him in his place without coming off like an ass myself.*

Stranger7721: *That would be amazing. I don't think he's ever been put in his place in his life. I'd do it, but I have to a professional.*

Stranger88: *Happy to do it for you. It's not like they can fire me. I don't work there.*

Stranger7721: *Appreciate it.*

Stranger88: *Okay, so let's talk about what we'd do AFTER I put this douche canoe in his place. I'm thinking we go into your office? (Do you have an office?) Shut the blinds. Lock the door. I'd kiss you, soft and slow at first, and then I'd take you right there on your desk, ripping off your nylons so I could spread your legs wide and taste you.*

I swallow, my entire body buzzing. The idea of having sex on my desk at work is one I've never entertained in my life—now I can think of nothing I want more.

Stranger7721: *Sounds dangerous... what if someone heard us?*

Stranger88: ☺*That's why you'd have to be extra quiet. Can you do that?*

In that second, I make a decision. Screw BLIND LOVE's terms of service. If we want to arrange to see each other ahead of time, we should be able to. I bet this happens all the time—people hit it off but they want to meet ASAP.

Stranger7721: *I wish we didn't have to wait so long to meet.*

Stranger88: *Technically we don't have to... I'm sure we could figure something out. There's got to be a way around the messaging parameters.*

Stranger88: *Are you a rule follower?*

Stranger7721: *I tend to be, yes.*

Stranger88: *Me too. It gets exhausting. But we're both consenting adults. If we want to meet up, we should be able to.*

Stranger7721: *It's hardly been a week. Isn't this kind* *of fast? And doesn't it defeat the entire purpose of the ninety day rule?*

Still, the idea of meeting him sooner rather than later makes my heart kick it up a notch and sends a hitch to my breath.

I'm clearly under stress and not thinking straight.

Also, Stranger88 is my refuge from reality, but if we meet in real life, he'll become a part of my reality and then I won't have... whatever this is.

I type, erase, then retype words, to that effect, about five times. Doubt creeps in. Or maybe I'm simply trying to talk myself out of this. What if he's been lying to me all along, catfishing me? What if all of this is just in my head?

Do you want to meet now?

I type the words, wondering what he'll do.

BLIND LOVE'S terms of service state that if you violate their rules, they can immediately terminate your account. In a heartbeat, I could be disconnected from Stranger88 forever, without a chance to meet him or find out know who he truly is.

I can't take that chance.

I delete the message.

Then I type in my phone number.

What if they have software that blocks emails and phone numbers? They probably do. So I delete that too.

Stranger7721: *I need to think about it some more.*

We should let things simmer for a couple more months. If I'm right, it'll only get hotter, and we'll be even more connected.

As I'm staring at the screen, waiting for his response, my phone buzzes with a call from the Women's Center. It's odd that they're calling me this time of night, so I take it.

"Yes?"

"Hi, Tenley, it's Francine, at the center. I hope I didn't wake you?"

Wake me? It's not even nine yet.

Actually, no, it's after eleven. Where did the time go?

And my voice probably did sound rather breathless and out-of-it, the result of too many hot texts with my stranger. I swallow and try to sound more professional. "No, of course not. What can I help you with?"

"I just wanted to tell you that Rhonda called. She's moving out of state."

"*What?*"

"Yeah... apparently her boyfriend is moving to Alabama, and she's going too."

I let out breath. Rhonda didn't have a boyfriend. At least, not last week. Or maybe she did, and she didn't tell me about him. Maybe there were a lot of things she didn't tell me. When I ask my clients to place her absolute trust in me, sometimes, they can't do that. They're ashamed of their behaviors, of the choices they made to put them in dire straits. I can just imagine Rhonda telling Francine this story. So happy and full of excitement for the future. But Rhonda didn't tell me directly, because deep down, she knows what I'd say and she knows this is a bad choice and that I'd try and talk her out of it. Her resources are here. Her life is here. The only support she has is here. Moving out of state could set her back... or worse.

It's not that I don't want Rhonda to be happy. But she has three kids with three different boyfriends, and each one of those men has chipped away at her, making her feel less than. She falls in love too easily, desperately wanting someone to depend on, because she feels she can't depend on herself. She's low hanging fruit and the men in her life take advantage of that.

But Rhonda is also brilliant. She's whip-smart, intuitive, and has a keen business sense. When it comes to work or studies, she can do anything she sets her mind too. It's those damn boyfriends who are her kryptonite.

A while back, I'd gotten her training at the career institute, and she was passing every class with flying colors. For the past six months, we'd been making so much progress, getting her that new job, standing her up on her own two feet... and now this.

Rhonda's a lovely person. But she trusts too easily.

I work in a place where marriages go to die. I volunteer at a women's center, seeing women stripped of their choices every day. I have no memory of my deadbeat father.

Not all men are bad, of course. There are plenty of good ones. Amazing ones, really. It's just that in my experience, they've been consistently disappointing.

I drag a hand down my face. "Oh no."

"Yeah, I thought you'd be upset."

"I am."

"But listen. I have a new mentee for you. Her name is Ellie. You have a meeting with her this Wednesday."

"Okay. Thanks. I'll be there. Have a good weekend."

I end the call and stare into space, thinking of Rhonda and her kids. Maybe they'll be happy in their new life. Maybe this time she's finally leapt with a man who will treat her well. I want to call her, but that isn't protocol. We can only help people who want the help. I can't make her do anything she doesn't want to do.

The only thing I can do is hope that she made a good decision, and that it all works out for her.

Sometimes I have to wonder if I'm really making a difference after all. Sometimes it feels like banging my head against a wall over and over. I have to wonder if Ruth ever felt that way.

I want to share my frustration with someone. Thankfully, I know someone who will totally get it.

But when I toggle back to the BLIND LOVE app, I see:

Stranger88: *You there?*

Stranger88: *Hello?*

Stranger88 has signed off.

It's probably for the best. He is a man, after all. And if I can't trust any man in real life, what makes me think I can trust one online?

12

Brooks

"You're doing it!"

The delighted cry comes the second I hear Jace shuffling down the stairs.

I can't see him though, because I'm underneath the air hockey table, tightening the last of the screws.

"Told you I would," I say as I spin the screwdriver.

I am a man of my word, even if that word's gotten pretty dusty, sitting on the shelf as long as I've left it there. At least I managed to do it before Jace started getting interested in girls.

"Let's play! Let's play! Let's play!" He's dancing around, chortling. I hear something that sounds suspiciously like an air-hockey-puck, hitting my wall, and I think he probably doesn't even need the table.

"Hold on, dude. Just a little more..." I finish tightening the last screw and wiggle out from under the table, then set it straight as I notice several dark scuff marks on the otherwise white baseboard. Perfect. "And... done. What do you say I plug this in and we give it a whirl?"

He claps his hands. I find the outlet and make the connection. Then I flip the red on-switch as he gets the paddles ready.

We both stare, expectant, waiting for something to happen.

Nothing does.

I flip the switch, again and again, as if that'll do something. Then I check the outlet, the fuse box, everything. Meanwhile, Jace is having a bang-up time, playing hockey on my floor, banging the puck against the white baseboard incessantly, leaving a little black dent every time.

By the time I decide the thing's just broken, he's lost interest, staring out the window. "Can we go outside and play frisbee?"

I'm still staring at the busted air hockey table. Can I return it? The box is in pieces on the ground. I don't have the receipt, and it's been over a month. Probably not.

Fantastic.

I rake my hand through my hair and look over at Jace, who's bouncing like he needs to go to the bathroom. "Sure. Yeah. Let's go."

We go out to the common area. Our condo complex includes a huge grassy field with tennis courts, a pool, a picnic tables, a gazebo. It's early June and not quite warm enough to use the pool, but there are a few people hanging out at the picnic tables. Frisbee with Jace involves me lightly tossing the disc to Jace, only to have it go through his hands. Every. Single. Time. Then he'll rush to retrieve it, and try to throw it to me, and it'll go three feet and land between us. Predictably, he gets out of breath and bored in about five minutes, so we decide to walk to the park, where he gets on the jungle gym and meets another kid who wants to play pirates.

It gives me some time to sit on the bench at the perimeter of the playground and check my phone. The first thing I do is go to BLIND LOVE to see if Stranger7721 is on.

She's not. And she hasn't replied to my last message.

It makes me a little antsy. We have to keep their streak going so we can hit the ninety days in a row and unlock the ability to exchange numbers and photos. If one of us misses a day, we have to start over. And we've already gone fifteen days. I don't want to reset the clock back to zero, because the truth is, I think about her.

A lot.

Way more than I expected to think about someone whose face I've never seen. I love how she makes me feel whenever we talk. She can brighten my day unlike anything or anyone else, and when I'm talking with her, I forget about the stress of the job, my home life, everything. When I haven't talked to her, I feel on-edge.

Which is probably why, though I'm sitting in the sun on a perfect June day, I can't stop checking my phone, wondering what she's up to at this moment.

Maybe she isn't thinking about me nearly as much as I think about her. Maybe this is all a joke. I know very little about her.

She could very well be some dude catfishing me for the fun of it.

I might not know her... but I feel like I do. And I know she's a sweet, intelligent, very feminine workaholic who turns me on more than I expected to be from a simple online message. I've never had this kind of banter with anyone. She matches my energy. She has an actual personality. She doesn't hold back. There's depth to her and every time we chat, that depth becomes deeper.

"Aargh!" Jace rushes me with a stick he's pretending to use for a sword, stabbing me in the chest with it.

It's surprisingly painful, catching me off guard.

"Whoa, kid. You got me." I look around for his buddy. "Where's your first mate?"

"He had to go to baseball practice."

I scan the area. He's really gone, no trace of him around. I need to pay better attention to my nephew.

"Aw, too bad. What do you say we go get those smoothies?" I ask.

He jumps up and down, pulling on my arm.

We return to my condo, climb into my car, and head out for the closest smoothie place, in downtown Yarmouth. Sahara Smoothie Café is hopping when we pull into the parking lot. Everyone's taking advantage of the nice weather and had the same idea we had, because there's a line out the door. I bet it's at least an hour wait.

Even so, I can't tell Jace no, so we get out of the car and stand at the back of the line on the sidewalk. I check the menu on my phone.

"What do you want... strawberry banana? Or... there's one here with orange juice and pineapple and mango?" I ask.

He nods right along with every suggestion.

I forgot I'm talking to a six-year-old. It's better not to give him too many options.

"I'm going to get the Sunshine. It's pineapple and mango and strawberry. You want that?" I nudge him.

"Yeah!"

"Cool." Great, so we know our order. I look over the heads of everyone, toward the front of the line. It hasn't moved. Apparently, people up at the front of the line aren't as well-prepared as we are. It's going to be awhile, and Jace is already jumping around, as antsy as I am to get another message from my stranger. I clap my hands together. "So..."

He looks at me.

"You make your move on the girl that sits next to you?" I ask.

He shakes his head, staring at the floor. "I think she likes Jackson."

I can't take the kid getting down on himself.

"What? Why? What's this defeatist crap? You're twice the man Jackson is." Okay, I don't know who Jackson is, but it doesn't matter. "You just need to go there and tell her—"

I stop when he gets this petrified look in his eyes.

"Let me guess. You still haven't talked to her yet?" The expression on his face tells me everything I need to know. I crouch in front of him and take his shoulders in my hands. "Dude. You need to talk to her. School's going to be out soon, and if you want to see her over the summer then you need to ask her soon. If you do, and she says she's not interested, okay. At least you know. You don't want to spend the whole summer living with regret. Do you?"

It's strange, giving dating advice to a kid, but I'm trying to teach him a valuable lesson—the importance of being yourself and going after the things you want in life. The worst thing that could happen is she shrugs him off or says no, and in that case, he'll learn another valuable lesson about how to handle rejection.

"Okay. I will." His voice is quiet.

"Good." I pat his shoulder and stand up as the people in front of us take a step—actually, more like a half-step —forward.

Progress is progress.

Glancing at the gas station across the street, I notice a woman with a dark ponytail, in yoga pants and a form-fitting hoodie filling up her car. A guy with a mustache is at the next pump over, leering at her as she ignores him, studying the rising numbers on the display. Another guy in a Mustang drives past, watching her so intently that he goes through the red light.

She looks familiar, but I can't place why.

In another life, I'd have run across the street to chat her up. It wouldn't have taken much. I'd have told a few jokes, worked my charm, and walked away with her number. One, maybe two nights later, she'd be under me, screaming my name and clawing the hell out of my back with her nails.

But things are different, now...

The woman behind me clears her throat and I realize that the line has taken another single step forward. I pull Jace along with me and he starts to play with the old free newspaper dispensers outside the shop's door. "Sorry."

Then I look back at the beauty across the street. She's heading inside to pay for her gas, all male eyes on her, and that feeling of familiarity grows. It's her walk. Long, fast strides. Purposeful. Driven.

Holy shit. Is that Tenley?

It is. I can tell by the *stay away from me while I accomplish my goals* scowl on her face.

I can't stop staring, even after she goes inside. Probably because I have never seen her outside the office or in anything other than those frilly, high-necked blouses. It's like when you're in high school and you accidentally see your teacher in the supermarket and realize they actually have a life outside of the classroom. It opens up a whole new world, and so many questions. You see them in an entirely different light and it's never the same again.

She comes a minute later, sipping on a giant red slushie.

Shit. Why didn't I suggest slushies to Jace? We'd be in and out by now and I could've run into Tenley, and...

Actually, let's be real—she would've growled at me and told me to get the hell away from her.

But I have to admit, she looks damned good in that outfit; it's hugging that tight body she always tries to hide under thick fabrics and bland, neutral colors. She's turning even more heads as she opens the door to her car, and part of me wants to storm over there and tear those losers new assholes.

Hell. Why do I care?

The woman behind me clears her throat again, and I take another step, so we're almost through the door.

By the time I look back again, Tenley's gone.

13

Tenley

Stranger 7721: *I got it in, 21 minutes under the wire!*

I breathe a sigh of relief as I hit "send." I'd almost let twenty-four hours pass without talking to Stranger88, and I can't let that happen.

I've been so busy with this case that as much as I wish I could have a nice long conversation with him, our schedules haven't been meshing. It's been a message here, a message there... but no deep, all-night-long back-and-forths.

Unfortunately.

We have sixty days left.

As I'm thinking about him, I hear the elevator doors ding. Shocking since most people don't start arriving until closer to nine. But it's an even bigger shock when I look up and see Brooks walking off the elevator car.

To top it off, he doesn't swagger past my office with his *I'm better than you* smirk. He actually stops and deigns to look in on me. "Hey."

I put my phone aside and glance up at him before going back to my work. "Hey."

"Good weekend?"

What part of us working together says that I'm open to casual chit-chat? That's not what we do. It's not what we've ever done.

"Our meeting's not until nine," I remind him.

There's that smirk. I know what he's thinking, *There's such a thing as tact, and you don't have it.* But he's wrong. I am sure I could be lovely at small talk, if it mattered to me. But I don't care about it. Where chatting with Stranger88 means something because it helps lift my spirits, the same cannot be said for chatting with Brooks.

Meaningless small talk is a waste of time, and I have things to do. So many things, in fact, that his simply being here, smirking at me, is an obnoxious distraction.

I wave him off. "Please. Go."

He doesn't. Instead, he gives me a mock-surprised look. "You don't want to discuss the Courtney Perry situation? Thought it was a pretty big deal. But okay..."

He starts to walk away, leaving me to wonder what the hell he's talking about. Courtney Perry is *our* client. Of course I want to discuss her situation. But I thought I had everything with the case under control.

"Right. We're meeting at nine to discuss that," I say.

It hits me then, how invisible I'd felt at that last client meeting. How well he and Courtney had jived. How happy she was to have him—and only him—in her corner, making her coffee, telling her everything was going to be okay. I've always prided myself in being a doer, an advocate. I'm not a hand holder. I'm a no-nonsense shoulder to lean on. I've always intended for my demeanor to empower women, not coddle them.

With Courtney, I'd done everything right, gone above and beyond, and yet that morning I was reduced to an invisible and useless third wheel.

Courtney Perry has both our business cards, but if she needed her attorney, there's no doubt who she'd call first.

"Wait." I jump up. "What situation are you talking about?"

He stops. Turns. And puts on this confused act, "You haven't heard?"

"Obviously not. What's going on?"

"I spoke with Courtney yesterday evening," he says. "She called me in a state. Needed to talk."

Of course she considers *him* her shoulder to cry on. Not me. He's the cute one, the charming one, the one who was acting like her lap dog, fetching her coffee and snacks. And being tall, dark-haired, with an athletic shape—he's not all that different from her soon-to-be ex, James Perry. If she's looking for a replacement, she's found him. A mix of unexpected jealousy and rage bubbles in my veins, but I inhale deeply, trying to keep it from unleashing. "And what did she say?"

"She found out that before they got married, James transferred all of his property and assets into his mother's name, making it look like he owns nothing."

"Okay, but the two of them built Periwinkle—"

"Yeah. But he bought it all before. It's in his mom's name. The whole business is."

I gape. Somehow, all this non-stop research I've been doing didn't reveal that nugget. It's not like me to miss something so huge. I blame the stress of the promotion and the excitement of my online stranger.

"Damn it." I exhale, massaging my temples."

He nods. "She could get royally fucked in this."

Over my dead body will I let another manipulative man rake his partner over the coals and walk away a winner. I grit my teeth and point to him and then my desk.

"In. Now. Close the door," I say. "Malicious intent. We've got to prove malicious intent. That's going to be key here."

"I knew you'd be pissed." He sits down and draws the chair closer to my desk. "I was as well."

Wow. First time we've ever agreed on anything.

"You could've called me. You have my number," I say.

"I thought I'd let you enjoy the rest of your weekend."

I snort. "I never enjoy my weekends. Remember?"

"Right. I forgot," he says, and to my surprise, he motions to the file, ready to get down to business. "The only thing she has as a bargaining chip in this deal is custody of her kids and she's not going to give that up for anything. She wants full, sole custody. She told me that, over and over. I don't know if that's realistic, and I told her that, but she's beside herself. If she wasn't in battle mode before, she is now."

I look up at him. I can't blame Courtney for feeling that way, but what gets me is Brooks's delivery. He sounds not just like her attorney, but like her friend, someone personally invested. "She told you all that?"

He exhales and nods. "She's losing it, T."

That pulls me right out of the case. "Did you just call me *T*? Like the letter?"

He frowns, as if he's having trouble thinking back to the last thing he said. "What's wrong with that?"

I could say I don't like it. I've never had anyone use a nickname on me. Even to my friends, I've always been Tenley. But oddly, I kind of like it, though I'm not sure why.

I let it go.

"We've got to take this guy down," I say. "It's the kids who are going to suffer here, being used like pawns. Cases like these, it's never about custody. It's about not having to pay alimony and child support. It's about having the upper hand. My dad did the same thing to my mom. He left her, she refused to give him the full custody he was demanding, so he checked out completely. It was never about me or the custody. Anyway, after that I was raised having absolutely nothing. It was the worst. I don't want that to happen to Courtney's kids."

Brooks tilts his head.

"Yeah, agree. I know what that's like though I wish I didn't." He points to the file. "You ever get that police report for the DUI in?"

I stare at him, dumbfounded. *He* was raised by a single mother with absolutely nothing too?

And here I've been loathing how easy everything comes to him.

How does one come from absolutely nothing and wind up going to an Ivy League college?

Is Brooks Gentry... an underdog?

Our eyes connect for a beat too long, and his start to fill with confusion, then concern. That's when I realize he asked me something, and like a spaz, I'm just staring open-mouthed at him, lost in my own thoughts.

"Oh. Yeah." I rummage through the papers and find it. "It's kind of bare. Says they were coming home from a wedding in Kennebunkport and got pulled over on the Maine Turnpike going ninety, weaving all over the place. She had a blood alcohol content of .16, which is twice the legal limit."

He reads it. "She told me he was driving."

I blink. "What?"

"He made her switch because he was fall-down-drunk, way worse than she was. She didn't want him to drive, but he insisted. They were arguing and he wouldn't give up the keys. And she was terrified. There's abuse there—not physical but emotional. He's a typical asshole, control-freak type, taking advantage of her."

I grab the report and look at it. "So she was afraid to disobey him. Afraid of losing everything."

He nods, looking down at his hands. "It's a shitty position to be in."

I watch him as he says those words, and now I'm starting to understand why he connects so well with Courtney. At first, I'd thought it was a romantic thing, which is completely inappropriate. But now, I suspect it may be something different.

No wonder he'd been so incensed when I assumed he'd been given everything in life on a silver platter. Sounds like maybe life hasn't been all privilege and ease for him like I thought?

"You were raised by a single mom?" I ask.

His eyes meet mine and for the first time, there's nothing smug or arrogant about the way he's looking at me.

"Yeah," he says. "I was."

"She put you through Yale?" I ask.

"Harvard," he corrects me, "Then Yale. And no, she didn't. She would have if she could have. I got a full ride for playing football."

"Huh." Crossing my arms, I lean back, studying him in a slightly new light, imagining him pulling himself up by his bootstraps, working his ass off at a top university, and landing a good job.

Why does that sound like someone else I know?

Oh, shit.

I refuse to even entertain the possibility that Stranger88 is Brooks Gentry, so I push the thought as far away from my mind as possible. "All right. What's our next move?"

14

Brooks

The call comes in while Tenley and I are working in the conference room.

"We should just go through it all, line by line." Tenley drops a giant binder in front of me.

I grimace. If there's one sure way to bore me to death, it's that. Apparently, James Perry was involved in a lawsuit with a couple of his waiters a few years back who alleged he wasn't paying them fairly. It's a stretch, but anything we can do to throw shade on his character at this point is a win.

We've been balls-to-the wall all week, getting everything ready for the courtroom.

So much so, the only times I've been able to converse with my stranger have been after midnight. We've been keeping the streak up, though I can't say either of us have been getting much sleep.

It's okay. When I'm talking to her, it's just as invigorating as sleep. It's refreshing and relaxing all the same.

But damn if I don't drag through most of the day when I'm supposed to be dazzling the partners for this promotion.

Doesn't matter. Being in the courtroom invigorates me, too. With the case we're building, I know I'll knock 'em dead. And that's what matters. Results. That's what's going to get me this partnership.

"Brooks?" Shelly, the executive assistant, pokes her head in.

I look up, everything swimming around me. I didn't shave this morning because I finished talking to my stranger at seven and I needed to get Jace up and to school because Ellie was hungover again. I can usually hide the lack of sleep, but I'm going on my fourth day of hardly any sleep and it's catching up with me.

"Yeah?" I ask, which turns into a yawn.

"You have a call. From a Mrs. Johnson."

I blink, and it takes me a while to process the name. Mrs. Johnson, from Sapphire Shores Elementary. Jace's school. Why is she calling my office? She usually calls my cell if she needs me which is rare since she's supposed to call my sister first.

My sister. Who is...

Connecting the dots doesn't happen automatically, but eventually understanding trickles in. Where the hell is Ellie? I'd left her hungover in her bed three hours ago.

And my cell phone is off. I've been turning it off every day while working with Tenley. It's a requirement to be in a conference room with her.

"What's the problem?" I ask. "Did she say?"

She shrugs. "She wants you to call back. She said it was urgent."

Tenley gives me a concerned look as I get up and go

outside, grabbing my cell phone from my pocket. I switch it on and go into a stairwell before making the call.

"Mrs. Johnson. It's Brooks Gentry. You called about Jace?"

"Yes, he threw up today at recess. He has a little fever. He's with the nurse now, but he needs to be picked up within the hour."

"I see," I say, relieved that's all it is. This should be no problem. Ellie can go and pick him up. Which reminds me. "Ellie should be able to—"

"I called your sister. Three or four times. There was no answer."

Shit. She was still drunk this morning and smelled like a human Oktoberfest. I don't know when she stumbled to bed, since I was chatting with my stranger, but if it's like the past few times she's gone out, it was probably after four.

She could be sound asleep. But this late? My mind goes to all sorts of bad outcomes. Traffic accident. Alcohol poisoning. I've heard of that, of people going to sleep after a long night of drinking and never waking up. Or someone could have slipped something into her drink and she's out cold. "All right. Tell him to hold tight. I'll be there."

I end the call and try my sister. Once, twice. Nothing.

My mind spirals to an image of her lying cold and dead in her bedroom.

And here I am, at work, as if nothing's wrong.

The alarm bells going off inside build as I go to my office, grabbing my things in a whirlwind. As I'm about to leave, Tenley pokes her head in. "Half day?"

I ignore the fact that she seems so triumphant over giving me a dose of my own medicine and shake my head. "Emergency at home."

She leans against the jamb. "Really."

"What's that supposed to mean?" Because, color me shocked, but it sounds like she doesn't believe me.

She shrugs. "It's just funny how conveniently you get called away for an emergency, right when we have all those depositions to slog through."

I suck the inside of my cheek. I don't have time for this. And I know what that look she's giving me means, but I don't have time to give her an explanation, nor do I need to. It's a private family matter.

"I'm working from home the rest of the day. Call me if you need me." I stalk over to the conference room and pile the giant binder into my arms, then turn around to find her watching me. I maneuver past her, trying to tuck the unwieldy thing under my arm. "I'll be back in tomorrow bright and early with my thoughts."

She says nothing, though she doesn't have to—her stiff posture says it all, but she can believe what she wants. I know she thinks I'm a slacker who's always had it easy, but I don't have to prove anything to her. Despite our miniature heart-to-heart earlier, when I swore she was looking at me in a totally different way than ever before, she's not as unthawed around me as I'd hoped.

If she only knew that I never talk about my past to anyone.

At least, not in a professional setting.

Honestly, I'm surprised I opened up to her at all. I was just thinking about the Perry kids, and how awful this divorce could go for them, and I guess I was musing out loud.

I'm waiting for the elevator, when I catch her still sitting in the conference room, watching me, a look of mild concern on her face. It's small, but it could be a sign she's wondering if she misjudged me. Or maybe she's trying to figure out what she thinks of me, processing what she wants to believe with what she's starting to see.

Either way, I don't have time to think about it.

I manage to wrangle the binder from Hell into my car and drive all the way to the school, picking up my ailing nephew from the nurse's office, who falls like a rag doll into my arms.

Once he's in the car, Jace leans his head back, breathing hard. I put a hand on his forehead. He's hot, clammy. I don't have a barf bag and he looks like he might puke again. "Just take it easy, Bud. I'll get you home in a jiff."

I do, thankfully, without incident. Gathering the kid's dead weight into my arms, I go to the front door and push it open, looking around.

No Ellie.

The place is exactly as I left it.

"Brooks?" Jace moans, his eyes closed, his breath hot on my neck.

"Yeah. I'm here. Let me get you to bed."

He mumbles something as I'm bringing him upstairs.

"What's that?" I ask.

"I talked to the girl."

I set him up in his bed, bringing a trash can over, in case he needs to puke again. "Who's that, Bud?"

"Peyton. The girl I was telling you about."

"Holy sh—*shizzle*. You did? My man." I hold up a hand for him to give me five but he's too out of it. "What did she say?"

"She said she'd think about it. But she's going to be in my class next year. And she said if she was going to marry anyone, it would be me."

"Hey, that's good!"

He doesn't seem nearly as excited as he should be. Then

he starts mumbling some gibberish, which can't be good. I feel his forehead, wondering what a mom would do in this case. It's really hot. Do we have medicine? Unfortunately, I have no clue where the medicine—or his mom—is, and I'm woefully uneducated when it comes to these sorts of situations.

I go to the bathroom and rummage around the medicine cabinet, finding a bottle of children's Motrin. I read the fine print on the bottle but the font is impossibly tiny and it may as well be in another language. I have no idea how much to give him. I don't even know what he weighs. Forty-five, fifty pounds maybe?

I need Ellie.

In the reflection of the mirror, I notice the door to her bedroom is closed.

Walking across the hall, I crack it open to find it dank and stuffy inside. It also smells like stale beer and cigarettes. She's in bed, face down. I creep over and hover above her form, trying to see any sign of life. But there is none. Her blonde hair is splayed over her pillow and her skin is pale.

My heart stops cold.

Until she lets out an enormous snore.

I exhale a huge breath.

"Hey," I say, pushing aside her blankets to find she's still wearing her clubbing outfit. She even has one shoe, still on. I nudge her. Then louder, "*Hey.*"

She moans a little.

I nudge her harder. "Your son is sick. How much Motrin do you give him? Or..."

I trail off. Maybe Motrin isn't right? Can he have Tylenol? No idea if kids can swallow gel caps at this age or how much of that to give him.

Her left eye cracks open, and then she suddenly sits up in bed. "What?"

"Yeah. Hello? The school has been calling you. He threw up at recess."

That startles her into action. "Why didn't anyone..."

"Trust me. We did."

Popping out of bed, she runs to the bathroom, grabs some medicine and heads into his room. The next thing I hear is her talking baby-talk to him, "Hey, baby, you're not feeling so well? Let's see if we can get you better!"

That's good. The kid needs his mom. I'm a poor substitute.

With that handled, I go downstairs, take a seat at the kitchen table, and grab the binder. I open it and scan the first page, my eyes crossing as I start to read.

A little bit later, I'm about to get up and make some lunch when Ellie comes in, scrolling on her phone.

"Jes-us. You'd think that he was suffering with the plague for how many times they called me. Heaven forbid he sit in the nurse's office for an hour."

"You weren't around," I say evenly. "I had to clean up your mess. Again."

"I'm doing the best I can. I'm working, at least."

It's true, she is. But Ted's only gave her two nights a week. The rest of the time, she's going out with friends. Guess who has to stand in and babysit? I turn to her.

"Listen to me. When you work, I watch Jace. But when I'm working, I need you to step up and be his mom. Half the time, you're acting like someone with zero responsibilities. I don't know what's going on lately, but this has to stop."

She snorts and sulks, just like a sullen teenager I accused her of being. "You want me out of here? Is that what you're getting at?"

"No. I want you in here. But only because of Jace. If it was just you, I would've kicked you to the curb weeks ago. You're acting like a privileged little snot, you know that?"

She cocks her head, arms crossed. "Would a privileged little snot work for crappy tips?"

"Two nights. Two nights a week, Ellie. That's hardly working. Someone has to be the adult around here. I'm not having Jace suffer for your poor decisions."

"Fine, *Dad*," she mutters, storming off.

Sometimes that's exactly how I feel.

I stalk to the fridge and open it, finding it empty. So much for Ellie going grocery shopping like she promised. I always leave her enough cash, and there's a shopping list on the fridge, but does she ever take the initiative? No.

This is how my mom must've felt as a single mother with two kids and zero help, but at least she always made sure we got to school on time and had food in the house.

I'm too tired to order in, so I rifle through the pantry but nothing whets my appetite.

Grabbing a nearly full bottle of Johnnie Walker, I pour myself a glass and take a drink, letting it calm my nerves. Then I go to the couch and open up BLIND LOVE, hoping that Stranger7721 is on.

But of course she isn't.

It's mid-day.

She's probably nose-to-the-grindstone, like I should be.

I look over at that binder and groan, rubbing my hands down my face.

This is my life—for now.

Maybe for the next twelve years.

Playing Most Important Person in the World to a kid I didn't have any say in bringing into it. And while I'll never resent him for it, I can resent the people whose poor choices and inability to accept responsibility got us here. I'll be damned if I let any of them hurt him.

I scroll up to past conversations with my stranger, wondering when she'll finally pop on.

Because right now, I feel the full weight of being alone against the whole damn world. And though I know damn well it's not realistic to want someone I've never met... I kind of need her.

15

Tenley

This is out of control.

I tap my fingers on the conference room table and check the time on the clock over the door again.

Now, he's *ten* minutes late.

Typical Brooks, only on time when a partner's involved and he can ingratiate himself so they'll offer him the partnership. In other words, *when it matters*. And clearly, I don't.

He was supposed to read that binder and report back to me. I trusted he'd do that. I bet he didn't. He'll probably waltz in here, thirty minutes late, and try to work his charm on me. And when I get upset, he'll turn it around and tell me I need to loosen up, and *I'll* be the bad guy.

I drag in a haggard breath and let it go.

Shooting up from my chair, I walk out into the hallway, expecting to see him chatting up one of the interns. Only he's not. I go to his office next, but the door is closed.

Asshole.

My face is hot and I'm sure I look like a witch as I storm down the hallway because several co-workers turn and stare and a couple of guys chatting in front of me quickly move aside as if they don't want to be caught in my destructive wake.

I don't care. This is unacceptable.

I'm trying to do the best for our most high-profile case and he's dead weight. I knew this would happen. I knew I'd be doing most of the heavy lifting here. Just like with school group projects in the past, I'm the one doing everything while other people get the credit.

I've never been one to snitch, but given the promotion on the line, the partners should know about this. I'm done being a doormat. And I deserve this partnership, not Brooks. If I don't speak up for myself, no one will.

Only when I reach Ed's door, it's closed.

I head to Tom's office next, only his door is shut too.

Lisa's my last resort, just because of the way I saw her succumbing to Brooks's charms in that last meeting. But still, this is nothing personal. It's business. She wants the best for the firm, and she'll be pissed as hell if anyone jeopardizes this case for us. His dimples and disarming gaze won't be so charming after that...

Not that I've been looking.

Unfortunately, though, her door is closed too. When I reach it, Shelly pops out from her desk. "You need something, Tenley?"

"I was just..." Where are they all? Is Brooks with them? Why do I get the irrational feeling that they've prematurely handed him the partnership and they're all out celebrating together on someone's yacht? That's just the type of thing that would happen to me... and him. "Are all the partners out today?"

She nodded. "They're in Barbados. For ILC."

"Oh. Right." The International Law Conference. The partners always spend a week in June in some exotic locale for it. I've never even been out of the country, so I'd kill for something like that. It's another dangling carrot I don't need, since I'm already chasing this partnership as hard as I can.

I turn to leave, then realize that Shelly can help me. She might not like me much, but she's the first contact with the partners, and will be keeping them apprised of the situation here. If I put a bug in her ear about Brooks slacking, it'll get back to them.

"Oh, um, did Gentry call in? We were supposed to have a meeting and he didn't show. After leaving early yesterday... I just hope he's okay?" I ask with forced concern.

She nods. "He's out today. He didn't cancel the meeting?"

I sigh deeply, really milking it. "Oh. No. Oh, gosh, that's terrible. We have a lot of work to tackle for the Perry case. That's a shame. I guess I'll just try to power—"

"It was an emergency so he probably forgot. Sick kid."

"Oh, I'm sure," I say, feigning sympathy. "I know how—"

I stop.

What was that?

Sick *kid*? Since when did...

My mind spirals out. Kid? Okay, I've joked about his way with women, but nowhere in our banter has he ever indicated that he wasn't every bit a single, unattached bachelor.

I'm picturing Brooks Junior, a smaller, cuter version

with a matching that smirk. Maybe he has a wife? *No...* not possible. I've worked with this man for a year. Surely he'd have mentioned it by now or at least have some kind of photo displayed where all the cute interns could see it.

I'm probably still gulping like a goldfish, because she says, "So... he's probably at home, if you need him. Do you have his number?"

I nod my head and wander back to my office, so deep in thought that it's a miracle I find it.

There's something off about this.

Is it possible he's lying? Could he lie that big just to get out of work because it's a beautiful day, there are still a few women left in town he hasn't conquered, and he doesn't want to tackle that binder? Truthfully, *that* sounds more plausible than Brooks Gentry, the consummate Casanova, having a kid.

After handling a myriad of divorce cases, I've learned sometimes men do ridiculous things to cover up their transgressions. My mother never talked about my father very much, but one thing she did say was that he was the worst of liars. He was a charmer, but he lied as naturally as he breathed.

Is this a lie?

By the time I get to my office, the curiosity's practically clawing at me, so I decide to take the bull by the horns and text him.

Tenley: *Sorry about your sick kid.*

Tenley: *Did you manage to read the file you brought home?*

I gnaw on my lip, wondering if I should have sent that second message. I probably could've eased into it a little better. *There's such a thing as tact, and you don't have it.*

Oh, well. Too late now. I watch for a few moments,

waiting for a response, but it just shows as delivered, not read.

Somehow I can't imagine him sitting at a kid's bedside playing nursemaid. The image is actually comical, like an octopus wearing gym shorts.

I manage to get through as much as I can with the case before I have to leave. It's my first meeting with my new mentee, Ellie. Apparently, Ellie is in her mid-twenties, and grew up in Sapphire Shores. She's a single mother who has been living with family and trying to get her life back together after a devastating fire ripped through her apartment last year.

As I walk to the Portland Women's Center, I imagine what my mother would've done, had a fire taken away what little we had. If it had happened while she was putting herself through paralegal school and trying to raise me? She'd been at the end of her rope and would've likely just let go. A tragedy like that is terrible, but when you're scratching and clawing to earn a living and barely making it in the first place, it's enough to make most women give up entirely.

My job is to make sure that doesn't happen to Ellie.

When I get to my makeshift office at the center, I go through her file. Ellie Garner. The writing on the application for assistance is shaky, as if we're her last hope. She's twenty-four. Has a son who's six. Father unknown. Dropped out of high school when she was eighteen. Works part-time waiting tables, not nearly enough for anyone to make ends meet or dig themselves out of their circumstances.

There's a knock on the door, and Francine pops her head in.

Francine is big, blonde, full of energy, and always smiling. Despite the sad cases that come in here, she's always a ray of sunshine, instantly putting everyone in a better mood.

"Ellie's here," she says. "You ready?"

"Sure." I rise. "Send her in."

The young woman comes in right behind her; a slip of a thing with dark-blonde hair in a ponytail, an Under Armor T-shirt, sweatpants, and Converse high tops. She looks like she borrowed her clothing from the teen boy's section at a department store. There are dark rings under her eyes, which don't meet mine as she tentatively perches on the edge of the chair across from me.

"Hi, Ellie," I say with a smile.

She piles her hands in her lap and sighs. "Hi. I don't know why I'm here. You probably can't help me."

"I've never met a person I couldn't help," I tell her with a smile to hopefully put her at ease. Pointing to her file, I say "I know you've been through a lot, and it might seem like you're at rock bottom and there's no way of climbing out. But there is a way, and I'm here to help you find it. You don't have to do this alone."

She finally meets my eyes, though there's doubt in hers.

"It says here, you live with family, is that right?" I ask.

"Yep," she says, biting her lip. "I think they want me out sooner than later though. I feel like a burden. Can't do anything right. Makes it stressful, you know?"

I nod, "Completely understand. It certainly doesn't make any of this easier feeling like you don't have a place to call your own."

She gathers a long breath. "They think I'm a failure who'll never amount to anything. I want to prove them wrong, but... it's hard."

"You will. You'll prove them wrong. I'll make sure of it."

"Yeah." Her posture softens, a sign she's growing more comfortable with me. "I was working so hard, trying to get ahead. And every time I see a chance when I might finally be able to breathe, something comes along and punches me right in the gut again."

I give a sympathetic smile. "I know exactly what you mean. I'm here to make sure those punches don't knock you out next time. But you have to promise me that you're going to keep fighting, all right? You only lose at the game of life when you stop playing."

"Did you read that on a calendar or something?" She cracks a sly smile at my cheesy saying.

"Probably," I chuckle. "I find when this whole thing feels overwhelming, sometimes it helps to think of your why. You have a son. Is he your why?"

Ellie nods. "My *only* why."

I think of my mother, and how she once told me I was the biggest motivator she had, something Ruth had kept pointing out every time it seemed insurmountably difficult to push forward. Right now, I want to be Ellie's Ruth.

I reach over and touch her hand. "And I'm going to help you do that."

Tears fill her eyes, but she blinks them away. "Thank you."

And that's why I do this. Not for the fame or notoriety. I don't need to be a figurehead on anything. I just want to give other struggling women a hand up so that they can push back against all the hands that are continually holding them down.

In order to do more of that, I need resources. I need the flexibility and the extra money that making partnership is going to give me.

The second I show her out, I check my messages. Gentry still hasn't responded. I can just imagine him hung over, lying in a bed in a room that smells like sex and perfume, milking this "kid" excuse of his for all it's worth.

He probably doesn't even have a kid.

16

Brooks

"Brooks?" a voice says, weak, timid.

I look up from the screen of my laptop and find Jace nestled among the pillows on the other side of the sectional. The hair over his forehead is spiky with sweat, and his cheeks are two apples. He looks miserable. Guessing his fever hasn't broken.

"Yeah, Bud?"

He doesn't say anything. I think it was more that he just wanted to know he wasn't alone.

Ellie would be here if she wasn't working her shift at the pizza place. It's been a couple days since I picked Jace up at school and had that little come to Jesus talk with her, and she's been on her best behavior since. She hasn't gone out clubbing, at least. I'm not sure how long it'll last. Probably until this weekend, when her drinking buddies text her about the next big party.

Whatever. Baby steps. She's working, so that's promising.

I reach over and massage Jace's little foot. "You want something? More Motrin? An ice pop?"

He shakes his head and his eyes drift closed again.

I turn back to my laptop.

I've been messaging with Stranger7721 for a couple hours. A rare treat, since it's not even nine yet. I was so excited when I got on and saw the green light by her name. Apparently, she decided to call it an early day today.

Stranger7721: *You've been on early, these past few days.*

Stranger88: *Yeah. Taking a few days off.*

Stranger7721: *Must be nice... can't remember the last time I had a day off.*

Stranger88: *You never take vacation or anything?*

Stranger7721: *Vacation? What's that?*

Stranger88: *What's that saying? All work and no play...*

Stranger7721: *I'm not dull. I'm just busy. It won't always be this way though. One day, I want a husband, kids, and complete control over my schedule, workload, and free time.*

Stranger88: *The American dream. How many kids do you want?*

Stranger7721: *At least six.*

Stranger88: *Six? Kids? Seriously?*

Stranger7721: *I'm kidding. At least two. Maybe three. I was an only child and alone a lot while my mom worked so I always wanted a big family. What about you?*

Stranger88: *I basically helped raise my younger sister. I feel like I've already had the 'dad' experience.*

Stranger7721: *So you don't want kids then?*

Stranger88: *Maybe one. Someday. Not any time soon.*

Stranger7721: *Why's that?*

Stranger88: *With my work schedule it wouldn't be fair to the kid or my spouse.*

Stranger7721: *Ah. True. But you could cut back on your hours. If I had the right partner, we could make it work. Might be hard, but I think it'd be worth it. But it should be a 50-50 deal. The woman shouldn't have to do it all.*

I couldn't agree more. So many divorces happen because the woman gets stuck doing it all, only to wake up one morning and realize it's not worth it anymore and she might as well do it on her own anyway. In every case, the husband almost always acts blindsided despite the writing being on the wall for years.

I don't ever want to be *that* guy.

I look over at Jace. There's so much that can go wrong when it comes to raising kids. So many ways to scar them for life. Jace is a good kid, perfect even. And yet, every day, there are arrows flying right at him. Even the best guardian can't shield him from all of them.

Stranger7721: *After seeing my mom do it alone, I know how hard is. I don't want to do it alone. I need a man who will be my equal partner, and those types are hard to find.*

Stranger88: *My sister's a single mom too. It's not easy.*

Stranger7721: *But would you do it? Would you be a single dad?*

I look over at Jace. Sometimes, you just have to.

Stranger88: *Yeah.*

Stranger7721: *I'd even give up my job for my child, if I had to.*

Stranger88: *Looks like you finally found something you'd love more than your job.*

Stranger7721: *Don't tell my boss.* ☺

I laugh so loud that next to me, Jace lets out a moan and rolls over.

Stifling it, I type more.

Stranger88: *What day are we up to?*

She responds almost immediately.

Stranger7721: *Only 56 left. I'm keeping count.*

17

Tenley

Highlighter in hand, I groan as I page through the binder, shaking my head.

Across the conference table, Brooks is calm, almost amused, leaning back in his chair as if he's proud of himself. "I take it you're not happy with my performance?"

I snort. "Are you serious?"

"Entirely."

A bitter laugh escapes my throat. I don't care that he said he came from a single mom—this is what happens when you grow up being told all your life that your bare minimum is worthy of a trophy. I jab the binder with the cap of my pen. "Did you even read through this whole exchange here on page 326?"

I take his silence as a no.

That's what I get for trusting it to his quote-unquote *capable* hands, for thinking he was going to take care of things. He's been out of the office for two days, and from the look in his eyes when he stuffed that binder under his arm, I thought he was really going to try to show me how dedicated he was to this case.

I couldn't be more wrong. He's nothing but a slacker who thinks he can cover his many, *many* inadequacies by pouring on the charm.

Not this time.

Sick kid. The more I've been thinking about it, the more I'm certain that the *kid* was an eighteen-year-old co-ed he picked up at a club somewhere. And sick? He probably couldn't look at the binder because he was too busy giving her sexual healing.

I throw the highlighter down. "This is just shoddy work. I'm going to have to go over it myself."

He crosses his arms. "I beg to differ. It's solid work."

I laugh again.

"But enjoy. If you want the torture, feel free to go over it line by line." He presents it to me like it's some prize I won on a game show.

"I don't want to. I *have* to. Because my partner dropped the ball." I glower at him.

He leans in. "Admit it, Bayliss. You're only finding fault with it because it's me and you don't like me. And because you can't bring yourself to admit that I did a good job at anything because you're convinced I'm a shit lawyer."

"Are you kidding me?" I scoff. "You did a terrible job."

He stares as if he's waiting for me to crack.

I will not.

An Ivy League educated attorney should be able to produce sterling work every time. And yet his is just... awful, like he was throwing together a homework assignment at the last minute hoping to turn it in for a passing grade.

I page through it a bit more, stopping when I see he used color-coded tabs to point out items of interest, and he made several insightful comments in the margins—things I probably wouldn't have thought of myself. It's all pretty damning to James Perry's case and makes him look like a real scumbag, which *should* make me happy.

But it took him three days to deliver this to me, and when he did, he slid into the conference room like an oily snake and said, "Thank god I'm back, right?" as if he'd been the one holding things together in *my* absence.

Earlier today when he stepped off the elevator, you'd have thought George Clooney had waltzed in the way everyone was making a fuss. I kept expecting someone to pop a bottle of Cristal or throw an impromptu welcome back party.

Brooks is still looking at me. Arm propped on the arm rest, holding his pen, clicking the button on the top of it. Not rhythmically though—sometimes fast, sometimes slow, no rhyme or reason, as if he wants to keep me guessing.

Click. Click-click. Click. Click-click-click.

I meet his steely gaze with one of my own. We stare each other down so long I swear the temperature in the room skyrockets.

He's not going to stop, is he? He's just going to keep staring like that, forever.

Clicking.

Does he blink?

Why the hell won't he blink?

He's definitely not stopping. The clicking is tortuously obnoxious, and I can't hold much longer without going off on him.

I blink and look away. "I have to get to work to fix this."

He stands the second I do. "Where are you going?"

"My office. I don't need any distractions." I head for the door.

"So I'm a distraction?"

I glare as I pass. "You and that pen of yours."

"I'm the bane of your existence?" He asks, a hopeful tinge to his voice.

"Worse than that."

"Great," he calls after me. "Mission accomplished."

I slam the door to my office. Instantly I regret it. I don't want anyone to know he's gotten under my skin. I stalk to my email and see a message from my paralegal.

Excited, I click on it, until I read her message: *Nothing interesting to pin on James Perry. All seems perfectly in order so far. Still digging...*

Bleh. We have a decent start on establishing James' character, but it's not enough. I was hoping the financial records would hold the smoking gun and I could wave it around in triumph, especially in Brooks's smug face. I'd used my connections at the women's center to find a pro-bono forensic accountant to help with the case, and she's been going over the numbers for me, partly so I won't have to bother the partners, and partly because it'll give me a leg up on that promotion.

Unfortunately, it doesn't give me that much of a leg. Yesterday, as I was going through the files, I found that Brooks has been emailing a professor at his law school for advice on the case. The two of them are tight. And the insight he's been providing? Pure gold.

I can't help but wonder if this is his strategy—make me think he's slacking off so I don't try as hard.

I knew this would become a pissing match, but I never thought we'd sacrifice our client's humanity and our professionalism in the process.

I type in a quick thanks to my assistant and lean back, staring at the binder and thinking about all colorful little tabs Brooks placed inside.

Sometimes I wish I didn't hate him so much. It'd make all of this easier.

Last night, I took out Old Reliable again, except once again, as soon as I came, I saw Brooks's face. I'm still trying to understand why. I've always been attracted to him. Physically, anyway. He's easy on the eyes—any woman alive could tell you that. I suppose there's nothing wrong with having a fantasy about a completely made-up man that happens to look *slightly* like Brooks Gentry...

It's just a harmless fantasy, after all.

As I open the cover of the binder, a text comes in.

Brooks: *Come on back. I found something.*

I jump up and practically trip over my feet to get to the conference room, where he's sitting, phone out, smirking, feet actually crossed and on the table. That takes balls. I don't even think I've seen the Fosters do that.

He looks up as if surprised to see me.

"What?" I demand.

"What?" He looks confused.

Okay, this is bullshit. "Are you in third grade? Didn't you just text me you found something?"

He shrugs. "Oh. Right. I didn't find anything. I just knew that was the only way to get you back here. And I'm lonely."

He's doing this on purpose, trying to annoy me. First it was the pen, now it's this. What's his angle? What's his game here?

I cross my arms and just stare at him. Seriously? He's going to play it this way?

"I'm not an intern," I remind him. "I don't delight in keeping you company."

He pouts. "I know. But they're all gone. Everyone's gone. And I can't work alone."

"You are a child."

"Perhaps. Or perhaps I just know that if the partners see us working separately, they won't be happy with either of us."

He has a point. I roll my eyes, then go back, get the binder, and throw it down across from him. "Happy?"

He nods, but I don't think he's happy I'm here—he's happy because he got me to do his bidding.

Trying to ignore him, I start to go through the binder. The closer I look, the more impressed I am at his comments. Maybe I shouldn't have snapped at him before.

I look up, wondering if I should apologize. But he's in the middle of reading something in the file.

I take a second to study him, truly study him. The man is so good-looking, it physically hurts. There isn't a single flyaway hair on his perfect head. His muscled shoulders strain against his suit jacket, like the thing can hardly contain him. And his lips are soft and on the fuller side, but not too full. For a second, I think about what it might feel like to have them on me. Then I shake the ridiculous notion out of my head.

I shift in my seat, trying not to think of last night's fantasy of him bending me over the desk and pressing his body against mine, but of course that's all I think about. I need to think of something else. Puppies. Rainbows. Flowers in springt—

His eyes suddenly blink up, focusing on mine.

Before I can look away, he says, "Why are you doing that?"

I wore a low ponytail today, and I realize I'm twirling a lock of hair, gaping like some lovestruck teenager. "Doing what?"

"Looking at me that way?"

"What way?"

He makes a face as if to say, *You're the idiot who was doing it.*

I make a clicking sound with my tongue, hoping my face isn't getting red and betraying me. "If you didn't notice, you're *right* in front of me. When I look up, I see you. *Unfortunately.*"

"Mm." He doesn't believe me.

I stand up. "Should we order food? I think we should."

He shrugs. "Might as well. Going to be a late night."

We get paninis from some place he knows, and then we burn the midnight oil, discussing the case. When we talk, which is seldom and only ever about the Perry case, it's weighted with tension.

Not sexual tension.

Just regular tension.

I think.

He's Brooks Gentry. If he wants to have sexual *anything,* he probably knows better than to do it with me. There's so much low-hanging fruit where Brooks is concerned, he never has to look up if he wants to get some. Plus, he knows he doesn't have a chance in hell with me. He's not about to waste his energy on a lost cause.

"You're doing it again," he says.

I blink and realize he's right. I'm staring at him, lost in thought.

What the hell is wrong with me? No, I don't have much sexual experience. Hardly any at all since I spent almost my entire college career holed up in the library studying. If I ever had needs, I had my vibrator to take care of me. I was perfectly fine denying that part of myself until the right man came along. Or if he never did, I was fine with that too.

But there's something about Brooks that both infuriates me and...

... gets me hot and bothered at the same time.

"I'm thinking," I say.

His eyes narrow. "About... ?"

This time, my face really does go red. I can feel it. I'm too flustered to think on the fly, and he can see it because the corner of his mouth quirks up into a half-smirk.

I need to take a break. To get out of here. To cool off. "Let's take five."

He's staring at me now, his gaze heavy, smoldering almost.

It's like a tractor beam, pulling me in. I can't move.

"You said you were going?" he asks.

His phone buzzes. He grabs it and smiles in a way that lights up his whole face. God, he's sexy as hell when he smiles. For a moment, I wonder what it would be like if he smiled at something I did or said. Then I realize he probably got a text from some girl he's seeing. Maybe it's the eighteen-year-old 'sick kid.'

Why does that depress me to no end? I have someone too. Even if it is Stranger88 and I've never actually met him. We have a deep, meaningful connection. A friendship, even if it's virtual for now. It's nothing like what Brooks and his flavor-of-the-week have, which is probably just sex.

Hot sex.

It pains me to think about how skilled he probably is in the sack. It'd be much more satisfying to assume he's a three pump chump who can't find the clit to save his life, but I highly doubt that.

For a second, my mind wanders into dangerous territory, imagining how steamy sex with Brooks would be.

What am I doing? I *shouldn't* imagine. Not here, of all places.

Which reminds me. I haven't checked BLIND LOVE all day. I'm treacherously close to ruining our streak.

I grab my phone and open the app, finding a new a message from Stranger88. My fingers fumble to open it as a grin spreads across my lips.

Stranger88: *Working late. Stuck working a case with that ass-kissing coworker I told you about. Wish I could be lying in bed, messaging you instead.*

I look up. Brooks is staring at his phone, as if he's waiting for something.

No. It can't be.

There's no way.

I've had inklings of it before, but always dismissed them.

Pure coincidence. Right?

It has to be.

I suck in a breath, trying to decide whether to respond right away. I don't want to make it obvious. And if I did... and then *he* started to respond?

I don't think my heart could take that.

Nope. No. Not happening. I tuck my phone away and get down to business, trying to keep that horrific thought out of my head.

My kind-hearted, compassionate Stranger88 is *nothing* like Brooks Gentry.

18

Brooks

It's after midnight by the time I get home. Tenley refused to quit until she could hardly keep her eyes open, and even then, I practically had to lock her out of the conference room so she'd go home.

"Hey." I set my keys on the table by the door.

Ellie yawns from the couch, where she's watching some late-night talk show. "Hey."

"Good day?" I ask.

"Same as always."

I head to the kitchen. There are cereal bowls in the sink—Ellie's go-to when I'm not around to buy or prepare dinner. But I'm choosing my battles here. At least she's not up in her room, getting ready for a night on the town. This is a step in the right direction.

I go to the fridge, crack a beer, and stand in the doorway, watching television. "Jace okay?"

"Yeah. He's back to his old self."

"Good. You taking him to school tomorrow?"

"Why wouldn't I?" She wrinkles her nose. I don't appreciate being gaslit or dismissed, but I don't have the energy for a battle right now.

"Cool."

I take a swill of beer when my phone buzzes. Fishing it out of my pocket, I find a message notification from the BLIND LOVE app.

Stranger7721: *I don't think you ever told me what you do. What kind of case is it?*

I take the steps two at a time, eager to get upstairs so I can start another all-night-long conversation with my stranger. After checking in on Jace, who's out cold, I power up my computer, strip off my button-down, pull off my belt, and get to work.

Stranger88: *Can't say much about it. Bound by confidentiality.*

Stranger7721: *Sounds important. What do you do anyway?*

Stranger88: *I can tell you but then I'd have to kill you and I really don't want to do that because I'm really looking forward to you screaming my name in a couple of months.*

Stranger7721: *Ah. Well, since you don't know who I am or how to get in contact with me until day 90... I'll take that chance.*

Stranger88: *Sorry. My lips are sealed.*

Stranger7721: *That's fine. So tell me about this ass-kissing coworker?*

Stranger88: *I don't want to talk about her. I've been working all day and I'd rather talk about anything but work.*

Stranger7721: *Same. Actually, I can't really talk. I'm exhausted. Just checked in to keep our streak going.*

She might as well have just told me she hates my guts and never wants to talk again, because disappointment engulfs me like a blanket, and all I can think about is this long, lonely night without her. The little somersault my stomach does every time a new message pops up is like a fucking drug. I can't get enough.

Stranger88: *All right. Let's talk tomorrow.*

Stranger7721: *For sure. Goodnight.*

Stranger7721 has left the conversation.

I stare at those words until they blur in front of me.

I can't shake the feeling that something's changed, though I can't imagine what it would be. Maybe she started dating someone in real life? I don't meant to jump to conclusions, but she's never been this distant. She's never turned down a late night chat.

Things in Ellie-land have been icy ever since I got pissed off at her over missing the nurse's call when Jace got sick. I need to smooth that over. No better time than now. Maybe it'll take my mind off the feeling that I said something wrong to my Stranger.

I go downstairs, where Ellie's sitting in the same position as before, mindlessly scrolling through her phone. Collapsing on the couch beside her, I try to ignore how she stiffens, and ask, "So how do you like the pizza place job?"

"It's a job."

"Are they nice there?"

She shrugs. "Sure."

"You get a lot of tips?"

This time, I get a grunt out of her. She's really not engaging, so I decide to switch gears.

"Hey, so, I saw this ad for community college. They have a medical assistant program. I think you'd be really good for it. I got the number of an advisor you can talk to, if you want..."

She looks up from her phone, the light from the screen illuminating the annoyed expression on her face. "What on earth makes you think I'd want to be a medical assistant? You know I get nauseous at the sight of blood."

Ellie lifts the remote, powers off the television, and storms up to her bed, mumbling something about how she's never good enough for me.

All I was trying to do was help...

I just want the best for her—and Jace.

I lean back against the cushions of the couch, pressing the palms of my hands into my eyes.

This day. Talk about hell. One explosion after another. And all I tried to do all day long was the right thing.

Hopefully one of these days soon, Ellie will get on her feet again and I'll be able to come home to a quiet house after work. I can't remember the last time I had a second to breathe in peace. And I can't remember the last time I wasn't constantly worried about making sure Ellie and Jace had everything they needed.

Squeezing my eyes closed, I imagine living alone again, and then I picture Stranger7721 waiting for me in the doorway when I arrive. She's smiling, holding a drink for me, giving me a kiss and telling me she missed me the second I walk through the door.

Everyone should be so lucky to come home to that.

I squeeze my eyes tighter and envision her with that smile and drink, nothing on but an apron...

I have no idea what she looks like, but it doesn't matter.

It doesn't even have to be sex.

All I know is that my life would be a million times better with her in it.

19

Tenley

"I just don't know what to do," Ellie says as she sits across from me at Beans Café.

I've often imagined the discussions my mom had with Ruth, back when I was a little kid, and my mother had no idea where her next meal was coming from, much less how she was going to keep a roof over my head. I think they might have gone something like this. With the fear. The indecision. The powerlessness of not knowing how to break free of the chains tethering her to poverty and hopelessness.

My mom did it though.

So that's why I know Ellie can too.

She looks different. Today she's in cut-off shorts and a big, chunky pink cardigan despite the heat. It's sagging off one impossibly bony shoulder, exposing her black bra strap. Her fingernails are bitten to the quick, and she's wearing at least half a dozen silver rings, spread out over fingers that are wrapped round her mug.

I smile at her as she sips her coffee. It's Saturday, and this is an informal meeting. I got the feeling that when I'd met with her, she was holding back because she was embarrassed to even be seeking help at the center—which is normal. Asking for help is hard and humbling. This time, I thought we'd take it someplace a little more casual and relaxed so I can get to the heart of the matter and make a plan to help her.

"It's understandable," I assure her. "The future is uncertain, and it feels like there are so many steps you need to accomplish. It's like looking up at Mt. Everest and trying to imagine climbing to the top. That's daunting. But you know, that's why climbers on Mt. Everest take it in stages, a little at a time. They don't do it all at once. They can't. They have to acclimate to each stage. And that's what you need to do. So what is your first step?"

She wipes her dyed-blonde bangs out of her pale blue eyes and shrugs. "I don't know. I don't know what I want to do with my life. I never have. When I think about picking something... I feel stuck. Like what if I'm no good at it? What if I pick the wrong thing?"

"Those are the kind of doubts that hold you back, and that's all they are—doubts. So what if you try and you fail? You'll be in no worse position than you are now. But if you succeed?" I lift my hand, gesturing.

"I know, I know. It's just taking the first step." She titters a little, wrapping her hands tighter around her coffee mug. I think if she didn't, they'd be trembling. She's so high-strung. Lots of nervous energy. I imagine one surprise would send her shooting up to the ceiling.

"I get it. But what is that first step? Just meeting with an advisor? The hardest part about that is going to be making the appointment. Action spurs more action. Once you do that, it'll set the ball in motion. And then you'll start gathering momentum and no one will be able to stop you. I guarantee it," I say.

She takes a sip of her coffee, studying me. "You know, you remind me of my brother. He's a lawyer too. People like you usually don't understand people like me. We're cut from a different cloth. He came out of the womb thinking and acting different than everyone else. Like he was *better* than everyone else. You're like him, but *so* much nicer. I can talk to you, and you actually listen."

"Well, maybe some of us can act like we're a different species. But I promise you, I'm not. My mom was a struggling single mom too, and I have what I have because someone helped her. That's all." I sip my coffee, realizing it's the first time she's talked about her family in an individual sense. Before she just said that her family was no help. "What kind of law does he practice?"

"Family law."

That's interesting. Maybe I know him. "Locally?"

She gives me a concerned look. "Look, I don't want this getting back to him. He has no idea I'm doing this mentor program, and I want to keep it that way."

I lift an eyebrow. "Why's that? Sometimes it's good to have extra support and encouragement, especially at home."

"Because he's a pain in the ass when he's right about anything. Which is all the time." She smiles. "He's always telling me what to do... sign up for this, take that class, try this program. I know he means well, but it's overwhelming. Plus, if I took one of those classes, I'd never hear the end of how right he was. He'd say, *Look at you now! All because of me!* I found this women's center program on my own, and so it feels like something *I've* done, not like something someone told me to do. You know? So I want to keep it to myself for now."

"I get it." Still, family law? Ellie's last name is Garner. Do I know any Garners who practice law in the area? No. Also, he could easily be a half-brother with a different last name. Or maybe she's been married in the past and changed hers? She doesn't want to discuss him, though, so I let it go.

That said, I know plenty of attorneys who love to rub your face in it when they're right. Brooks Gentry being one of them.

For a second, I imagine Brooks being Ellie's brother. They have the same blue eyes, dark arched, almost-black eyebrows. But it's easy to connect dots when dots are all you see. As a lawyer, I'm trained to look for those connections. It's a habit.

And not really helpful in this situation. Because she's a Garner, not a Gentry. I need to quit thinking about my annoying co-worker, who has been occupying far too much of my headspace lately.

"I'm sure you've given lots of thought to what you should do and what would be a good career to make some money. But what would you do if you knew you couldn't fail?" I ask, hoping it's different enough to distinguish me from her pushy brother.

"If I couldn't fail?" Her eyes light up, telling me that it is. She answers at once: "Culinary school."

"Really? You like to cook?"

She nods, then gnaws on her lip slightly before explaining. "Bake. I did. When I had my own place, I was always in the kitchen, making pies. I was good at it, too. I'm nervous about it now, though. The fire in my apartment was because I was stupid and left the stove on while I was making a glaze. There was a potholder too close, and..."

"Oh. That's awful. I'm so sorry."

"I can't even go in the kitchen, now. I keep thinking of how I failed. And poor Jace—that's my son—I haven't made him a real meal since the fire. My brother doesn't understand. He thinks I'm being lazy."

"We all make mistakes, Ellie. You need to give yourself grace on that. I was in a car accident last year. Just a fender bender, but I didn't want to drive again after that. But you need to get in the car again. Eventually it gets easier."

A smile touches her lips. "I actually saw there's a baking program at the local community college. It sounds amazing."

My jaw drops. Not just because it's nearby but because of the spark that flashes in her eyes when she talks about it. "That's perfect!"

She sighs. "It's fifteen-hundred dollars for the classes, but I can't afford that. I can barely afford the gas for my car."

"Oh, forget that," I tell her. "You're going. Sign up for it. I'll pay."

She looks at me in shock. "Oh no. I couldn't—"

"Oh, yes you can. This is an amazing opportunity. Just make me a triple-layer chocolate cake for my birthday and I'll consider your debt to me repaid." I grin.

"Okay... great.. Let's do this!" This time, when she smiles, it lights up her entire face.

I drive home later with the windows down and the radio up, thinking of Ruth, hoping she's looking down on me with pride, pleased with the way I've carried on her legacy. It's not going to be easy for Ellie, but I feel like we've made a huge step forward. Like things might finally start to turn around for her and her son.

My drive takes me past Foster & Foster. It's empty, since I'm the only one who ever goes in on the weekends.

Briefly, I wonder what my co-worker is doing. When we left last night, I spotted him sitting in his phone, grinning at something, probably planning an evening of debauchery at the clubs with his boys or texting some girl for a booty call.

I force all thoughts of him out of my mind though. I'm having too good of a day to let anyone throw a wrench in it.

When I get home, I'm feeling so good that I actually start to tackle some of the boxes in my condo.

I start with the ones in my bedroom. They're full of clothes I haven't worn since law school—mostly sweats and hoodies. But there are a few interview outfits and nicer clothes I wore when I was about to graduate and was interviewing at law firms. I doubt they'd fit me anymore.

But they'd fit Ellie.

And if she has any interviews for jobs coming up, it'd be a godsend. I grab my phone to send her a text.

Tenley: *Hey, I just found a whole box of dress clothes I don't wear anymore. You want them? I can bring them by tomorrow afternoon.*

A moment later, she responds.

Ellie: *That would be so great. Thanks! I'm home all day tomorrow.*

She texts me her address a second later. It might not be what the average twenty-something is doing, but I'm happy to be able to spend my weekends like this. Changing the world, one good deed at a time—which is more than Brooks Gentry could ever say.

20

Brooks

"Love the suit, Brooks," Kenzie says, her voice a low, sexy whisper as she stands at the fridge in the break room, grabbing her snack. "It's really flattering on you."

I focus on pouring my coffee. Kenzie's been after me since the day she showed up for her internship. I'll admit, attention from a young, pretty college student is hard to ignore and it doesn't feel... bad. But I'd never touch her. It's best not to feed into any delusions she may have about me.

"Thank you," I keep it short, sweet, and neutral.

"The blue really brings out your eyes." Her blouse is undone an extra button today. I know this drill. In the past few months, she's gone from buying my lunches to flirting with me—subtly at first, growing more aggressive each time.

Sorry to break it to her, but *this* isn't going to happen.

I point to her blouse. "Think you missed a button," and start to spin on my heel to walk out, when I realize Tenley is behind me. She has her back to me and is staring at the vending machine as if to decide what she wants.

The glass of the machine is reflective, so she can probably see me in it. Tenley has never struck me as indecisive, so that begs the question: is she listening in to my conversation with Kenzie? Is she stewing over the attention I'm getting for simply existing?

In that case, I decide to milk it just to mess with her.

I can't resist.

It's so easy to wind Tenley up, to get under her skin, and some days any kind of a reaction from her is better than being on the receiving end of her ice cold shoulders.

Turning back to Kenzie, I say, "By the way, is that a new bracelet?"

I take her hand, and she giggles. "Yeah... I got it when I went to..."

Kenzie rattles on, telling me some long, involved story about her trip to the mall, but I'm not listening. Near the door, Tenley has finally made her selection. She feeds her dollar into the machine, presses a button, and a bag of veggie chips falls. I watch as she leans over to retrieve it, and with the slit in the back of her pencil skirt, I can almost see up to her mid-thigh.

Scandalous.

My mouth goes wet and it's all I can see, even while holding Kenzie's wrist in my hand.

Kenzie sidles closer to me, narrowing the space between us and tucking her hair behind her ear. She's so close I can smell the cinnamon gum on her breath. I was only trying to screw with Tenley since she was eavesdropping, but I can't lead Kenzie on. It's not right.

"Hmm. It's nice," I say, still watching Tenley as she opens the chips. "Email me the name of the store when you get a sec. I think my mom would like something like that for her birthday."

Tenley gives me a single, almost disgusted glance, pops a chip into her mouth, and power-walks out of the room.

Meanwhile, Kenzie's still rambling on, saying she could help me shop for my mom sometime. We both know that's *not* the type of help Kenzie is interested in giving me.

"Thanks," I say, dropping her hand and heading out the door in time to catch Tenley walking into her office.

Damn, she looks good today. It's warmer, so she's traded in her blazer for a little blouse with pearl buttons. It's puritanical, but the blouse is so sheer I can see the same camisole from my fantasies under it. The entire ensemble hugs her curves like nobody's business—the perfect combination of sexy and sweet.

I can't take my eyes off of her.

In a perfect world, Stranger7721 would look exactly like Tenley. *That's* my ideal type. Not only accidentally scorching hot, but poised and put-together. Unapologetically ambitious. Whip-smart. Takes no shit from anyone.

While I'm salivating after her, Tenley turns in the doorway, almost as if she knew I was there admiring her. "I hope you can take enough time away from your *other business* to talk about the case today?"

She glowers past me. I look over my shoulder to see Kenzie, looking like a wounded fawn as she watches us.

Other business? Nice.

In my attempt to get under Tenley's skin, I reinforced her belief that I'm the resident intern-fucker. Not my smoothest move, but nothing I can do about it now.

"I have no other business. This case is my number one priority," I tell her. "Is that not obvious?"

She clears her throat, looking me up and down. "Not at all."

Our hate-sex would be off the charts.

As I'm picturing how Tenley would gasp as I bent her over my office desk, Kenzie slips by, placing a finger on my forearm. "See you later, Brooks?"

I nod, ambivalent, my gaze still honed on Tenley. "Sure."

Tenley's crossing her arms, revulsion etched on her face per usual.

I'm half tempted to ask her why she hates me so much. Not that she'd answer it. I've asked her before only to get the run around. But I have to know. Not knowing is torture.

The words are on the tip of my tongue until Lisa steps off the elevator, the picture of professionalism in her dark pantsuit, leather briefcase in hand.

She smiles at the two of us, as if she can't see that we're about ready to pounce on each other and draw blood. "Hey, you two. Great to see you working together."

In an instant, all the fight inside me dies. I don't know how I do it, but I swallow the bile in my throat. "Lis, good to see you."

"Everything going well?" she asks.

Tenley doesn't miss a beat. "It's always a little bumpy working with someone new, but we're finding our way."

"And the case?"

"Great." I grit out the words and look at Tenley, who nods.

Lisa pats me on the shoulder. "Wonderful to hear. All of the partners have been saying how well you've been working together. I know I speak for all of them when I say it's still going to be difficult choosing between the two of you."

I might be wrong, but I'm pretty sure she gives me a wink as she heads to her office.

When she leaves, I turn back to Tenley, who looks horrified. She must have seen the wink, too.

I thrust my hands into the pockets of my slacks and saunter closer. "You know she only said it's going to be really hard because she doesn't want you to feel bad when they give me the partnership, right?"

I'm digging again.

I can't help it.

She makes it so easy.

Tenley leans back, glaring. "It must be exhausting, being so ignorantly self-assured all the time."

I chuff. "I'm sorry. Did you not see her two minutes ago? She was practically giving me the partnership with her eyes."

"She was giving you *something* with her eyes, but it wasn't the partnership."

She can't just end the conversation like that. It's clear she has more to say. I lean in. "Clarify?"

She gives me a glance. "Leave."

"Not until you clarify. Just what were you insinuating she was giving me, Bayliss?" I ask, mostly because I just want to hear her say it.

She glances past me, toward the door for a split second, and then her eyes land on me. "A visual blow job, to match the eye-fucking you keep giving *her*."

I stare, sure she didn't just say that. "What?"

Tenley gives me a superior look. "You heard me. You eye-fuck every female in this place. Even me. That's how you get what you want. Like I said, you don't even have to touch them. Maybe you don't even know you're doing it. But you are. But the difference is, I don't buy it. And I never will. You make my skin crawl when you look at me like that. To me, you just look like a smarmy used car salesman. If you could spare me going forward, that'd be great."

Holy shit.

There are few moments I'm rendered speechless, but this is one of them.

Hearing those wicked words coming from that pristine mouth? It's enough to knock me sideways. Because Tenley Bayliss isn't nearly as innocent as her façade would imply. All those f-bombs from that soft, sweet mouth of hers?

Talk about hot.

21

Tenley

I never realized rush hour traffic sucked this bad.

Of course, I'm never usually in it. I always get to work too early and leave too late to ever be a part of the long line of cars leaving Portland.

But today I'm in the thick of it as I haul the box of clothes over to Ellie's along with an envelope with fifteen hundred dollar bills for her tuition—my investment in the future of her family. I know, as someone who has lost everything, she'll be able to put all of these things to good use and chase her dreams at the same time.

When I get off I-295, though, and the GPS takes me through a relatively upscale section of Sapphire Shores, I start to wonder if all is not as it seems with Ellie Garner. A few minutes later, I pull into a new-looking complex called The Portside, parking in front of a gorgeous building with shiny black framed windows and modern, clean lines.

This place is better than mine, with a view of the Maine

coastline. Ellie said her brother's a family law attorney, but if he can afford a place like this, why can't he give her tuition money?

I decide it's none of my concern as I pull into a parking space. She obviously feels as though she's outstayed her welcome here, and she needs to get back on her feet. That's where I come in.

I wrangle the box of clothes out of the passenger side of the car and head to the front door of condo number 112, ringing the doorbell. A second later, a little boy with dark hair and a chocolate milk mustache answers in a Portland Pirates jersey. It's got to be Ellie's son.

"Hi, there," I say with a big smile.

He's eyeing me with suspicion. I'm surprised he's allowed to answer the door for strangers, but I'm not here to judge.

"Is your mom home?" I ask. "I'm a friend of hers."

He shakes his head warily.

"Oh, okay. Well, I just brought her something. Do you think you coul—"

I stop when a male voice inside says, "Hey. You're not supposed to answer that. Who is it, Bud?"

Before I can react to the familiarity of the sound of his voice, he appears.

Brooks Gentry.

When she said her brother was a family law attorney, the last person I expected it to be was him.

He's still wearing his button-down shirt and slacks from work, where I left him not an hour ago. He looks slightly more deconstructed, though, more rugged, his hair tumbling more into his face, his shirt unbuttoned to the breastbone and untucked, his shoes off.

I hate that deconstructed Brooks is even hotter than office Brooks.

It's not fair.

Also, what are the odds?

Slowly, my mind works through the irony and impossibility of the situation.

Brooks seems just as shocked as I am, but he manages to speak first. "What are you doing here?"

I hold up the bag. "I'm dropping off some things for Ellie."

His eyes narrow. "How do you know my sister?"

He looks down, his hands on Jace's shoulders, and in that moment I think someone is playing a cruel joke on me.

"We're friends," I say. It's protocol not to reveal how we know our clients at the women's center unless they give us the go-ahead.

"This is... Ellie doesn't... you don't..." He lets out a long breath, and now he just looks angry. His voice doesn't match his expression, though, when he pats a very confused Jace on the shoulder and says, "Hey, Bud, go on inside and watch the end of Paw Patrol, okay?"

The little boy nods, still looking suspiciously at me, and runs off.

So that must have been the kid that was sick the other week...

He steps toward me, pulling the door shut behind him, and lowers his voice to a whisper. "I'm sorry, this isn't making sense. I've seen the kind of people Ellie's friends with and you're not it. What's really going on? Are you stalking me?"

I sniff, tempted to throw a "you wish" in his face.

"I have some clothes to give her," I say, "interview clothes. Professional clothes."

He squints, confused. But I can't betray her trust.

But before I can say anything else, he notices the envelope of cash in my hand. "Why are you giving her this money?"

"Because she needs it," I say, not wanting to disclose the culinary school thing. Ellie made it clear she wants to prove she can do this on her own, without his help or judgment.

"Damn it, Bayliss." His voice is still a whisper, but I've never seen him so pissed before. "Tell me why you're suddenly showing up at my front door with money for my sister? And don't bullshit me either."

"That's rich coming from you," I say. "Why don't you ask her yourself?"

He drags his hand through his already-messed up hair, like he's done that a few other times since he's been home from the office.

"Ellie's been through a lot," he says, "I'm the only thing she's got. If she's asking for money from people she hardly knows..."

"It's not like that."

"Then what's it like?" His hardened gaze pins me into place. He's not going to let this go. If he doesn't get it out of me right here, right now, he's going to pester me at the office until I cave.

"She's taking steps to better her life. That's all you need to know. You should be proud of her. That's all I can say," I tell him.

He looks surprised, but only for a moment. "And the check is for...?"

"Tuition." I leave it at that.

"*You're* paying for it?" He says it like it's a bad thing.

I shrug. "It's what I do. If you took a second to get to know me, you might learn a thing or two about me."

He lets out a bitter laugh and shakes his head. Then he steps aside. "Come in."

He says it like he wants to give me a stern talking-to. As if I did something wrong. I follow him anyway, because I know what Ellie told me about her brother. She said he doesn't understand how hard it is for her, for single moms. If I can *make* him understand, then I'll have done my job and things will be even easier for her from here on out.

As pass the dining room, there's an air hockey table where a dining one should be, and moving onto the living room, I'm stepping over toys that are scattered everywhere.

He leads me into a kitchen full of stainless steel and dark wood, masculine and modern except for the kids' finger-paintings on the refrigerator, dirty sneakers on the counter, and a dinosaur book bag piled by the back door.

He pulls out a chair for me. "Sit, please."

Very polite of him. What a great host. I lower myself into the chair, cross my legs, and lace my fingers together on my knee, as if this is business meeting. Then I say, "I hope you're not going to try to talk me out of it."

He tilts his head. "That's exactly what I'm going to do."

The impertinent bastard. He thinks he knows what's best for her, just because they're related? No wonder Ellie didn't want to tell him about this or ask him for help. He's impossible.

I stiffen and move my legs away, so I won't accidentally brush against anything of his. "Good luck. I'm in Ellie's corner, not yours. I'm here to help her."

The superior look on his face gives way to annoyance. "You don't know Ellie, not the way I do."

"And?"

"And this is a private family matter."

"Maybe she doesn't want your help, ever thought of that? Maybe you're just another man limiting her options."

"Limiting her options?" He repeats.

"Yes! She wants to be a chef, and this opportunity is perfect for her because—"

"She's lying."

I stop. "What?"

"Ellie is messed up. She has been, ever since she was a kid. She's a compulsive liar. There likely isn't a training program. And a chef?" He winces. "Ellie couldn't boil water if she tried. She can microwave some Easy Mac, that's about the extent of her abilities."

I blink. "She doesn't bake pies?"

He shakes his head. "*Pies?* I wish. This kitchen is perpetually empty of things to eat."

"She said her place burned down because she was making a glaze on the stove..."

"I'm sorry you believed that," he says. "She left a candle unattended on her nightstand. The heat kicked on, blew her curtains into it. Just lucky no one was home when it happened. Feel free to Google it if you don't believe me. Search up Sapphire Shores apartment fire, you'll find an article."

Suddenly I feel stupid, like I've been knocked off the high horse I rode in here on.

I stand up. "Tell her to keep the clothes. They'll be good for interviews or office jobs or whatever she wants to do."

"I appreciate that." He hands me the envelop of cash.

I hesitate in the doorway of the living room. I thought Ellie and I were starting to connect, that she trusted me. When she told me about her struggles with her brother, about her personal tragedies, I believed her. And yet, it was all a scheme to get money and sympathy.

"I'm sorry," he says, and I believe him. "Ever since the fire, she's been on a bit of a downward spiral. She and Jace been living here while she tries to get back on her feet." He seems genuinely affected by it, scrubbing a tense hand down his stubble-covered jaw. "I'm doing what I can to help. But it's not a straight path out of the hole, you know?"

I know. I absolutely know.

"Thanks for trying to help, Bayliss," he says as he walks me out.

In the parking lot, as I'm sliding behind the wheel of my car, something comes to me.

Sick kid.

Brooks wasn't lying about that. He was taking care of his nephew.

And what did I do? Instead of offering him sympathy, I insisted he bring a slew of work home and then bitched at him that I didn't think he'd done it well enough.

Oh god.

But how was I supposed to know? He's an arrogant bastard at work, constantly doing everything he can to get under my skin (when he's not schmoozing). Now I'm thinking I had him all wrong. Maybe that charming façade and over-inflated ego are nothing more than a mask, hiding his soft, gushy center.

Could it be?

Is it possible that Brooks Gentry actually has a heart?

22

Brooks

I'm sitting in the conference room, going through some last-minute details we need to firm up in our 9 AM meeting with Courtney Perry, when in walks Tenley with two steaming mugs of coffee.

I stare at it skeptically, even when she sets it down next to me. It's black, just like I drink it. Coincidence or has she been paying attention?

"If you were getting coffee for our client," I say, "This'll probably be cold before she gets here. She texted me saying she's running late."

She gives me a look like I'm an idiot. "It's for you."

"Oh." Because of that, I help her push the unwieldy chair out from under the conference room table. Then I stare into the mug's black-brown depths. "It's not poisoned, is it?"

She doesn't crack a smile. "Why don't you drink it and find out?"

Still, it's progress. "Thanks."

"Mm hm." She walks the chair in under the table and picks up her pen, opening a file, ready to get down to business. But I see an opening. And when was the last time I saw one of those? I have to keep the good vibes going.

"How was your night?" I still can't believe she showed up at my door, that she knows Ellie. When Ellie came home from work, I immediately asked it about it, before she had time to slip off her shoes. She filled me in, but only because I wouldn't let her go until she did.

She looks up. "Fine."

"How long have you been volunteering at the women's center?" I ask. It hadn't have been easy to find out Ellie tried to swindle her. I'm sure it stung, especially since she thought she was paying her tuition out of the kindness of her heart.

"Sorry about Ellie."

"I know you are. You told me last night. No need to apologize again," she says without looking up. "No need to apologize for her either."

"I appreciate how generous you are—I mean, were going to be. Can't think of anyone else who'd have helped her like that, no questions asked."

Her face softens and she puts down her pen. "She wasn't playing me entirely. She still needs help. I'm not giving up on her. Won't be giving her any money, of course. But I can give her my time if she needs it."

"She could use a good role model. I'm the only thing she's got and I'm not exactly a strong, female figure," I say. "I mean, there's our mom, but the two of them aren't really talking right now. Long story. I think you'd be a good influence on her."

"That might be the nicest thing you've ever said to me, Gentry."

"Don't get used to it." I wink. "Look, she and I don't get along all the time. But I'm trying. I really am. I gave her and Jace an open invitation to stay with me as long as she needs to. But I know she'd be happier living on her own. She's just having trouble taking those first steps, and I don't know how to help her. She doesn't want to listen to anything I say. Funny. I can win a court case like no one else, but when it comes to her, it's like I'm hitting my head against a brick wall every time I open my mouth."

"Maybe it's your approach. All that charm and wit is useless on family."

I sniff a laugh. "True."

She nods. "Let her know I'm still here if she needs anything."

"Will do."

"Tell me about Jace," she says, a small smile on her lips. I could tell by the way she was talking to him last night that she loves kids.

"Jace? Oh, he's my best bud. He's six. In kindergarten— well, he's graduating tomorrow. So he'll be in first grade. Loves playing with cars and airplanes and trains. And he plays baseball."

Her smile widens. "He's really cute."

"And he knows it."

She rolls her eyes. "Must run in the family."

That's an insult, but she's also smiling, so I don't bother to search for a witty comeback. For once, the mood is actually light. It feels good to have something other than tension, simmering between us.

"I thought—" She stops suddenly, her face turning pink.

She gives me a small, sheepish smile. "When I heard you had a sick kid, I thought—"

There's a sharp knock on the door. I don't even look at it, because I want her to continue. She was thinking about me? She thought the kid was *mine*? Did that make her jealous? A thousand thoughts swarm me, but her eyes are now on the door as Shelly opens it.

"Hi. Courtney Perry's here." She seems concerned.

Tenley checks the clock and stands, smoothing her skirt. "She's early. I thought you said she was going to be late?"

"That's what she told me..."

Shelly tucks her chin. "She's... on her third tissue."

"She's crying?" I ask, as Tenley looks at me, alarmed. "I've got this."

I stride out into the lobby to find Courtney hunched on one of our leather sofas, sobbing, a pile of tissues in her lap. Interestingly enough, her social media pages never feature *this* side of her. But it's a side I'm familiar with, after God-knows how many times coming in from school or waking up in the morning to find my mother in the exact same position.

So I don't hesitate to put a hand on her shoulder and crouch in front of her. "Hey. Courtney. What's going on? Did something happen?"

She sniffles. "Did you find anything, Brooks?"

We were hoping for something big. It seems, as sleazy as her ex was, he should've left a paper trail. But though Tenley's accountant friend has been going over the numbers for weeks, she hasn't found anything untoward. Everything is squeaky clean. "We're still looking."

"How hard are you looking?" Her tone borders on anger. "He cheated me. Again and again, that bastard cheated, and not just with Raul. All those sneaky tactics he's used to hide his assets? It's got to be all over the books. We have to make him pay. I don't care how much it costs or how long it takes. We have to ruin him."

That's a surprise. Not that James isn't a sleaze, but this vindictiveness is another side of my client I've never seen. "Courtney, the first time we met, you told us that if all you did was walk away with primary custody of you kids, that would be enough."

Her face morphs to sheer, rabid rage. "It's not enough. Not nearly, for what he's putting me through."

I look back, wondering if Tenley's hearing this. Sure enough, she's standing a few paces behind me, looking just as concerned as I feel.

"So are you going to tear him a new one, or what?" Courtney demands, scrunching another tissue in her balled fist.

"The goal is always to get you the most equitable settle-ment possible, Courtney. So—"

"—Equitable? Bullshit, he's never been equitable to me," she snarls, standing up. "Forget it. Let me know when that accountant of yours finds something. And if they *don't*... I'll be finding another attorney."

She storms off, slipping into the elevator at the last second, before the doors closed, leaving Tenley and me staring after her, stunned.

"*Ohhhkay*," I say, drawing the word out and clapping my hands. "That went well."

Tenley barks out an uncertain laugh. "What do you think got into her?"

"Probably something her asshole ex said." That's always how these things work. Divorcing couples go into it wanting the least amount of drama possible. But almost always harsh words and truths are unleashed, and it isn't long before the claws come out. "I think we all want to ruin that asshat, but I don't know that a judge will care. Marriages end every day. People cheat. It hardly affects the division of property and assets."

"She's thinks more money would put her in the best position to care for her children without having to involve him."

"Ordinarily I'd agree with you, but she made it pretty clear that her goal is to ruin him." The price for that is that the kids get a front-row seat to their parents' smackdown. Never a good thing, especially since when there are kids around. No matter how much a parent wants to, you can never fully extricate an ex from your life. Because the Perry kids are young, James and Courtney will have to be dealing with one another, *frequently*, for the better part of two decades. Better to be on friendly terms.

Or... not. Based on what I just saw, that's looking less and less possible.

"You might be giving our client too much credit. She talked a good game, but she's used to presenting a façade. She did it every day on social media. You never know a person's true colors."

She tilts her head at me. "Even when you're family."

I know what she's thinking about. I follow her into the conference room and sit down. "Just so you know, I told Ellie she was wrong to exploit you like that, and that she needs to drop out of that program."

She gives me a look that tells me she wishes I hadn't. "Don't. There are other ways we can help. I have a lot of resources at my disposal."

"I can help her, too. I have—"

"Don't you get it? She doesn't want *your* help, Brooks.

The least I can do is find an apartment in her budget so you two don't constantly lock horns."

"We don't lock horns."

She cocks her head at me in disbelief.

Maybe it's true that Ellie and I are at each other's throats more than we're not. If it was just Ellie, I'd have probably told her to move out by now because she's abused my hospitality the way she abused Tenley's generosity. But I have Jace to think about. As much as I want my freedom, I can't get it until I know Jace will be okay. As much as I want to provide for him, it can't be good to see his mom fighting with me all the time.

"Yeah, but why would you want to—" I ask until she cuts me off.

"Look," she says, pointed. "This is what I live for. What I need to do."

I snap my head up to look at her. "You *need* to?"

"Yes. It's important to me. Very important. I guess you can call it paying it forward for something that happened to me. Anyway, that's why I want the promotion. So I can make more money and have more time to help more people."

She's speaking from her past hurts, trying to make a difference and help save people from having to go through what her mother did. That's respectable. Refreshing as hell too. Definitely better than wanting it for the prestige. Like me. Growing up struggling, I simply wanted to secure my future, to ensure I'd never have to struggle again—and that Jace wouldn't either. I've already started a college savings account for him.

But all of this doesn't mean I need to bow out hand her the promotion.

After all, you never know a person's true colors.

"For the record, while I find that all incredibly admirable, I'm still not going to hand over my chance at the partnership," I say.

"Wouldn't dream of it," her words are cutting but there's a gleam in her eye that I've never seen before.

Are we... *flirting?*

Regardless, I didn't make it this far in life by letting my guard down every time a beautiful woman waltzed into my life.

And I'm not about to start now.

23

Tenley

I sip my tea and lean back against my headboard, my laptop propped on my knees as I consider the question from Stranger88.

Stranger88: *If you could choose your manner of death, how would you die?*

Stranger7721: *Obviously I'd just have my heart give out while I was with the person I love.*

Stranger88: *You want to die during sex?*

Stranger7721: *I never said anything about sex! I'd just like to be with the person I loved most... and just kind of fade away. What about you?*

Stranger88: *I think I'd probably want to be alone, and have it be really fast. Like getting hit by a train.*

Stranger7721: *?? Masochist!*

Stranger88: *I read somewhere that your body starts shutting down before your brain does. Like 30 minutes* *before. They say during that time, you're aware of everything happening. So you know you're dead, but there's not a damn thing you can do. I don't want to spend my last 30 minutes watching that.*

Stranger7721: *So you'd rather have your brains splattered all over some train tracks. Makes sense.*

Stranger88: *It beats the alternative. Watching the people I love suffer over something I did.*

My heart does a little dance over that. He's so honest, so sensitive, so deeply concerned for the people he cares about. It's that part of him that tells me it can't be—it's absolutely not—Brooks Gentry.

But then I think about him, taking in his sister, wanting the best for his nephew... and I think maybe... just maybe... it is him.

Everything else checks out. I've gone through our messages a few times, trying to remember different conversations I'd had with him, at the office. He was on early when Jace was sick. He's on late whenever we stay late at the office to work on the case. And he mentioned a case, an ass-kissing co-worker. It all seems to fit.

I can't bring myself to believe it, though.

I want him to tell me something that assures me this isn't Brooks Gentry I've been pouring my heart to every night.

Stranger7721: *My turn. Have you ever been in love?*

Stranger88: *Absolutely*

That takes me by surprise. He responded so easily, with no hesitation. So good. This can't be Brooks. The only person he loves is himself.

Stranger7721: *More than once?*

Stranger88: *Twice.*

Stranger7721: *That's twice more than I've been.*

Stranger88: *Because you love work and not much else.*

Stranger7721: *I guess. I am hyper-focused on work. But also—I never really found anyone I wanted to play hooky with. Or they never liked me. I was kind of an outsider in school. Late bloomer, too. I never did my hair right and I wore Salvation Army clothes and had thick glasses for amblyopia, and I had horrible buck teeth I hadn't grown into yet.*

Stranger88: *Amblyopia?*

Stranger7721: *Lazy eye.*

Stranger88: *That sounds hot.*

Stranger7721: *Oh God. I grew out of it! I wear contacts and got braces. You probably think I sound like a total troll.*

Stranger88: *Do I sound like I care what you looked like when you were 17? I told you, I don't even care what you look like now. All I know is that I can't wait to kiss you.*

I smile at that.

Stranger7721: *Me too. I bet you are a good kisser. But I am worried I will disappoint you.*

Stranger88: *Not possible. Why?*

I stare at the computer, crack my knuckles. Am I going to admit this? Okay, yes. Why not? If we really are going to meet, he's going to find out sooner or later.

Stranger7721: *Well, I'm not very experienced. I've only had sex once.*

Stranger88: *Once?*

I wince. He's obviously horrified.

Stranger7721: *Yep.*

Stranger88: *So you lied. You said you didn't do one-night stands.*

It gets far more pathetic than that. But what the hell? He hasn't run away yet, even after I divulged my most embarrassing secrets.

Stranger7721: *It wasn't a one-night stand. I was dating him three weeks. We had sex on prom night, and then he dumped me.*

Stranger88: *Prom night? So you haven't had sex in... 10 years? :o*

I'm not about to tell him about my constant need to replace the batteries in my vibrator lately because of him.

Stranger7721: *Yep. So you have had serious relationships before? With whom?*

Stranger88: *I went out with a girl in high school for 2 years. Thought we'd get married. But then I went away to Harvard and she stayed at home, and when I got back, she was engaged to my best friend.*

Stranger7721: *Ouch.*

Stranger88: *Not really. Then I dated a girl at Yale Law, and same thing.*

I stare. Law school. He just said he went to law school... Yale Law?

Quickly, I open a tab and pull up the Foster & Foster website, finding the About Us page. I scroll down to the list of bios, past my own, to the one with the smiling, gorgeous photo of Brooks Gentry. Underneath it, it says: *Brooks K. Gentry is an associate who focuses his practice on family and civil law. Mr. Gentry is a graduate of Harvard University (magna cum laude) and Yale University School of Law (magna cum laude). During law school, Brooks clerked for the...*

Oh shit.

My fingers shake on the trackpad as I navigate to back to the conversation, doing my best to ignore the massive elephant in the room that's sitting on my chest.

Stranger7721: *She got engaged to your best friend, too?*

Stranger88: ☺ *No, we just dated two years. And then she decided she didn't want to be on the East Coast. I didn't want to be in California, where she was from—and so we went our separate ways. Since then, I haven't even dated.*

Stranger7721: *So you're a lawyer! Mr. Stranger88, Esq.*

Stranger88: *I thought I already told you that.*

Stranger7721: *You didn't confirm. You just said you were working on a case.*

Stranger88: *Ok, you got me.*

Stranger7721: ☺ *By the way, how is that ass-kissing co-worker of yours?*

Stranger88: *Strangely, she's starting to grow on me. She's not as horrible as I thought.*

A frisson of electricity makes its way down my spine. It's him.

I wiggle my fingers over the keyboard, itching to ask, *Brooks?*

But what if I confirm it? What then? Is that a good or a bad thing?

Right now, my brain can't process it. Because of all the things we've told each other, in confidence, never expecting...

My mind hitches on that running office fantasy. Sex in a remote, unused cubicle. To think we were both picturing Foster and Foster...

And whenever I had that fantasy, I saw *his* face.

I'm not foolish enough to think he saw mine too. Didn't he say something about not dipping the pen in company ink? And what if I reveal myself and he's disappointed?

Stranger7721: *That's nice.*

Stranger88: *Are you jealous?*

Stranger7721: *Should I be?*

Stranger88: *No. Not at all. She's not you.*

As I let those words sink in, a little voice inside me says, *But what if she was?*

No. No. No. This is all wrong. It can't be him. He's not expecting it to be me. If he knew, he'd back away. Far away.

Which is what I need to do.

A full-body shiver grips me at that moment, and without a word, I close the lid on my laptop. The war inside me is practically nuclear. Deep down, I think I always wanted it to be him. And now... I don't. I *can't* have it be him, because when he does find out, I'll never recover from that loss.

How can Brooks Gentry, a man so wrong for me, so insufferably arrogant, be the man of my dreams?

24

Brooks

Friday afternoon, something happens that never has before.

Tenley Bayliss knocks on my office door with a giant smile on her face. "Guess what?"

I've been smiling all day, as has most of the office, simply because it's the start of the weekend. But knowing how dedicated Bayliss is to the job, the rest of the office's Friday is her Monday. So I'm at a loss. Unless... "Something came through on the case?"

She nods. "Sandra thinks she found something."

That is worthy of a smile. "I thought it was going to take months."

"Apparently, it's something pretty big too. I just got the file. It's in the conference room. You want to have a look with me?"

I'd been dragging, counting down the minutes to quitting time. This changes things. "Absolutely." Instantly, I spring up and follow her down the hall.

She shows me the files. Apparently, all the way back to when they were first married, there were quite a few personal transactions attributed to the restaurant and a number of huge withdrawals totaling over one million dollars that were moved out of the restaurant and sent overseas. It definitely smacks of something illicit.

"You think he knew he wanted to leave her, and so he was shielding his assets from her? Even years ago?" I ask her.

"That's what it looks like," she says with a shrug.

It might be Friday, but this is too good to wait the weekend on. This time when we decide to stay late and work on the case, I'm actually okay with it.

Of course, Tenley is, too. But it's different. She's lit up. Excited. Exhilarated. She's driven, focused, concentrating so hard on the files in front of her, she barely looks at me. She's also wearing these thick, nerd glasses with round frames.

And it's as sexy as hell.

She once called me a distraction, but now I'm the distracted one. There's an electricity in the air, and most of the time, all I can do is sit back and watch her work. Every time she looks up, I expect her to say something snide, like, *Are you going to help?* Instead, she bites her lower lip, which I think might be the hottest thing I've ever seen.

If this were one of my fantasies, she'd get up on the table, rip that clip from her hair and the glasses from her face, and cat-crawl over to me with a wicked look in her eyes.

After a few hours, sometime after midnight, she closes the folder and taps it with her pen. "That's it. I think we've got him."

I'm not sure. Not because I don't believe in Tenley;

actually, quite the opposite. I've just been so mesmerized by her that I couldn't even tell you what was in those files. "I trust you."

"You do?"

I shrug. "Sure."

She pulls her glasses off and sighs, and that fantasy of mine edges a bit into reality. She just needs to take out that clip, shake her hair a bit...

It makes me think of my sweet Stranger. I have to wonder why she thought I would care what she looked like. Does she really think I'm that shallow? Okay, maybe I am—I'm here, gawking at my sexy-librarian coworker. But while I'm a sucker for a pretty face, and I have had long-term relationships before with beautiful women, I've never shared as much with another person as I have with my Stranger. It's only thirty more days until we can see each other, and I don't even care. I won't ever connect with anyone like I have with her.

But I am hard up. Really hard up.

Not to mention, hard. And it's all my ass-kissing coworker's fault.

Tenley pushes away from the desk. "Ready to head home?"

She seems perplexed that I'm not doing my usual bit of trying to be the first to leave the office. Instead, I push my chest up against the table and motion to her glasses. "I never knew you wore those."

She blinks. "Oh. Yeah. My contacts were bothering me."

I inspect them. They're thick, which reminds me of my conversation with my Stranger. "Lazy eye?"

"Mmmhmm." She suddenly looks up at me, and something in her expression changes. The bleary-eyed exhaustion goes out, and she's left looking... alarmed.

Before I can ask her what the problem is, she says, "It's you. You're him."

She's playing some sort of game with me. There's a punch line at the end of this. "I'm who?" I mumble, shifting under the desk to get my cock to behave, because I think she's on to me.

I expect her to say something like, *The pervert who's hard for me while I'm trying to conduct actual business.*

Instead, she says, "You're Stranger88."

My mouth opens, but nothing comes out. Nothing can come out. Two worlds I've kept perfectly separated are now suddenly thrown together, and the result is a combination that makes no sense whatsoever.

"Stranger77211?" I finally spit out.

She nods slowly.

Holy shit.

"I didn't want it to be you," she says, her voice a whisper.

Oh, I can tell that. She looks horrified, now. But I'm too shocked to be insulted. And now that I think about it, it makes perfect sense. Of course she's my Stranger. I might have tried to keep those two worlds separate, but they always kept colliding. Again and again in unexpected ways. In a lot of ways, it was completely natural, completely meant to happen, like fate.

"And now that you know it is?"

She shakes her head and starts to pack her things up. "I have to go. I don't want to talk about this now."

She doesn't want to talk to me? After this bombshell? How can we not? I've been saying she'd be my perfect girl if only she wasn't such a bitch, if only she'd let me get close enough to peel back her layers. And now that I know she's been the one chatting with me... that does it.

This was meant to happen.

She turns away from me, as if she can't stand to be near me a second longer.

I'm not going to leave it like this. I can't.

"Why do you hate me so much?" I call after her, stopping her in her tracks.

When she turns to look at me, there's softness there, indecision. She's gnawing on her lip again, and I think it might be my undoing. "I don't hate you," she says quietly. "But I don't like you either."

"After everything we talked about? You told Stranger88 you couldn't wait to see me. Well, I'm right here."

She closes her eyes. "But that was before—"

"And nothing's changed."

"*Everything's* changed!" She hoists her bag onto her shoulder. "We *work* together. When I told those things to you, I never thought anyone would... it's so inappropriate. And it can't continue."

She stalks for the door but hesitates when I call her name.

"For the record," I tell her. "I never thought it was you. But now that I know, I'm not mad about it. I'm sorry you don't feel the same."

And she must really not. Because she doesn't turn back. She continues on, and a few moments later, I hear the elevator doors slide closed, leaving me alone in the office.

25

Tenley

I never thought it was you. But now that I know, I'm not mad about it. I'm sorry you don't feel the same.

Those words keep playing in my head again and again as I drive home.

How can he not be mad about it? This is Brooks Gentry. He's all about appearances—which is why he flirts hardest with the hottest interns.

Somehow, I just can't reconcile the man from the office with the one I've been messaging with. The one who said, *I don't even care what you look like now. All I know is that I can't wait to kiss you.*

Lies. They were all lies.

They have to be.

If he couldn't wait to kiss me, why did he let me go? Why didn't he make me stay?

Well, maybe that's on me. I did tell him I didn't like

him. I skirted away from him like he was infected. I probably had a disgusted expression on my face.

The same expression I'd expected he would have.

And yet, he didn't. He was okay with it. *I'm not mad about it.*

So does that mean he still wants me?

I'm so deep in thought that I nearly cut off a sedan trying to make a lane change. Finally, I get home to the safety of my apartment. My dry cleaning is hanging outside for me as usual. Taking it in, I go into the dark living room and look around, a feeling of dread settling over me.

I'm all alone. I don't even have Stranger88 to talk to now.

Trudging to the kitchen, I come face-to-face with Bevin's wedding invitation. The wedding's in a couple weeks, but in all the chaos surrounding the Perry case, I'd forgotten to send in the response card. I suppose it's too late to respond now.

Bleh. I'm not sure what is worse, my lack of response, or that I feel happy that I don't have to go there alone and embarrass myself in front of my college friends.

I *could've* gone with Brooks. Maybe.

If I'd stayed there and we talked, maybe we could've come to some understanding. Maybe we could've agreed to —I don't know—start seeing each other for real?

No, who am I kidding? That was one thing both Stranger88 and Brooks Gentry had in common—they both insisted they didn't date co-workers.

So what would've happened, had I stayed?

At best, more awkwardness. At worst, sex in an unused cubicle, which would most likely *never* be as hot as the fantasy, followed by me having to move out of state to avoid ever embarrassing myself by seeing him again.

No. It's good that I left when I did. And good that I'm not going to that wedding. I'll just send Bevin my regrets with a big check to make up for it. She'll understand.

I sigh and open the pantry, grabbing for my familiar cereal box. It's nearly empty, but I manage to pull out a handful of broken O's and Cheerio dust for my dinner.

This isn't going to work. I feel worse after eating the food. Hungrier, more unsettled. Grabbing my phone, I place an order on the mobile app for Shaw's, asking them to deliver bread, milk, eggs, coffee, and Cheerios tomorrow morning so I can at least have a good breakfast.

Done.

That gnawing feeling doesn't go away, though. Because it has nothing to do with food.

I collapse on the couch and try to unwind with a show on Netflix. But all the while, I keep thinking of Brooks saying those words to me.

You told Stranger88 you couldn't wait to see me. Well, I'm right here.

I remember what I said I'd do when I saw him. I said I wouldn't be able to stop myself from kissing him and touching him and wanting him closer, now that I had him in the flesh.

My face heats at the thought of having Brooks that close.

Just like in those fantasies.

I practically run up the stairs and strip off my skirt, climbing into bed and grabbing my vibrator from the nightstand drawer.

I'm about to bring it between my legs when I look at it and realize what I'm doing.

He didn't want to leave. *I* wanted that. Am I that lost that I'm giving up real human contact for something with batteries?

Shoving the vibrator back into the drawer, I grab my phone and pull up the BLIND LOVE app. I expect that now, Stranger88 will have decided that the app is for shit and disconnected his account.

But he hasn't. In fact, he's online now.

Probably messaging other women.

Just as that thought filters through my head, a notification pops up. *You have one message.* I open it. It's from him.

Stranger88: *I was hoping you'd pop on.*

I stare at it, my fingers trembling on the keypad. It was so easy to talk to him when I didn't know who he was. And now? I can't find the words.

But Brooks always has the words.

Stranger88: *So where do we go from here?*

A thousand ideas have been rattling in my head since I left the conference room—from ludicrous things, like leaving the country—to more sensible things, like telling the partners that we can no longer work together.

But all of them seem wrong.

Because none of them end the way I want them to.

It's so crazy because this is Brooks Gentry. The man I hate. The man I never saw myself with in a thousand years.

But when I line him up with Stranger88, I feel like all those things I thought I hated about Brooks were just my own false, preconceived notions about him, and that maybe I was wrong.

But he can't possibly feel the same way about me. Can he?

Stranger7721: *I don't know. All I know is that I am*

going to miss our messaging. I looked forward to it every night.

Stranger88: *Past tense. So you're saying you want to call it quits?*

Stranger7721: *I think we have to, don't we?*

Stranger88: *Is that a law? I must have skipped over that part in law school.*

He's toying with me. Because he's actually making it seem like he wants to continue. I don't—can't—buy it. Brooks lives to toy with women. I've seen the way he makes those poor interns twist in the wind. I'm not going to let it happen to me.

Stranger7721: *It's probably for the best.*

Stranger88: *If you think so.*

I really don't know! I expect to see the words: *Stranger88 has left the conversation,* and a bolt of alarm strikes me straight in the heart. I don't want him to leave. I don't want to be alone again.

As if he senses that, another message comes through.

Stranger88: *Can I ask you one question, though?*

Yes. Truth be told, I'd love it if he could ask me a thousand questions. But I can't—this is Brooks Gentry. I need to remember that. So I make my answer as short as possible.

Stranger7721: *Ok*

Stranger88: *If you hate me so much, why did you check the app? Why did you reply to my message? Why are you on here right now, talking to me?*

All very good points.

He's calling my bluff. And he's right. I'd love to stay up all night talking like before. Who cares if this is Brooks? Chemistry is chemistry—online or not. I want to take everything I said back. Let's keep this going.

But before I can respond, he beats me to it.

Stranger88 has left the conversation.

26

Brooks

She hates me.

Or she's convinced herself she does.

Either way, there is absolutely no sense in me trying to tell Tenley Bayliss otherwise. Her mind is made up.

And while I may be a pro at convincing a judge to see my side, I never thought I'd have to convince Stranger7721.

She knows me. Better than anyone.

But she's still holding on to that belief that I'm nothing but a thorn in her side.

In a way, I am. I am the guy standing in the way of her getting that promotion.

It's bullshit. I stalk downstairs and into the kitchen, pulling out food to make something to eat. A little while later, as I'm wrapping my mouth around a PB&J, Ellie comes in. "What's wrong with you?"

Her tone is accusing. I'm not in the mood. "Nothing."

"You looked pissed. Actually... not pissed. Just sad."

I don't look up from my sandwich. "Not sad."

This is why Ellie has annoyed me since my parents brought her into the world. You can swear up and down that things aren't the way she sees them, but once she gets a notion in her head, she won't ever let it go until she gets her validation.

"Yeah, you are." She sits down next to me—though I wish she'd go back in front of the television and leave me alone—and cranes her neck low to look into my eyes. "What is it? That lawyer chick? Tenley Bayliss?"

"I don't know who you're talking about."

She rolls her eyes. "Of course you do. Don't give me that. I could tell the moment you got on me for accepting her charity that you *loved her*."

My eyes meet hers. "What?"

"Otherwise, why protect her? You have a big ol' crush on her, don't you?"

I glare. "I don't know about you, but I graduated from the third grade twenty years ago. I don't care about Tenley Bayliss. I just don't want my dumbass sister to end up in jail for fraud."

She crosses her arms, playing with the pendant on her neck as she studies me. "Well, that's good. She's totally wrong for you, anyway."

I was about done with this conversation ten minutes before it started. I shove the rest of the sandwich into my mouth and say, mouth full, "Doesn't matter."

Although it kind of does.

We sit in silence as I chew.

By the time I swallow, my mild interest in her statement has inflated to a full-blown itch. Peanut butter sticks in my throat as I say, "Out of curiosity, why do you say that?"

She smiles, triumphant in the fact that she's succeeded

in getting under my skin. "Because Tenley is a nice person. She deserves a nice, boring guy who does nice, boring things, and doesn't turn everything into an argument."

I wipe at my mouth. "I don't turn everything into an argument."

She laughs. "Yeah, you do."

My voice rises. "No, I—"

Shit.

Forget it. "You done?"

"No. She also is way too pretty for your goofy-looking ass," she says, standing up and heading upstairs. "Now, I'm done."

I give her a middle finger she can't see, toss my trash away, and climb the stairs, wondering if Tenley is still online. Maybe she is. Maybe she's now on BLIND LOVE, seeking out a new love match.

A nice, boring guy who will treat her well. Who will have the honor of touching her, kissing her, making her smile.

The thought makes jealousy simmer in my veins.

Nope, no, can't think of that. Why should I be jealous over her? I've never even dated Tenley Bayliss. She's no one to me. Right now, all she is to me is the person I should be beating out for an important promotion. That should be at the top of my mind.

Not what I can do to make her happy so that I can be the one to see her smile.

Who cares? I don't care.

And yet when I climb up to bed and fall into it, all I can think about is our past conversations. How she used to call me on my bullshit, in real life as much as online. How she used to get that blush on her cheeks whenever I'd say something inappropriate, in the same way that she'd always pause much longer when I typed something inappropriate online. How every time I typed something to her and imagined the person behind the screen, I was imagining everything exactly right, because it was Tenley after all.

It's always been her.

We're perfect for each other.

Almost.

If I had never worked at Foster & Foster to begin with, we *would've* been. It's this fucking job that's in the way. I'm sure of it.

Because if I close my eyes and imagine the perfect life, it's not as partner at Foster & Foster.

No, it's coming home to that fiery brunette who ignites every one of my senses, again and again. Who tells it like it is, who isn't afraid of looking bad, who challenges me to be a better person. *That's* everything I ever wanted.

Not a stupid promotion.

Her.

27

Tenley

Of course sleep doesn't come right away.

Or at all.

I should be worried about the case. We have more work to do to get ready for the trial, but our late-night pow-wow wound up being cut short, for obvious reasons. There was no way I could stay there any longer.

But instead of running possible strategies for the trial through my head, all I'm doing is replaying conversations with Brooks.

If you hate me so much, why did you check the app? Why did you reply to my message? Why are you on here right now, talking to me?

Because I don't hate him, obviously.

No, not even close.

I open my eyes and stare at the moonlight, streaming through the blinds and painting prison bars on the ceiling of my apartment. The windows are open, letting in brisk night air, rustling the curtains. Propping my head up on the pillow, I imagine just what could've been, if I'd responded in the right way.

There is such a thing as tact, and you don't have it.

What I need to do is stop letting my head lead the way. Maybe I need to let my heart to the talking.

I've been denying it for far too long, but if I let it speak, I think it would tell Brooks that I was wrong in my first impression of him. That I actually do think he's one hell of an attorney, and the reason I've been so standoffish is because deep down, I know I've met my match. I've never had anyone intimidate and infuriate me quite so much, and that was why I had to shut him down.

But I was wrong. So wrong.

At least I have the weekend to think about how I'll respond to him.

As I'm trying to craft that witty response, my phone buzzes on my nightstand. I pick it up to see an unknown number with a 207 area-code. It could be someone from the women's center needing immediate assistance, so I answer. It's just the distraction I need. "Yes?"

"It's me."

Some distraction.

It's Brooks. I've rarely spoken to him on the phone—maybe only once or twice—and yet I know his voice instantly. "Hi?" I chirp out, sitting up in bed and looking at the glowing numbers of my bedside clock. It's after two. Why is he calling me now?

There's only one reason I can think of. It's something with the case. He had a late-night epiphany, and he needs to share it with me right away.

He says, "I can't stop thinking about it."

I sit up and turn on the light at my bedside, rubbing my

eyes. "Well, she did upend everything with her change of heart, but we're on track. We just have to—"

"What?"

I pause. "Aren't you talking about Courtney?"

"Screw that," he says, a hint of urgency in his voice. "I'm talking about what you said. I can't stop thinking about that."

Okay. I've said many things. I'm not sure which one he's thinking about, so I stay silent.

"The truth is, we *don't* have to call it quits. The only one saying that is you. So if you don't want to, then what the hell, why don't we just let it go and see where it leads?"

I blink, now wide-awake. "You want that?"

"Yeah. Remember all those things I said I'd do to you, after a long day at the office?"

I blush. How can I not? He had this fantasy about greeting me at the front door after a day of work, dropping everything and pushing me up against the door, lifting my skirt and... "Yes..."

My voice is barely a breath. His voice is low and controlled. "I still want to do those things for you. With you. *To* you."

My heart races like a motor, starting up. Goose bumps break out all over my body, suggesting I'm shivering, and yet I've never felt so hot. My body simply doesn't know how to behave with him.

I hesitate. Yes, we have insane chemistry. "But... this changes everything."

"It might," he says, and I can just imagine him, facing the judge, laying out his case just as levelly and coolly, without a single ripple. "But there is good change and bad change. What's the worst thing that could happen?"

"It won't live up to the fantasy, and we both go home

disappointed. And then we still have to see each other in the office."

"You really think that will happen?"

He's right. At least, for me. We've both talked about our past romantic relationships. I have a string of losers, none of which are worth writing home about. He had two serious relationships though. "Not for me. But you... what if—"

"No. I'm telling you right now, it's not possible. And the way I see this, it's all good. No downside. I'd tell you if I saw one. We're better together than at each other's throats."

He's right again. But I don't speak. I'm too afraid of something going wrong here.

"Do you agree?" he finally asks.

"You make a convincing argument, counsel."

He chuckles. "What are you doing now?"

"What do you think? It's late. I'm lying in bed."

I don't mean anything by it, but he groans as if I just described the most lurid, detailed sexual fantasy to him. "Don't do that to me."

I smile. "I did nothing to you. You're doing it to yourself."

"You have no idea," he says in a tortured, low voice. "Look. I don't know about you, but I've had one hell of a week. I could use a little company right now."

"It's Friday. You could've gone to the club," I point out.

"I don't know where you got the idea that I go to clubs anymore, but I promise, I haven't set foot in one since before I graduated from Yale. That's not my scene."

Right. Stranger88 had told me that. I'm having a hard time reconciling the ego-filled Brooks Gentry I thought I knew with the real one. Despite what I once believed, the real Brooks Gentry thinks clubs are too loud. The real Brooks Gentry doesn't like to party or get drunk. The real

Brooks Gentry dated two women seriously and has never had a meaningless fling.

And the real Brooks Gentry lives with his sister and her son, who he graciously took in when they were in need.

"I could use the company, too," I say, combing my fingers through my hair and searching out my reflection in the dresser mirror across the room. Much work to be done there. "You should come over here."

"I thought you'd never ask."

I give him the address and end the call, my body fluttering with excitement as I rush to get ready for him. He'll be here in ten minutes, maybe eight, if he rushes.

Oh my god. Brooks Gentry is coming over here. And I may be inexperienced, but I know that *company* isn't all he's going to want to give me.

We're going to have sex.

I'm going to have sex with Brooks Freaking Gentry.

Standing in front of the closet, I weigh my options. Dress? No, too fancy. Sweats? No, I don't want to look like a slob. I finally pick out a little romper and wiggle into it, then rush to put on some make-up and do my hair.

This is really happening.

I pinch myself several times in order to get it to sink in, but it still doesn't.

I can barely even think straight. All I can think about is him here... and I don't think I've been this giddy and scared and anxious and *what the hell am I getting myself into?* in all my life.

But I love it. I wouldn't have it any other way.

28

Brooks

I've never been to Tenley's apartment.

She lives on the other side of Sapphire Shores, in a modest but well-kept brick building, probably built in the 1970's. There are ten identical walkways to identical white doors, the bushes are manicured with pink flowers, and the lawn outside is trimmed with military precision. There's no flash, just a faded sign outside that says, "Now Renting! Lockwood Manor. 1, 2, and 3 Bedroom Efficiencies!" with a starburst that says, "Starting at $1150!"

Efficient. That's Tenley. She doesn't do anything overboard. She uses exactly the right amount to get the job done. She has no one to impress. She uses her leftover money to help other people at the women's center.

That's probably why I have a minor crisis of confidence while I'm sitting behind the wheel outside her door.

She's too good for me. I don't know why I'm here.

I have never in my life felt that way, except, maybe,

when I was growing up poor, letting my dad kick the shit out of me. Back then, I thought that I deserved it. But I realized I had to get over that real quick if I was ever going to make something of myself.

And I need to get over it now. If I want her, and she wants me, and I know we'd be good together, I need to haul my ass out of this car.

The fears all but disappear as I reach her door. I notice a plastic bag from Shaw's, sitting outside. She's ordered groceries. Milk... looks like eggs... Cheerios.

Telling myself I'm doing a good deed by alerting her to their presence so they won't sit outside in the warmth all night, I knock on the door.

She opens it almost immediately, as if she was waiting on the other side for me, which gives me a burst of confidence.

And she looks phenomenal. She's wearing a little get-up that bares her long pale legs, and her hair is loose on her shoulders. She's nothing like the Tenley from work, and I get this surge of excitement thinking that I'm one of the few people who gets to see this side of her.

I hold up the bag. "Groceries?"

She stares at them in confusion. "Oh. I thought I ordered them for the morning."

Reaching forward, she takes them. Sets them down. Returns her eyes to mine.

I've always pegged Tenley as someone who knows what she wants. And I'm right, because she doesn't hesitate. She pulls me to her, kissing me hard, taking my breath away.

Sweet, pristine little Tenley Bayliss. There's nothing soft, nothing tentative about it. And I love it.

"Is this what you wanted?" she groans, our noses touching.

No. Hell no. I want, need more. She's tugging at the hem of my shirt, which can mean only one thing.

She's not nearly as virginal as she said. She wants me, us, naked.

I am more than happy to oblige. I spin her around, pressing her against the door, just like in our fantasies. Still devouring her mouth, I reach down over her thighs and go for the hem of her little dress, but to my disappointment, it's shorts. Why the hell do they make clothes this way? Undeterred, my hands slide under the fabric, over her bare thighs, and up the delicate curve of her ass. There is nothing else there but a little piece of string masquerading as underwear. I'm instantly as hard as a rock, and I know she can feel my cock pressing against her abdomen.

Holding her up against the door, I press my open mouth against her neck, tasting her sweet skin.

"Fuck me," she growls into my hair, pushing her tits up against me as she scrapes her fingers through my hair. "Can you fuck me here?"

Yes. Hell, yes. Right now I *need* this.

But this damn outfit. I pull away, inspecting it. "How does this..."

She smiles. "Oh." She pulls the neck wide and lets it slip easily from her shoulders, leaving her naked except for her thong.

And for once, I'm speechless, that silver tongue of mine perfectly useless in my mouth. I've never seen a more gorgeous set of breasts in my life. Her whole body is a work of art—her breasts not more than a handful with perfect pink nipples I can't wait to suck on, her waist tight, her curves even more beautiful than all my fantasies had created. I'm like a kid in a candy store, hardly knowing what part of her to devour first. My cock strains against my pants, so ready it's about to burst.

Scooping her up from her tight little ass, I wrap her limbs around me as she takes my earlobe into her mouth, sucking on it. She lets out a gasp and tilts her head back, giving me access to her long neck as I feel for the fabric of her barely-there thong.

Her breath hitches when I hook a finger under the fine filament and easily rip them free, lowering my hands down her hips and caressing the full globes of her backside. And now she's naked for me. Tenley Bayliss is naked and wanting me. Incredible, is all I can think, and I might even say it aloud. She's incredible, a fantasy come true. It makes it impossible to believe I ever doubted this.

I nudge her thighs apart and run my fingers down her slit, finding her so wet and ready. For me. She wants me. I can't even get that through my head.

She gasps and shudders when my finger finds her clit, suggesting she wants more. I hungrily oblige by flicking my finger over it, making her moan aloud. "Brooks," she whispers. "Please... go slower, now..."

I can't even believe this luck. I'm finally going to be inside my sweet Stranger. My sweet Stranger, who right now I want to know as deeply as one human can know another.

"You want it here, or...?"

"Yes, please..."

"Do you want me to fuck you against the door?" I growl at her, to which she nods mutely.

I'm frantic with excitement. I want her. Every last bit of her. Now. But I'm too damn excited. Her breath is warm on my face. Her nose bumps against mine. I can feel her pulse fluttering under her skin against me.

I'd had it in my head that tonight we'd take it slow. I'd spend time getting to know the girl I thought of as a Stranger. But right now, I can't. All I want is to sink into her.

But I'm not sure once will be enough.

I'm hyperaware that her nipples are hard because I can feel them pushing against my T-shirt even through the layers of clothing. I press her harder against the door and rub a thumb over her nipple. Yep, already stiff. I suck on it hard.

Yes. Oh God, these are beautiful breasts, made even more beautiful now that I've tasted them and they're wet with my saliva. I tongue one nub, and then the other, again and again and again. She mewls at the sensation and tangles her hands in my hair. "God."

She reaches down and pulled at my belt buckle, wasting no time. My cock jumps to attention at once, thrilled to be in play so soon in the game.

In the darkness, we scrabble at each other's clothing. She grabs for my pants, dipping her hand inside and drawing out my cock as expertly as if she'd been imagining this moment almost as much as I've been. She's doing it all. When I bring my hand down lower, I feel her heat.

"Now," she orders, her heart beating a mad drumbeat against mind, her breathing shallow and raspy. "Now."

I hook her legs around my hips, press her up against the door, and drive into her so fast that it steals both of our breath.

She screams, a sound I stifle with a hot, open-mouthed kiss, to keep anyone outside from hearing.

And then I fuck her. Long, deep strokes into her. And goddamn, she feels better than I imagined. I feel myself losing it almost the instant I fill her warm, wet confines.

Either the door's shaking, or the whole world's shaking, because I get into a fast rhythm in the dark. She growls against me, begging, "Yes, oh, please, yes. You feel so good."

It's only when I'm coming that I realize I'd forgotten the condom.

I hold her against the door and pull out immediately, and to her surprise, I hunch over, catching my cum in my hands.

"What happened?" she asks in the darkness.

"No condom," I say, still hunched over, wondering what kind of mess I'm making. "I don't know where my head was. I wanted you too bad."

Her voice is a breath. "I'm on the pill."

"You are...? But you..."

"I've been on it since I was sixteen. For my periods."

I could've planned this better. "This is what I get from letting my dick make the decisions for me. Sorry."

She's still breathing hard, as she'd been teetering on the edge of orgasm when I'd suddenly brought that to a crashing halt. "It's okay." She points. "Bathroom's over there."

Collecting my jeans around my legs, I go in and close the door, then clean up, shaking my head at my reflection in the mirror. Our first time. I ruined it. Shit.

Ellie's words hang in my head. *She's too good for me.*

She is, but I'm not going to let myself fail at trying to be the kind of person who deserves her. I fail, I pick myself up. That's the way it's done.

When I come out, she's sitting, half-clothed, on the couch, looking a little embarrassed. "That was fun, but...um..."

I sit down next to her. "I'm not done with you. I've been waiting for this a long time. I want to see you. Come here."

I let her straddle me, her thighs on either side of my

hips. She's wearing this little jumper thing, but it's no impediment, because she's not wearing her underwear. I pull it down to her waist and just stare at her. "God, you're beautiful."

She smiles a little shyly. "I am?"

"Absolutely." I slip a finger up the leg of her shorts and between her legs, through the folds covered with her soft, downy hair, and hooking my knuckle, drive it into her warm, wet canal.

She gasps.

I kiss her, long and slow, as I fuck her with one finger, then two, feeling the pulsing ridges of her insides. All the while, my *thumb's* brushing her clit in soft, circular motions. She starts to sway against me, rocking on my hand, getting into it, her breathing coming shorter and faster now.

"You like that?" I say. Unbelievably, she's making me horny as hell again just by those sweet, sexy little sounds.

She nods, her head lolling against my shoulder. "So much. Keep going."

I start thrusting three fingers into her, my hand locked between the soft, sensitive thigh muscles, and she's grinding into me, a low moan emanating from her throat.

"This is too good. I can't..."

I kiss the doubts away, feeling her twitching inside, hot and wet and so fucking warm. "I've been thinking about you every minute, Tenley. You're so fucking gorgeous."

And she comes. Her insides contract around me, hard and fast, and she growls as she slumps against me, her tits pressed up against my chest.

"Oh," she whispers, still spasming around me as I slowly withdraw my wet fingers. "Oh my god. That was good."

I chuckle, bringing my hand to my mouth and licking

my fingers. She's incredible. I taste her musky sweet taste on my fingers, sucking them dry.

This was amazing, but... when I'd come here to see her, it wasn't for that. Well, it was partly for that. But that wasn't all of it. I simply hadn't been able to wait. She'd had me too out of control with desire.

Now, though, we have all night.

I know she has the same thought in her head as she takes my hand. We bump together in the darkness as she leads me up to her bed.

29

Tenley

I was having the best dream.

In the morning when I wake, for the first time, work isn't the first thing on my mind. I look at the sun shining through the window, listen to the birds chirping outside, and I feel so content. I wish I could wake up like this, every morning.

Then I look over at Brooks, and when I catch my breath, I realize it's not a dream. My former work enemy is tangled in my sheets, his arm curled around me, his body against mine.

I sit up, careful not to wake him, still taking in eyefuls of his gorgeous body. His tanned skin contrasts with the white sheets. The dip and curve of every muscle, the notch on his strong chin, the long lashes most girls would kill for.

With my eyes, I trace the lines of his pectoral muscles, right down to his navel, with a treasure trove of soft dark hair, trailing down to... oh.

I think of last night. The way his body was perfectly in sync with mine, the way we came together, performing like a well-oiled machine. Oh my god.

Well, the partners did say they thought we'd work amazingly together.

It almost feels a sin to tear my eyes away, but eventually, I manage to. I slip out of bed, go to the bathroom, brush my hair and teeth, and stare at myself in the mirror, wondering how *this girl* wound up in bed with Brooks Gentry. He has all those fans, can have any woman he wants, and yet... he chose *me*.

The thought makes those goosebumps pop out all over *again*.

Then I slip on my white terry robe and open the door, finding him just sitting up in bed, a sleepy look in his eyes. He yawns and his eyes fall on me, making my heart somersault in my chest. "Hey. You getting up?"

I nod. "I was going to make breakfast."

He grabs his phone and checks the time. "Good idea. I'm starved."

He probably should be, after all the work he put in last night. I've never come before when someone else was around. With Brooks? Six times. Six. He knew how to play my body like an instrument, like a world-famous musician.

I knew he'd be good, but now I can't help looking at him in awe, like he's some kind of god.

"Okay!" I say, way more chipper than I usually am. "Just give me a few!"

I sail out of the room, thinking, *Okay, that wasn't too awkward. He didn't say anything about regret.*

In the kitchen, I find the groceries that I'd put away while he was in the bathroom last night. I take everything out, trying to be blasé in the wake of last night, as if that kind of thing happens to me all the time. But as I'm cracking eggs for the egg-white omelets, I keep overthinking everything. All of last night. Every single word he said to me. All the times he told me how good I felt or how he groaned as he pushed inside me. It's enough to make those goosebumps multiply on my skin, making me shiver every two seconds.

I'm so deep in thought that I don't realize he's crept up behind me until I feel his presence, like electricity zinging between us, even though he doesn't actually touch me. "What are you making?"

I jump a little. "Omelets? Um, with just the egg whites," I stammer, averting his eyes. "In case you're into health. As you probably are, because..." *because you have the most beautiful body I have ever seen.*

Oh my god. Why am I so nervous around him?

"Need help?" He's so close I can feel his warm breath, fanning my cheek. It's enough to make me spin and beg him to take me right there.

I control myself.

"No. You just sit."

He pads over to the table, wearing just his boxer briefs, and slips into the chair, just as casual as can be. I crack an egg, and my fingers shake so much that I get a bunch of shell pieces in the bowl. I try to fish them out, again and again, but the shell keeps slipping away from my fingertip. "Ugh."

He probably thinks I'm a moron. "Sure you don't need help?"

"No. I'm fine."

"Smells good."

I turn to gaze at him, then stop myself. I don't need to make myself even more nervous by looking at his perfection. "I haven't even started cooking yet."

I venture a look as I reach down to grab the pan, using

my hair as a veil to hide it, and see him watching me, a hungry look on his face. Does he want another round?

Oh God. So do I. The second I think about it, my nipples pucker against the robe. I straighten, pan in hand, and go to the kitchen to pull out the milk for the eggs. I only realize I've pulled out the orange juice when I've poured it in with the eggs.

Gross.

I sigh and glance over at him. How can he be that relaxed? And why is it that I'm a bumbling idiot?

At least he doesn't notice.

"Hey, you okay?" he asks me.

I take it back. He's noticing.

I force a smile as I stare into the bowl, wondering if it can be salvaged. Probably not. Damn. "Oh, yeah. Never better," I say.

He cocks an eyebrow at me. "You sure?"

"A hundred percent." I'm not looking at him. I'm looking at my toaster and realizing I don't have any butter. Jelly. Or anything.

This is going to be the worst breakfast ever.

He pushes away from the table, manspreading on the chair. He hooks a finger at me, gazing at me in a way that makes fresh need bloom deep inside me. "Come here."

I toss the egg-mixture into the sink and reach for a couple of fresh eggs. "Why? I need to—"

"Later."

He's very convincing. I can't say no. I step over to him, trying to figure out what's on his mind.

When I get there, eyes still boring into mine, he takes the bowl and sets it on the table. Then he drags a hand under my robe, cupping my ass, pulling me toward him.

Closer... closer, until I have no choice but to mount and straddle his lap.

When I do, he casts a lazy eye down my body as he slowly opens the tie on my robe. "Tell me what's wrong," he coaxes, his voice husky as he rubs the pad of his thumb over my nipple.

"It's just... I don't know. I'm just wondering..."

But as I study his face, his full, kissable lips, parted just a tiny bit, the dark stubble on his strong jaw, the icy blue of his eyes... I'm speechless. Again, he's rendered me speech-less. But not like before. This speechlessness is from being in a perfect moment, and not wanting to ruin it.

So I lean over and let my hair fall around us so that it feels like we're in a world all our own. "I'm just wondering how many eggs you want?"

His lips twist into a smile. Then he wraps a big hand around the back of my neck, pulling me down for a slow, sexy kiss.

And—thank god—I get the feeling breakfast is the last thing on his mind.

* * *

I finally do make breakfast, though.

An hour later.

It's just as bad as I thought it would be, but at least it's food.

It's much easier to wrap my head around the act of cooking without him watching me. By the time I plate the omelets and finish making the toast, he's still in bed sleep-ing, so I decide to bring it to him. I pile all of the food on a tray with glasses of orange juice and mugs of steaming black coffee and carry it to my bedroom.

But he's not sleeping. He's stalking around the room in nothing but his jeans, looking for something, a phone tucked between his cheek and his shoulder. "Where are you calling from?" he demands, and his voice is nothing like the sweet, gentle hum he'd used in bed with me. It sounds alarming, like gunfire.

He doesn't even notice me when I step inside and set the tray on the dresser. He locates his t-shirt and barks, "Yeah. I'll be right there. Stay put."

He ends the call and throws the shirt on. "I've got to go."

For some reason, I feel like a stranger in my own apartment. "Problem?"

"Yeah. I guess Ellie went out last night and never came home."

I gasp. "Really. Where do you think—"

"No clue. I thought she was in for the night. I saw her. But she has these friends, and they're not the best influence on her. She goes out and..." He scuffs into his shoes. "Anyway, I've got to go."

Opening up my drawer, I find a pair of underwear. "Hold on. I'm coming with you."

He holds up a hand. "No. You don't have to—"

"I want to. And I insist, so don't bother with a closing argument. Motion denied," I say in my firmest voice, reaching for a t-shirt and shrugging out of my robe.

When I peek my head through the neck hole, he's gazing at me, a small smile on his face. "You're a ballbreaker, aren't you?"

"Yes, I am." I grin, pushing the shirt down, static crackling around my hair. "Deal with it."

"Yes, ma'am. Remind me not to be across the aisle when you're in the courtroom." He's smiling, but as he grabs his phone and checks it, I notice the worried crinkle there.

So I grab a pair of shorts and run to the bathroom. "I won't be long."

When I return, he's standing there, finishing up his eggs and washing it down with orange juice. How cute is he? He didn't want all my hard work to go to waste. Not only that, but he's also put my scrambled eggs in between slices of toast and wrapped it in a napkin, making me a to-go sandwich. He hands it to me. "Here you go. An Egg McMuffin. Sort of. You have a to-go cup for the coffee?"

"Aw." I take the sandwich. "Thanks. But I'm good. Let's go."

We go to his car. Before he backs out, he tries calling Ellie again. No answer.

"Where do you think she could be?" I ask as he sets out toward the coast, and the other end of Sapphire Shores.

"No clue. All her friends live in South Portland where she used to live. So that's my first stop."

There's bitterness in his voice, but something more than that. Exhaustion. And not just from what we did last night. Clearly, this isn't the first time his sister has let him down. I know Ellie's side of the story—she said that her brother didn't believe in her. I suppose it's a vicious cycle. When other people don't believe in you, it's easy to not believe in yourself. To give up.

And maybe Ellie has just given up. "You think she just walked out after you left?"

He nods. "She was in bed when I left. I don't know why... her friends were probably out. They stay out all night sometimes. And she never could pass up a good rager."

"She does this a lot?" I ask.

He exhales, rakes his fingers through his hair. "She

didn't used to. She's been doing it more and more, though. This is the first time she just left him."

Jace. Poor kid. "Maybe she thought you were home?"

"Yeah. I guess she did. Because I usually am at that time of night."

It's hard to believe that I used to think he spent the last nights of his twenties partying like a rock star in the club. That's not him at all. How wrong I was! I feel terrible for having all those misconceptions about him, so I reach over and put a hand on his thigh. "I'm so sorry."

He glances over at me. "You didn't do anything. If anything, you're saving me from having a meltdown right now. So I should be thanking you."

"Believe me. I know how it is. I've had plenty of family crises."

"Yeah. Well, all of mine these days seem to circle around one person. I didn't claw my way out of this shit to have her keep dragging me down. I'm supposed to be lifting her up, to be with me. All I want her is for her to get her act together, but..." He trails off, his fingers tightening around the wheel. "I get it. It's not easy. I feel like every card she's ever been dealt has been a bum hand. It sucks."

I'm silent, stunned by this admission. Now I'm even more sorry. It couldn't have been easy listening to me bitch about him goofing off and acting like an immature bachelor when he was doing nothing of the kind.

Why didn't he tell me off? Why didn't he set me straight? I deserved to be taught a lesson.

He slows to a crawl and scans through the windshield at a broken-down neighborhood. "Where the hell could she be?"

I give his leg a squeeze. "We'll find her."

But we don't. All morning we drive around Portland,

looking in places she once frequented, speaking with her friends. No one has seen her. Brooks is visibly upset, but he doesn't ever lose his temper. He just becomes quieter and sadder.

"Shit," he says, sitting behind the wheel after yet another strike-out. "I don't know where else to look."

"She works, right? Maybe we should go to her employer?"

He nods and starts the engine. "Only two nights a week. But I'm out of ideas."

He's pensive and silent as we drive. It's a totally new side to him, to add to all the new sides of seen of him lately. Every time I look at him, he surprises me, in a good way. Now, he's the caring family man, a loving brother who'd do anything for his sister, even when she's being a pain in the ass.

As we're driving into the lot of Ted's Pizza, the door of one of the shabby condos across from it opens, and Ellie's blonde head appears.

"Well, look at that," he mumbles.

As we drive closer, I notice that Ellie's limping, and her eyes are bleary, make-up smudged, and she's wearing a skin-bearing outfit that leaves little up to the imagination. I hate to say it, but this looks like the typical walk of shame.

She doesn't even notice our car until Brooks pulls right in front of her and powers down his window. "There you are."

She glares at him. "Why are you here?"

"What do you think? I'm looking for you. Get in."

Ellie looks up and down the street before starting to walk away. "I don't need your—"

"Get in," he says, voice louder, icy.

Rolling her eyes, she does as she's told. Brooks takes off, tires squealing, glaring at her in the back seat.

She lets out a little laugh. "Oh, so you *are* tapping that?"

I think she's referring to me. And if so, that's the absolute wrong thing to say, because at that moment, Brooks pounds the gas, his arms tight, his knuckles white on the wheel.

I feel like I'm in the middle of a powder keg. I know how this is going to go. He's going to give her shit for not being responsible, and Ellie's going to sink deeper, feeling like she's never going to live up to his expectations for her. No way is this going to end well.

When he opens his mouth to lay into her, I say, quickly, "We were worried about you, Ellie. We thought you were home with Jace?"

Thankfully, it works. Brooks swallows back his damning words and stares into the rear-view mirror, waiting for a response.

She shrugs. "I went out. I had a call from Dylan."

"So a booty call is more important than your son," Brooks says, almost to himself.

I glare at him, but she doesn't seem to have heard. She says, "Can we stop and get coffee? I need it. I think I'm still high."

He grits his teeth as he points the car toward the nearest cafe. "Your wish is my command."

"Thanks," she says, obliviously checking her phone. "Oh, wow, you called me a lot. So... Jace is at Kelly's?"

He grunts out a yes.

"Geez. What a ray of sunshine you are." She lets out a laugh.

This is like the calm before the storm. It's only going to get worse. So I turn around in my seat and say, gently, "Your brother's a little upset because he was at my place last night. He got a call in the morning from your son, who couldn't get in touch with you. He'd been home alone last night."

She stares, her smile fading to concern. "Oh," she says, sheepish.

"*Yeah,*" Brooks fills in, imitating her. "*Oh.*"

I put a hand on his arm before he can lay into her. By then, we're at the coffee shop. Since Kelly's taking care of Jace, I suggest we go inside and talk. The two of them look at me like they have nothing to say, but eventually, they agree.

We get our coffees and sit in a quiet corner. The two of them sit as far away from each other as possible, silently staring into their coffees, with me in the center. I bet if I weren't there, they'd come out punching.

I look between them, hoping one of them would be adult enough to break the ice, but it doesn't happen. Something tells me the ice is too thick.

Finally, I can't take it anymore. "Look. You each thought the other one was home to watch Jace. This is just a misunderstanding."

"We have a lot of those," Brooks says under his breath, shifting in his seat, still not looking at her.

Without warning, Ellie covers her face with her hands and begins to cry.

He watches her, unmoved. I glare at him, and he lets out a sigh. "Okay, okay. It's fine. I guess I should've told you I was leaving. I thought you were asleep."

Ellie doesn't say anything. She simply sobs quietly. I put a hand on her shoulder. "You're a good mom. You never would've left him, had you known."

"Never," she says, sniffling. "I think about how scared

he must've been when he woke up alone. Oh god. Kelly said he's okay?"

She finally looks to Brooks, who nods, and the next time he speaks, his voice is softer. "Yeah. He's okay."

They start to talk about taking him someplace fun this weekend to make up for it, and I smile. I think we might have just thawed the next cold war.

30

Brooks

I've never seen Jace smile so big.

It's a perfect summer day, with a cool breeze blowing off the ocean and copious amounts of cloudless sunshine. We're spending the Sunday at Funtown Splashtown, one of Maine's few amusement parks. It's our peace offering for the royal screw-up Ellie and I made Friday night. I think Jace forgot all about it the second his mom walked through the door, but I still felt like some retribution was in order.

Now Jace is riding a little boat on Cactus Canyon doing nothing but going around in circles, but he's pretending like he's the captain of this pirate ship and having a grand old time. "Ahoy maties!" he calls to us.

"Ahoy!" we call back from our shaded seats on a nearby bench.

I look down at my phone, and the message Tenley sent me.

Tenley: *I hope you two are still talking, and that wasn't a show for my benefit.*

I frown at the message. When we came off the BLIND LOVE app, I thought we'd just continue our flirty banter via text. Not so much.

Brooks: *Relax. We are talking. We're at the park with Jace right now.*

Tenley: *The three of you? That's great!*

Hmm. I've tried to sway her to other things, but she seems intent on discussing my relationship with Ellie, as if I'm just one of her cases from the women's center.

I can only think it means one thing—regret.

But I decide to test her anyway.

Brooks: *So when can I get you under me again?*

Nothing at first, and then the message switches from "delivered" to "read." Then, the ellipsis. It disappears and appears a few times before her response shows up:

Tenley: *Not sure. Busy.*

Okay. There's definitely regret at play here.

Before I can think of a response, Ellie jumps up and starts taking pictures of Jace, on the ride. "Jace! Jace, baby! Smile!" She snaps the pictures and stares at her phone. "That's a good one. He's so cute."

She walks back to me in her sunglasses and obscenely short shorts, grinning maniacally, oblivious to all the looks she's getting from fathers with their kids. Collapsing on the bench next to me, she shows me the photo. She's right. That's one cute kid.

"Thanks," she says quietly, as we're both staring at it. "For bringing us here. I know the tickets cost a fortune."

I wave her off. "Every kid needs to come to Funtown at least once in their childhood."

"But I couldn't do that without you," she says, her face tilted toward Jace. "It's all because of you. I know I need to get my act together. I know it. But..."

"I don't make it easy," I fill in.

She smiles. "You do not. But you never make *anything* easy. That's why I'm glad you're with Tenley. She won't take any of your shit." A blush climbs onto her cheeks. "She inspires me, you know."

I understand that. Tenley has a way about her. People might not like her, but they respect her, because she says what she means and means what she says. But I'm not sure I can trust Ellie to follow in her footsteps. She says a lot of things. And the last time Tenley thought she was helping, Ellie had only been trying to cheat her out of cash.

"You could probably learn a lot from her," I say.

"I think we all could," Ellie says as Jace comes bounding toward her, falling into her arms.

"Mom! That was so fun! There's no line. Can I ride again?"

"Sure, go ahead," she says, releasing him to rush off to the canopy where the ride begins. She smiles after him, waves, and then gives me a cheeky look. "So, why were you two together Friday night?"

I give her a hard glare.

"Oh, so you *were* tapping that?"

Again, I won't be dignifying that with a response.

She knows that, so she doesn't bother to wait. She says, "I still think Tenley needs a boring, safe guy. Not you."

I smirk at her. "And that's why I always tell you to keep your opinions to yourself."

"What?" She shrugs. "I can't help it. She's just so..."

"Out of my league?"

Ellie points forcefully. "Exactly."

She's probably right. I've had that same, niggling feeling, ever since Tenley and I decided to take it to the next level. Yes, we like each other. Yes, we have chemistry, and it was off the charts when we hooked up. But the future is anyone's guess. We could be nothing at all.

I glance down at the message Tenley sent me. I get the feeling nothing at all would be just fine with her.

"She's a good person. She's been sending me notes, you know, every so often. Just to make sure I'm okay."

I give her a sideways look. "Even after you screwed her?"

"I didn't screw her! I really did want to go for culinary—"

"Right."

She sighs. "Okay, okay. I wasn't sure exactly what classes I wanted to take. But I did want to take something."

"You need to focus. It's like I—"

"*Stop.* We're not talking about me. We're talking about you, and your love life," Ellie says, patting my arm. "Or lack thereof. Tenley is too good for you. But don't worry. All of my friends like you, for some reason I will never understand. Remember Raquel?"

I shake my head. I really have no clue.

"From Denny's? Remember? She has red hair? She was just telling me how she wishes you'd ask her out." When I stare at her blankly, she adds, "I'm just saying that, even if it doesn't work out with your lawyer friend, you always manage to land on your feet."

Land on my feet. Yes, I've always been good at that. Just call me the Bounce-back Kid.

Jace comes running up, into my arms, this time. "Arghhhh." I give him my best pirate impression. "Shiver me timbers... What do you say we go on the big log flume now?"

I point to the massive structure hulking in the distance.

He claps his hands, showing no sign of fear. Then he looks up at his mom. "All of us?"

Ellie smiles at him, then at me. "Yes. All of us."

31

Tenley

I can't believe I've slacked off this much.

Hunching over my desk, I page through mountains of never-ending dispositions and paperwork. Thanks to Courtney Perry's change of heart and new decision to go for her ex-husband's jugular, we have quite a bit more work to do.

My only saving grace is that I know the only other person going for this promotion has slacked off as well.

Not that I've really thought about the promotion that much. No, instead, my thoughts have been filled with other things.

Such as Brooks's washboard abs.

His perfect butt.

His...

I grit my teeth for the thousandth time and try to force my brain to behave. *It was nothing. It really meant nothing. What matters is that promotion. That's your key. You can't forget that you two are in a battle to the death for that partnership.*

Because I can guarantee, *he* hasn't.

No, this is probably the first rule in the Brooks Gentry playbook. *Disarm your enemy.*

And I hate to say it, but he had his dick in my mouth. And other places too. So... mission accomplished.

That's why I'm on high alert. This morning, I came in at six o'clock instead of my usual seven. I'm prepared for whatever attack he might launch because I know he's going to come at me even harder now. He's going to try to bring out the big guns, to level me until I scream for mercy.

Not. Happening.

So I'm a little pissed off with myself when Brooks appears, bright and early at seven AM, with two mugs of coffee.

He sets one down in front of me. "Two sugars, right?"

And I'm supposed to melt into a little puddle, just because he knows how I take my coffee? Drop my panties and spread my legs for a pre-office-hours quickie?

Okay, the urge is there.

Dammit.

I stifle it and continue to stare at the paper in front of me, though I've read the same word, *contested*, at least twenty times. "Stop acting all weird. We just hooked up once."

Make that twenty-one.

He chuckles and starts to close the door. "Relax. It's just coffee. It's not that deep."

I venture a glance up at him. Big mistake. It instantly makes me wet between the legs. How is it possible that he gets more and more gorgeous every time I see him? Same suit, same hair, tumbling over his forehead, same *I'm better than you* expression. And yet, now more than ever, I want to climb him like a tree. "You don't need to—"

My eyes fall back to the paper. This time, they land on the word *recurrent*.

No. It was just one night. It is most definitely not going to happen again. That's why I gave him his space for the rest of the weekend. I needed to process everything that had happened. And during those two lonely nights, I determined that it was best if we stopped this cold.

I also masturbated more than any human being should, all to thoughts of Brooks's hard body over me.

Sitting across the table from me and sipping his coffee, so relaxed, so confident about himself... he has no idea that when he sent me that message *When can you be under me again?* I'd salivated like one of Pavlov's dogs. It had taken every ounce of restraint left within me to tell him I was busy.

And I'd convinced myself it was for the best.

But even now, I can feel my resolve weakening.

And he hasn't even said a word about it yet!

So when he leans in and says my name in a way that makes it sound unspeakably sexy, I already know I'm in trouble.

"What?" I snap.

"We have a lot to do," he says, in a voice that tells me exactly what he's thinking about. And it has nothing to do with the Perry case. "We should work late tonight."

My mouth goes wet, because it's so much easier to picture exactly what will happen, now that I know him intimately. Before, that empty-cubicle fantasy was just that—a fantasy.

Now it's so real, I can taste it.

And he's used to women falling at his feet. Obviously,

by the way he phrased it. There was no question. He might as well have said, *You will stay late with me tonight*. I'm sure any other woman would eagerly accept.

I can't be another one of those.

Luckily, I remember I have other plans, which makes denying him so much easier.

I swallow, hard.

"C-can't." Oh my god, did I just stammer? What's wrong with me? I take a breath to collect myself. "I have to work at the women's center. I'm helping a new client."

Of course, Brooks Gentry isn't one to be shattered by a single denial. He barely registers a ripple. Instead, he makes a tutting noise and taps the file. "Shame. We have so much work to do."

Who does he think I am, an idiot? I'm not so naïve to think he's *actually* thinking about work.

Although ... maybe he is. He is right. We do have a lot of work to do. And if I deny him the chance to meet together and tackle it, it could get back to the partners and make me look bad. "I'd have to check my schedule," I say in a business-like, wooden voice. "But I think I have a few free hours tomorrow morning. We can work on it then?"

He pulls out his phone and starts to go through it. "Tuesday... morning?" He shakes his head. "No, that's not going to work for me."

I blink, wondering just what else he has going on then. It's probably an actual work meeting. No reason to be jealous over that.

And yet I am.

Because I'm an idiot.

I force myself to shrug with indifference. "That is a shame. I guess—"

"I have your schedule here too. And it looks like we're

both free Wednesday night. I'm putting you down." He jabs in something with his thumb.

I'm putting you down.

My phone beeps with a meeting request. For me. And him. The purpose of the meeting? That's blank. Allowing me to fill in all sorts of lurid details. Location? Empty also, but I can't help thinking of an empty cubicle.

I glare at the ACCEPT button.

I'm not going to accept. I'm not going to accept. I AM NOT GOING TO ACCEPT.

Of course I'm going to accept.

Oh God. I really do suck.

"It could run pretty late," he says with a wink, sweeping out of the office.

"We'll see!" I call after him, but who am I kidding?

I'll be counting the moments.

32

Brooks

Tenley taps on her keyboard, a thoughtful look on her face. I keep looking over the screen of my laptop, wondering when she'll break her concentration and look up at me.

She doesn't.

I've got to give her credit, because the tension in the room is electric. And yet she's still poised, intent on her work.

It's sexy as hell.

Not to mention it's distracting. But it's not entirely her fault. Ever since last Friday, I've been thinking about things a lot. Rethinking my priorities.

Foster and Foster might be the best law firm in downtown Portland. But there are others. I have a ton of connections from Yale who'd jump to have me if I wanted. I have other options.

But more than that, if I want to be there for Jace—and it

feels like I need to be—then putting in the hours of a partner is not what I need right now.

This might be fate.

Impatient, I look up at the clock. I've counting the moments, and I'm about to explode. Kurt the janitor was the only person still in the office, but I'm pretty sure even he's left. I haven't heard him whistling in the hallways in over an hour.

That means we're alone. And since we've been working for a long time, I think we could use the tension breaker.

Tenley looks up from her laptop. "Okay, I just finished. Unless there is something else you're working on, I think we're through here."

I shake my head slowly. "We're not done."

She gives me a curious look, all innocence. But she's no idiot. She knows exactly what unfinished business we have. "What are you working on?"

Pushing my leather executive chair away from the table, I point to the carpet in front of me. "Close your laptop and come here."

She gives me a doubtful look. "Brooks ..."

"You know you want to."

She looks out toward the hallway and bites her lower lip. "It doesn't matter what I want. We're at work. And the promotion—"

"Hey." There's that word again. The one I've been hearing constantly. It gets my blood boiling. I fix her with an intense stare. "I know you and I have been going hard at that partnership for months. But what about—for one night —if we just *don't*? Frankly, Tenley, right now, I don't give a shit about it."

"Right *now*..." she repeats, as if I'll change my mind the second I pull out of her.

That might have been me a month ago. But now? Things have shifted.

And I'm ready to accept that.

I smirk. "Fine. You want the partnership? You can have it. The only thing I want is you."

The doubt on her face deepens, but I shrug and pull my laptop toward me. I dictate the email as I'm typing it. "Dear Partners. I have decided to respectfully bow out of the partnership promotion. Thank you for the opportunity, but let Tenley Bayliss have it, because not only is she an incredible attorney, but she also looks fan-fucking-tastic on my cock. Sincerely—"

She rolls her eyes, arms folded. "You're so full of it."

"And send." I press the button and grin triumphantly. "Sent."

Her mouth falls open. "You didn't."

"I did." I spin the laptop toward her. "Come see for yourself."

"You couldn't have. About me on your—your—" She jumps to her feet and practically throws herself across the length of the table to have a look. Frantic, she reads what I'd written, her eyes darting back and forth.

"Okay, fine. I left out the part about you looking fantastic on my cock, even if it's true. But I sent the rest of it."

She eyes are wide. "I can't believe you did that."

I motion her forward. "Come here."

I'm expecting sass—this is Tenley, after all—but I don't get it. She nods, almost as if she has no other choice. It tells me she knows just what I want, and that she wants it too.

She snaps her laptop shut and slides from the chair across from me, then saunters toward me, standing next to the arm of my chair. There's a sly little smile on her face, like she's trying to figure out what I'm up to and is game to find out.

"Why would you do that?" she asks.

I spin to face her and stand. The momentum backs her up, so that her bottom brushes the edge of the table. There's a strand of hair loose from her ponytail, and I pull it down, coiling it around my finger. "Oh. Did I not make myself clear before? I don't want the job, I want *you*."

Tenley squints, her head tilting. She doesn't believe me. Which is fine. Talk is cheap. I'm more than happy to let my actions to the speaking from here on out …

I stretch an arm out behind her, move my legal pad, and close the laptop. I lean forward, inhaling the floral perfume of her hair, giving her even less space. She makes no effort to move back, but she doesn't lean into me either. I slide the laptop from the surface of the table onto the seat of one of the chairs.

There. My half of the conference room table is bare.

Just like she will be in a moment.

I lift her gently, placing Tenley on my desk.

She's figured it out. I can see it in her eyes.

"Wh—what are you doing?" she asks.

I lean down. My lips hover just in front of hers, but I don't brush them. I need to know she wants this and when her mouth moves on mine, I'm convinced.

Her arms close behind my neck. Her kiss is urgent and at the same time somehow sweet.

I pull away. "You mean what are *we* doing?"

She nods.

"I think you know. I think you've wanted it as much as I have."

My palms drop to the smooth cherrywood of the table, fingers kneading her firm ass.

The kiss is long—longer than I mean it to be—and deep. In my fantasies, there was something fast and rabid about it, quick and dirty. But I can't fight the need to want to savor every moment with her. When I'm finally able to break my mouth away from hers, she gasps as I kiss down her jawline and her neck.

I kiss back up her jawline to her lips and take her mouth with mine again. My hands roam down the sides of her body to the hem of her skirt. God. This is the skirt from my fantasies—tight and yet somehow demure. I clutch the fabric in both hands and start to yank it up.

She pulls away from me and throws a hand up. "Brooks, wait … stop."

Damn. Did I read her wrong? I let go and straighten up. As soon as my breath is no longer frantic and ragged, I ask, "What's wrong?"

She raises an eyebrow. "Are there … security cameras here?"

I laugh, planting my hands on the desk and kissing her forehead. "No."

"Are you sure?" She looks around. "No one will see us?"

I move one hand and comb it through her dark, lush hair. "The only security cameras are in the front lobby. I made sure."

"Really sure?"

In my fantasies, we never had to worry about this. But in the past few days, since I started thinking about how to make it a reality, I've done my homework. "Absolutely."

She studies me for any hint of a lie, then, satisfied, leans in kisses me.

And this time when my hands clutch the hem of that skirt, she doesn't stop me. In fact, she helps with the zipper, and soon, it's puddled at her feet. The pearl buttons on her blouse are so small and delicate, but she helps me with those too. I unclasp a nude-colored lace bra, edging it off of her bit by bit.

Helping her back onto the slick cherry surface of the enormous table, I take a moment to take her in. Tenley Bayliss, wearing nothing but a little black lace thong, nylons, and high heels, sitting atop the conference room table, her legs spread for me.

As she beckons me, I'm positive I've never seen anything so sexy in my life.

My breath hitches as I bridge the distance in record-time, ready to kiss and touch and suck everything in my sight. Reminding myself not to get too excited, I take my time.

I kiss down her jawline, neck, and cleavage, then take a pert pink nipple in my mouth as I roll the other between my fingers. Her legs swing wildly around me, so much so that she kicks me once or twice.

It's hard not to chuckle even as badly as I want to take her. I take one last taste before laying her back, then I grab her legs and gently pull her so her ass is at the edge of the table and her legs are wrapped around me. With my fingers tucked into the waist of her nylons, they roll down. I remove them so her feet are bare, kneel on my knees, and press a kiss to the bottom of each foot.

Her feet flex as my lips brush against the soles of her feet.

I kiss her ankle then up her shin to her knee, and up her thigh to her hip. When I come to the lace panties, I press my tongue against it until both my tongue and the cloth sink in.

Her thighs squeeze around my neck. "Oh my god ..."

I move up and sink my teeth into the purple panties

pulling them off, and then I kiss down. This time there is nothing between her opening and my tongue. She quivers. I don't need to linger. One stroke of the tongue lets me know she's ready.

I've been ready.

But I also love her taste. I can taste her all day long, every day. I lap at her, listening to her sweet sounds, holding her body still as she attempts to writhe under my control. I feel her body tensing as she whimpers, begging me for more.

"Tell me what you want." I exhale my warm breath against her sex.

"You." Her voice is tortured. "Inside me."

She doesn't have to ask twice. My pants drop to the floor, followed by my briefs. I loop a hand around each thigh anchoring myself to her and thrust into her.

She covers her face with her hands and screams.

"Tenley ..." I sigh, holding her in place as I thrust.

Her legs wrap tighter around me as she matches my momentum, and then her hooked legs climb up my back as I fill her to the hilt.

She's shaking, bucking, clawing my back. "Brooks ..."

I explode as she comes, then I scoop her up off the desk and sit down in the chair letting her straddle me, her hair falling over my face.

"Thank you." She drops her head to my shoulder.

"For what?"

"The way I feel right now." Her voice is still low, the words a moan.

I hold her tighter.

"That isn't something you need to thank me for. You were an equal player." I kiss her. "You deserve better."

She giggles. "I'm not sure how that could have been better."

"No... I mean, you're right," I say with a smile. Hell yes, it was perfect. "But what I meant is that I want to take you out. On a proper date."

She tilts her head. "A proper date? You mean, with clothes on, other people around? Without us clawing at each other like rabid animals? You think we could do that?"

I shrug. "I'd have to clear it with Ellie, obviously, make sure she's not working, but... yeah."

She gasps, mock-surprised. "What would other people say?"

I kiss her chin. "Who the hell cares? Are you in, or not?"

33

Tenley

Are you in, or not?

Of course I am.

I was into going on a "proper date" with Brooks just as much as I was in to fucking him on the conference room table. Anything involving him, I'm game for.

I still can't believe we did that, by the way. No, it wasn't an unused cubicle... but it so many ways, it was hotter than even my most lurid fantasies.

So hot, I'd spent the rest of the week, salivating for the chance to do it again. But Brooks was every bit the gentleman the rest of the week. Every bit the professional. Every time we were in the same room together, he barely afforded me a single sexy look.

The good thing? We got a lot of work done.

The bad thing? All we did was get a lot of work done.

I'd like to think he was being respectful, because, as he

said, "I deserve better." So now, as I get ready for our *proper date*, I'm so excited, I can barely think straight.

I clip on an earring, studying myself in the mirror and making sure I look perfect for him. I'm wearing a little red sundress that probably shows far more skin than most people have seen on me—but not him. I know he'll be blown away because it's sexy and short and cleavage-bearing, nothing like what I wear to the office.

Somewhere in the back of my mind, I know I'm a glutton for punishment. He might just be playing me, but I don't think so.

He has no reason to now.

The promotion is mine.

It hasn't been officially announced, no. But yesterday, Lisa pulled me aside and said it was mine, if I wanted it.

As if she needs to ask.

I can't even explain the burden that was lifted from my shoulders, when Brooks did that for me. I was so uptight, so nervous. And now, I feel relaxed, happy... like a totally different person.

It's all because of him.

Of course, I feel bad that there can't be two partnerships, because Brooks deserves it. But he told me why he made the choice. For Jace. For me.

And so, yes. I am absolutely, one-hundred percent, falling for Brooks Gentry. How can I not? I keep telling myself I need to guard my heart from getting it broken, but I can't help it. Every time I look at him, I want to fall so fast into his arms and never let go.

He rings the doorbell right at nine on the dot, which makes me happy. *He's on time when it's important.*

I scuff into my sandals and rush downstairs, opening the door with a breathless excitement. "Hi."

He gives me a once-over, then leans in and takes my hand, kissing my cheek. "Wow. You're gorgeous."

He doesn't look so bad himself—he's wearing slim khakis and a button-down shirt and loafers, and he smells delicious.

"Ready?" He tugs my hand outside, but I want to tug him *in*. I give him a mischievous little smile and he gives me a stern, warning look. "Proper date. We'll miss our reservations."

I pout. "Oh. Okay."

I follow him out to the car, where, like a true gentleman, he opens the car door for me. He even puts the seatbelt on for me too, as if I couldn't do that myself. I don't mind it, because as he leans over, I get to inhale his yummy after-shave and let his stubble tickle my face. Once it's clipped in, he gives me a chaste kiss on the lips.

When he takes off, headed for Portland, I say, "I'm thinking we're *not* going to Periwinkle."

He chuckles. "No way in hell."

"Good choice. Fore Street?"

He shakes his head.

"Street & Company? Scales?"

"Nope."

I wrack my brain, thinking of the many better restaurants I've taken clients to in the downtown area. "Please tell me you're not taking me to that place with the oysters."

He gives me a look. "They are an aphrodisiac."

"I don't think we need any help where that is concerned."

He laughs and snakes a hand over the center console, setting it on my thigh. "No, we do not. But, my curious one, you're just going to have to sit your little ass tight and wait until we get there."

I pout again.

If it has any effect on him, he doesn't show it. He adeptly changes the subject. "You spoke to Lisa this morning, I saw. How did that go?"

I can't fight the ear-to-ear smile that spreads over my face. "She told me they're giving me the promotion. They're not going to announce it yet, but... yeah. But..." I look over at him. "It doesn't feel fair. We should've fought each other to the death."

"Oh, yeah? I told you, though. You deserved it, fair and square."

"That's not true, and you know it. Did you talk to any of the partners? They must've wondered why you were backing out?"

He nods but doesn't say any more.

"Well? What did they say?" I goad.

He shrugs. "Guess they wanted us to fight to the death, too. But I'm glad we're not," he says, his fingers making lazy circles on my thigh, flirting with the hem of my dress. "I'm a pacifist. Make love, not war."

I snort. "Right."

I get the feeling there's something he's not telling me. Lisa was happy for me when she told me the good news, but there's no question she was pulling for Brooks. And maybe the other partners were too. They had to be shocked when he pulled out. Maybe they even tried to convince him to reconsider.

Then I look out and realize he's exited 295 before reaching the Portland city limits, and is now heading east toward the coast. When he pulls down a dark, wooded road that is little more than two tire ruts in the ground, I wonder what he's really up to.

"So... did you let me have the promotion because you

expected to drive me out into a remote place and push me off a cliff?" I wonder aloud, looking out the window and seeing nothing but darkness.

"There's a thought."

I punch him, just as the trees part, and the moonlight catches the glimmering ocean below. We must be up pretty high, because it feels like the sea is all around us. He brakes and I catch a look at his face. He's smiling, leaning over the wheel and gazing at the gorgeous seascape. "I wanted to bring you out here. *Not* to kill you. I thought we could have a picnic."

A picnic? I stare at him in shock. That's the sort of thing from romance movies and novels. Do guys really do things like that? The Brooks Gentry I thought I knew never would have. But this one?

Yes. I guess he would. "Did you bring strawberries?"

"Why? You like them?"

I nod. "*Love* them."

"With whipped cream?"

"Yes!"

He frowns. "They're an aphrodisiac, though. And this is a proper date."

"Oh." So that's a no. "So what did you bring for this picnic, then? Finger sandwiches and tea?"

He pulls off his seatbelt and opens the door, then turns to wag a finger at me. "You're just going to have to wait."

He goes around back and opens the trunk, and then he opens my door and helps me out. He's holding a little wicker basket. I don't know many men who have a wicker basket like that on hand, so I'd like to think he bought it just for me. "Look at you, boy scout."

We walk along a wooded path to a stone outcropping, overlooking the mirror-calm ocean. The sun has long-set behind us, but the lights from ships passing on the horizon, and from the busy Portland harbor in the distance, provide a light show as beautiful as any sunset or fireworks display. It's a little chilly, so when he sets out the blanket and opens us each a beer, Brooks wraps an arm around me and we just sit there, snuggling and taking in the view.

"So this is a proper date," I muse.

He nods and says, "Don't you think so? Or would you have rather gone to Fore Street?"

I shake my head adamantly. Not just because this is a beautiful view, but because that restaurant is a favorite of my co-workers. If anyone saw us there, it would be all over Foster & Foster by morning. Most of them already don't like me, so I can just imagine what the rumors will be when they see us together.

"You don't have to worry about that," he says, as if reading my mind.

"Easy for you to say. Everyone loves you. If anything negative is to be said, it will be on me." I raise the pitch of my voice, impersonating them. "*She made him give up the promotion. She insisted he bend over and take it. She knows she's not nearly as good as him. It's all her fault.*"

He gazes at me. "Are you kidding? First of all, I never cared what any of the people in the office said. And secondly, you're twice as good an attorney as I'll ever be."

"Oh, please," I argue. "You're—"

"No. Listen. Yeah, I wanted the promotion, sure. Mostly to prove to myself I wasn't a complete fraud."

I stare at him in shock. "What?"

He nods. "I think that goes with the territory of being abandoned as a kid. It doesn't really matter how high you soar—it's never enough. You never get over the fact that the person who was supposed to love you most... left."

I nod sadly. I know that feeling. So deeply, I feel a stab of pain in my chest for him. I put a hand on his and squeeze it. "You are not a fraud. Everything in your life, all the things you've done... how can you think that?"

He shrugs.

"If anything, I'm the fraud. I've always had imposter syndrome, like I needed to prove myself. You know the first thing that happened to me when I stepped inside my very first law classroom? I *cried*."

He looks at me. "You cried?"

"Yes. The professor put me on the spot, and I couldn't think, and I ran out, crying. After that, I thought I'd never be a lawyer. But then I talked to my mom, who told me something Ruth had told her—that it's business. Women can't be emotional in this business, or they will get torn apart. *Strike first,* my mother said. *Put them on the defensive.* So I buried my emotions. I steeled myself. I told myself I wouldn't let anyone get too deep inside me to see that weakness. That's why no one likes me at the firm. I've been so devoted to getting that partnership at any cost... I guess I forgot... like you said. *Tact.*"

He gives me a small smile. "I was wrong to say that. You wouldn't have won so many cases if you couldn't win the judge. I was just envious over your record. And how you're always so perfect and right."

"Of me? I hated how everyone loved you. The partners love you most, you know. I was sure they were going to give you the promotion," I say. "Are you sure you—"

"Absolutely. Look. I had it in my head I'd be able to afford a better life for Jace. But I realize that what he needs right now isn't a bigger bedroom or for his uncle to be some big, high-powered partner at a law firm. He doesn't give a shit about that. What he needs is more time with me."

I stare into his eyes, wondering if that could be true. He'd seemed too ruthless before, so wholly devoted to getting that partnership, whatever the cost. I remember those words he'd said to me as we left Lisa's office. *Good luck. You're going to need it.*

"Really?" I squeak out.

He nods. "That partnership... it's just not the ideal time. Besides, I love working at Foster & Foster, doing what I'm doing. It might not be a lot of money, but you know what? There are other things more important than that. It's a good firm. I'm happy there. They like me. It's... all right."

All right. But not ideal.

In that moment, I can see it so clearly.

He wants more. He wants his chance. But he's letting me have this one.

"You know, you're a lot nicer a person than I thought, Mr. Brooks Gentry," I say, kissing his cheek. "Mr. Stranger88, Esquire."

His arm is around my shoulder, but he shifts slightly so he can dig into the picnic basket. Then he pulls out a white container, sets it on his lap, and pulls off the lid. He holds something up to my lips and I smile against it before taking a bite.

Strawberries.

34

Brooks

Turns out, the picnic wasn't strictly necessary. We don't do much eating on our date, save for the strawberries.

Just a lot of cuddling, kissing, and talking. By the time we get back to her place and she invites me in for a night cap, the picnic basket is still full. "Can I bring this stuff in and put it in your fridge for tomorrow? Do you have space?"

"Oh, sure." She opens the door to her place, and we go inside, straight to the kitchen.

I didn't have to ask if she had the space. Her fridge is nearly as empty as mine is. I start pulling sandwiches and desserts out, feeding them into the shelves, as she watches, standing behind the open fridge door. "Oh God. I feel bad! I didn't know you had all this!"

"Hey. I don't feel bad at all. I liked what we did a hell of a lot more." I grin at her, remembering it, and lean in and kiss her.

When we break the kiss, she grabs the front of my shirt

and yanks me to her, kissing me harder and with all of her strength, so surprisingly hard that I stumble back and almost get trapped by the door.

I step around it and, rapping my arms around her, I walk her back from the refrigerator, closing it with my foot. I hoist her onto the center island, helping her take off each of her shoes, then dropping them to the tile floor. Then I ease her toward me, so that my waist is trapped between her knees. I urge the dress up on her thighs, placing my hands on her bare hips. "Well, look at you. You look good enough to eat."

She licks her lips in anticipation.

I pull her close to me, my hand trailing under the loose, silky fabric of her dress, and up the warm, smooth skin of her back, feeling the angled rise of her shoulder blades. God, she's gorgeous, and smells like dewy fresh air and ocean breezes.

Then I kiss her, softly, tenderly, savoring the sugary sweetness from the strawberries on her tongue. I delve a hand around her front, cupping her full, round breast.

She heaves in a breath, and her ribcage pressed against my wrist. "Oh," she murmurs. "I love that."

The thin straps of the dress fall down over her shoulders, exposing her to me. Every time I look at her breasts, they're better and better. Pale and sweet, the nipples already pebbling in the cool air. I rub a thumb over the tips, and they respond, growing harder.

She starts to let out a low moan but catches herself, sucking her lower lip into her mouth self-consciously.

I'll have none of that. I maneuver her closer to me, bringing my hands down the small of her back to her round ass.

Pulling her body toward me, I take her breast in my

hand and run my tongue along the hardened nipple. "I can stay here all day, Tenley, sucking on you like this. Do you want me to suck on them some more?" I breathe into her skin.

"Oh, yes," she says, inching forward, offering them to me. "Please."

Holding them both in either hand, I bring one to my mouth, taking it in, moving my tongue in slow circles around the puckered flesh. She presses her palms onto my shoulders, hard. letting out a little squeak of exhilaration as I thoroughly explore the skin. It's as sweet as the rest of her, tasting faintly of the sea air, and just her. Just that sweet, uniquely female scent that intoxicates me.

I move to the other breast, getting my fill of that one, before switching to the next, all the while molding her ass cheeks.

Though my cock is straining against my pants, wanting to pick things up, I'm in no hurry. I could stay here, trapped between her legs, sucking on her tits, caressing her perfect ass until sun-up.

"You're fucking perfect, you know that?" I growl, never stopping lavishing attention on her breasts. "I can't get enough of you. Lie back."

She does, sitting up on her elbows to lift her ass so I can help her lower the dress down over her hips, then gaze at her body, clad only in a small black thong. God, she's more than gorgeous. She is a work of art. It's almost enough to make me forget myself. A second passes, two, with me just staring, until I sense her unease and break out of my trance, letting out the deep breath I've been holding.

She smiles unsurely.

I come up close to her, hovering over her. I kiss her then,

close to but not touching her naked body. She reaches out to undress me, undoing each button on my dress shirt with slow, deliberate movement.

I explore her mouth, nibbling on her lips, letting her tongue dance with mine.

I nearly growl from the pleasure of her hands when they land flat on the skin of my chest. Eagerly, I rip the rest of my shirt off, letting her concentrate now on getting me naked.

When I pull off my pants, she wastes no time in getting my underwear down too. She gazes at me as I stand before her naked.

But I can barely wait anymore.

I reach forward, without warning, taking her legs and spreading them wide, hooking my arms underneath her knees. She gasps as I lowered my face to her thighs and slowly began to lick every inch of her skin. She squirms, her thighs trembling, her breaths coming in fits and starts. I try to be as thorough as could be, lapping everywhere.

She arches her back off the granite countertop, urging me on.

When I ask, "Do you want my tongue on your pussy?" that she bobs her head in desperate anticipation.

Slowly —too slowly for her liking, I can tell—I lift her legs and lower them down on either of my shoulders. She closes her eyes, and I can tell from the tortured look on her face and the way she reaches for my head that she's just as excited as I am.

But I want her to plead. I want her to beg me, because she has me begging for mercy every minute I'm away from her. It's a sweet pain, knowing we're this close to getting what we both want. So I take my time, timing the assault for when she's at her most desperate. When she's trembling uncontrollably, nearly sobbing, her hands scrabbling at her sides, reaching for my head, I know she's ready.

There's no tentative tasting, no nibbling. With no warning, I plant my open mouth, full on her clit, and suck her hard.

She cries out, bucking against me. "Oh, god ... Brooks ... maybe we should slow down?"

Her hands fly to my head, but I grab them and hold them together, rigid against her belly.

"Slow down?" I stop. "Does it not feel good?"

"No, it feels incredible, I just—"

"There's nothing wrong with letting yourself enjoy it."

I take my time, drawing out every lick, every flick of my tongue on her folds. I move my hands to her thighs, which are now moist and sticky with her arousal, spreading her apart. She relaxes, letting my tongue slide slowly and languorously up the crease of her folds.

Her head falls back, and she whimpers with a combination of relief and delight. "That's so good," she moans. "Oh God, I've never felt anything like this, Brooks."

Encouraged, I lick upward, slowly, fully, from bottom to top, tongue darting in and out of her. She gasps again and again, her sounds coming deep from her throat, primal and uncontrolled. Then I dig in with my tongue, pressing against the nerves of her sensitive nub, and I feel her whole body begin to twitch and tremble.

She moans louder. "Brooks... I don't know if I can take much more of this."

My tongue circles her clit and pushes inside. I wrap my arms around her thighs, tight, and caress her ass. Whatever fire I've lit, it's building.

But just as I feel her beginning to fall over the brink of ecstasy, I let go. Not yet. Not yet. I want this to last.

She opens her eyes, exasperated. Those deep brown eyes met mine, and she pleads desperately, "Please, Brooks. Please..."

"What do you want?" My voice is more breath than sound. "Say it."

"Make me come."

I attack her clit again, this time my tongue relentless, flicking over her clit, bringing her close again, teetering on the edge. She arches up against me, meeting my tongue, writhing now. Sucking her clit, pulling on it gently with my teeth, I give it everything I have.

The orgasm rips through her in such a way that it feels like an earthquake beneath us, a seismic shift that sends the world spinning end-over-end. She comes so hard that I think she might explode in my mouth. I suckle her clit deeply as she screams loud, throwing herself forward on the counter.

"Oh god ...," she sighs.

I pull her legs off my shoulders, smirking with satisfaction.

But I can tell from the wolfish look in her eye that she's far from done. She sits up on the edge of the counter, her legs still trapping me, wrapping around my waist. She takes a single finger of the whipped cream and trails it through the hair on my chest. Then she licks her fingertip thoughtfully, her tongue dancing over it in a way that's so goddamn sexy.

I grin as she leans in and begins to lick the icing off my chest. She threads her hands around my neck and her tongue making designs on my pectorals, making *Mmmm* noises as she presses her wet core into my rock hard erection. I can't say I object. I want as much of her skin against mine as possible.

Then she looks at me, eyes dark with desire. "Fuck me," she says, surely and shamelessly.

God, this woman is my undoing. I nearly lose balance, it's so damn good.

This time, I'm ready. I scoop a hand under her ass and drag her to me. I run a hand down her breasts, cupping them, then pressed my chest toward her, flattening her breasts against me.

She takes my cock in her hand, holding it still and ready at her entrance.

I lean forward, capturing her face in my hands. I kiss her almost gently. She thrusts her tongue desperately into my mouth.

I move my hands to her shoulders, down her arms, and hold her wrists on the counter, at her sides. I want her so badly that I took in a shuddery breath. "Ready?"

She nods and guides my cock to her entrance. I give a gentle nudge, and she pushes the rest of the way onto me. Feeling her slide on inch by inch, I teeter on the edge of madness as I strain to make it last, to make it significant. But the feeling of my cock filling her, stretching her, fitting into her so perfectly is almost enough to make me lose it.

"You're so good inside me," she breathes in awe, her forehead falling down and resting on my shoulder.

"You're so tight and sweet," I breathe into her skin. I plant my hands on her hips and pull her closer to me, until she's flush against me and I'm buried as far as I could go.

I slide out, leaving just the tip inside her, then plunge in deeper. She lets out a hardened moan.

"You okay?" I ask, stopping.

"Yeah, yeah, it's good. Just like that. Keep going," she whispers to me. "As fast and hard as you can."

I let out a surprised groan. Her wish is my command. So I do it again, my tip nestled at her entrance, then thrusting in harder, revving up.

It doesn't take long to get into the rhythm. Soon I'm pounding into her, making her whimper with every thrust. It's so intense, so perfect, the way we work together, with her meeting each one of my thrusts with fervor. All I can do is hold on tight to her hips.

Whatever chord she's hitting inside me, it's a chord that has never been struck, ever. An orgasm is building inside me, and I can feel that it was going to be a tidal wave. I can feel her insides twinging and spasming inside me, and I know I'm not feeling it alone.

The rhythm increases to a frantic pace, and my hovering climax crashes down around us, enough to shake the complex off its foundation. "Come, Tenley."

"But I want you to..." She protests.

"Don't worry about me," I growl, and next second, she comes hard, so hard that she screams loud enough that I'm surprised the granite slab beneath us doesn't break in half.

Groaning, I lift her and tip her back so that I'm supporting her whole weight, hovering above her. I drill my cock into her, kissing her neck, her gorgeously swaying breasts. She wraps her legs tight around me, and our eyes lock. My muscles flex and tighten, and I crash into her, growling, rough and hard, body jerking and raw, fingers digging into her ass as I milk my orgasm.

When the last waves subside, I set her back down on the counter, and draw myself out slowly. She strokes my back, running her fingers down the contours of my body to my ass.

She smiles at me as I kiss her shoulder. It's dark in the apartment, the only light the moonlight and streetlights, filtering in through the open glass door to the balcony. "Ready for bed?"

She smiles, and I help her off the counter. She takes my hand, leading me upstairs.

In the morning, I wake up feeling like a million bucks, with her wrapped around me. I quietly disentangle myself from her and take a shower, and when I return, she's still sleeping peacefully. So I go out to the donut place on the corner and return with two tall coffees and a selection of pastries.

When I step inside, she's coming down the steps in her robe, twirling her hair into a messy bun. "Oh! Donuts? I thought you left me without saying goodbye."

"Hey. That's bullshit. I'll always say goodbye," I say, going to the kitchen and setting the donuts down on the counter where we'd just made love. "I hope you like Boston cream."

"*Love*," she says, so I pull one out of the box and feed her a bite.

As she lets out a little orgasmic moan that makes my cock dance in my pants, I take the next bite. I'm just starting to chew when she grabs my hand.

"Hey. Hello? You're taking all the custard! What's with that?"

"What are you, the donut police? I bought these," I remind her.

She's grabbing my hand at the wrist, licking the cream from the center of the donut in a very suggestive way. I'd tell her I have another two in the box, but I'm enjoying this too much.

"Happy?" I say as she finishes the donut, licking my fingers clean.

"Mmmhmm."

I reach into the box and take out another one, shoving the whole thing in my mouth. The cream oozes out between my lips, and she smacks me. "You slob! Why didn't you tell me?"

I hold up a finger, chewing, chewing, and finally swallow. "You can have the other one."

"Thanks..." She lifts the lid and frowns. "They look so good. But one is enough for me. How do you eat like that and keep those abs?"

"I'm just naturally... incredible." I push her coffee over to her and take another donut.

She rolls her eyes. "I don't think that excuse is going to work with the partners." She opens the lid and peers inside, and, satisfied that I got her order right, fixes the lid on again. "Geez. This is nice. It feels like we're dating."

I nod. It certainly does feel that way.

"Are we?"

I look up. She looks a little worried. "Yeah. I guess we are. I mean, is that not what we're doing? We're together. Right?"

She smiles. "Yes. But...what about work? Company policy..."

Ah, that's the problem. She has that new promotion now. And secretly dating me is probably not going to do her any favors with the partners, especially now that she's a part of that upper echelon who both makes and keeps the rules in the firm.

"We should disclose it to HR first thing Monday morning. Is that what you're thinking?" I ask her.

She nods. "Yes. I think that would make me feel better."

"Then that's what we'll do." I reach into the box and take the last Boston cream out, setting it on a napkin in front of her, and fix her with a wolfish grin. "Eat up. You're going to need your energy today for what I have planned for you."

35

Tenley

At seven AM on Monday morning, I arrive at the office building, practically dancing on air.

That all comes to a crashing halt at 7:01 when I try my key card.

Bzzz. Denied.

I try it again. Same thing.

Then I tug on the door handle helplessly, wondering if I left it too close to something magnetic, and that screwed it up.

Shelly comes by a few minutes later. I've never said good morning to her, so she doesn't bother saying it to me now. Instead, she just says, "You forget your ID?"

"No." I hold it up. "It's just not working."

She tries her card, which she perpetually keeps on a beaded lanyard on her chest. But that doesn't work either. "Odd."

She tries it again. And again. Nothing.

"It has to be a glitch, right?" I ask.

"Probably." She sounds doubtful as she shields her eyes and presses her face to the window, looking inside. She knocks hard.

Thankfully, one of the lobby security guards jogs over and opens the door. I don't know him by name—never bothered to find out—but Shelly does. "Thank you, Bruce. Something's going on with our cards."

Bruce lets us in. "Well, that's not good. You two go on. It's probably something with the door."

We watch as another person from one of the other companies in the building swipes their card and passes right through. "Is it happening to anyone else?" I ask, starting to worry.

Even though I asked the question, the guard speaks to Shelly as he guides us to the elevators. "Don't be alarmed. I'm sure it'll get sorted out."

Of course we only wind up getting more alarmed when we reach the floor of Foster & Foster. We're the first ones there, as usual, so we turn on the lights, go toward our respective offices, and turn on our computers, but a few moments later, we're back in the hallway. Shelly has her cell phone to her ear and looks just as confused as I feel. "When did you last speak with the partners?" she asks me.

I shrug. I used to get one of them on the horn almost every weekend. But not this time. This weekend was delightfully partner-free. Stress-free.

But now I feel the stress pouring back in, tightening my shoulders. "Have you spoken to any of them?"

"I've been trying to call Tom. No answer. I'll try Ed next. I guess." She looks at her phone and presses a single button.

I grab my phone. "I can call Lisa."

I punch in her number, but it rings right through to her voicemail. I leave a message, then end the call, just as Shelly ends hers. "Anything?"

Shaking my head, I say, "Bill Lindsey?"

She nods and starts to punch in the call as the bell above the elevator dings. We both turn, hoping for the solution to our problems, but it's just Mike. I'm surprised he's here this early. He looks worse for wear, as if he had a tough weekend —his eyes are bloodshot, the lower half of his face is covered in raw razor burn and his tie is loose and crooked. He's carrying a giant metal commuter mug.

"What the hell's going on?" he says, more to Shelly than to me since he still doesn't like me. "Why didn't my card work? Did someone fire me when I wasn't looking?"

"No. It happened to both of us, too. We're trying to figure it out," Shelly says, lifting the phone to her ear. She shakes her head. "Another voicemail."

"Shit. This isn't good," he says, more serious than I've ever seen him before.

"Hold on. Don't get worked up. It might be nothing," I tell him calmly.

He scowls at me and says, "Shelly always knows where the partners are. Don't you, Shell? If you don't know..."

Shelly retreats to her desk, and we follow her over there. She starts going through the schedules of the partners, since she coordinates all of their appointments. "Hmm. Well, Lisa has a meeting in Falmouth at nine. And Bill's clear... but he doesn't come in Monday mornings. He has a lunch later in the afternoon with Lisa..."

"And the others?"

She frowns. "They're supposed to be in. This is very odd. I don't know what to say."

I don't, either. I grab my phone and text the only person I can think of, right now. Brooks.

Tenley: *Something's going on. Our keycards didn't work, and the brothers are missing. Where are you?*

He responds almost instantly.

Brooks: *Are you serious? I'm on my way in. I'll stop by Tom's place—it's on the way.*

Leave it to Brooks to know where Tom lived. I always got the feeling the brothers were inviting him on upstate hunting trips and schmoozy little backyard barbecues with clients. I'm no idiot—I know it's because he knows how to schmooze and I don't. He's pleasant company, and I never have been. But this time, I'm not jealous. I'm thankful.

My man is a man of action. *He* will be able to get to the bottom of this.

"Hold on. Brooks is going to stop by Tom's place before he comes in," I announce.

We all retreat to our offices, but of course, no work gets done. Every time the elevator doors open, new rumors fly. I try to concentrate on tying up loose ends with the Perry case, but it's practically impossible. Especially when Brooks texts me.

Brooks: *HOLY SHIT. You are not going to believe this.*

I wait on pins and needles for about five seconds, before I decide I need to know.

Tenley: *Tell me.*

Brooks: *I'm almost in. I'll be up in a minute.*

True to his word, he's up in a minute. The non-working keycard is no hindrance whatsoever—he probably charmed someone into opening the door for him. He strides in, and though by now there are a dozen people gossiping in the hallway, passes them without a look and makes a bee-line for my office, closing the door behind him.

His face is grave. I know something is wrong. "Is Tom okay?"

"No. It turns out, no one's okay." He's not just upset. He's shellshocked.

"What do you mean? Did you talk to Tom?"

He shakes his head. "I spoke to his wife. She was on the way to the hospital so she couldn't talk. Apparently, on Saturday, Lisa and Bill cleared out Foster and Foster's bank accounts and skipped town."

"*What?*"

He nods. "Apparently, they were lovers. And they were planning this for a long time. Tom was so distraught by the whole thing that he had a minor heart attack. And Ed... I don't know where he is."

I'm still trying to digest the first part of the story. Lisa and Bill, lovers? Bill was sixty-five, heading into his golden retirement years. I knew his wife had passed a few years ago, but... Lisa? I say her name out loud.

"She has a husband. Young kids," I say. "Why would she...?"

"Your guess is as good as mine." He leans against the desk, as if he needs it to support him.

I put a hand on his. "Okay... this can't mean anything good for us."

"It means that Foster & Foster is done, that's what it means. They're going to have to shutter us. And it also means that we're out of jobs."

My mouth gapes. It's bad enough that I won't get the partnership. But we won't have jobs? Exhaling shakily, I scan my tiny office. I'd been taking it for granted, thinking a big, window-filled corner office was everything I wanted—

and now, as I look around, I realize even this small desk and chair won't be mine anymore.

But it's worse than that. An invisible hand clutches at my heart as I think of my rather empty checking account. I might have a month of rent and expenses saved up, but... more than that is pushing it. "But we'll get paid, right, for..."

I trail off. The accounts are dry. He already told me that. Brooks confirms it with a terse, "Wouldn't count on it."

I look out the window of my office. People are congregating out there. They know Brooks was the one who was going to get answers, and now they're looking to him.

Pushing away from the desk, I stand. "We'd better go tell everyone."

He nods, and I follow him out the door, the dread in my gut slowly building.

* * *

Interestingly enough, though it's barely noon, most of the office ends up at Houlihan's, a dive bar on Commercial Street, drinking their worries away. The mood is like that of a funeral luncheon.

"Lisa... and *Bill?*" Mike grumbles, shaking his head. He's by far the drunkest of us, but he's echoing the question most of us have had since the news broke.

I always saw Lisa as living the perfect life. Family, great career, success. She had it all. And yet, she'd thrown it all away. For what? Was it the money? Was she in love with Bill? Or had she been secretly so dissatisfied with her seemingly perfect life that she needed to shake things up?

It makes me think of Courtney Perry, of Brooks, of all the people I'd misjudged.

"You just never really know a person," I mumble, staring into my now-warm beer.

"It does make sense, now that I think about it," Shelly says with a sigh. "She was always scheduling off-site meetings with him to go over his retirement plans. It seemed like overkill, but I did what I was told. And usually I'd hear her laughing on the phone with him. All the warning signs were there, but I ignored them because it seemed so unbelievable."

"I wouldn't beat yourself up," Brooks says. "She fooled us all."

Shelly gulps her beer. "Well, I don't care about me. I can find another job. Or I'll just retire. But you all? You're all young, at the beginnings of your careers. What are you going to do?"

That's the question. I'm sure most of the young attorneys in the firm have big-time student loans they're chipping away at. And there are only so many firms in the state of Maine. "I'm moving back to Georgia," Mike says, surely.

We all stare at him.

"Since when did you make that decision?" Brooks asks.

He shrugs. "I've been wanting to go back, anyway. My family's there. All my friends. A buddy who owes me a favor just started his own firm. And the weather up here sucks."

Brooks and I wind up trading glances, silent. If only it was as easy for us. But I've never had a back-up plan. I was too busy building my career at Foster & Foster and working with the women's center to even think about a back-up plan. I don't even know what the job market is like, but it's probably not good. There are only a few local firms nearby, and most of them are small and I doubt they're hiring. The thought of sending our resumes give me hives.

Finally, Mike says, "What are you thinking of doing, Gentry?"

To my surprise, Brooks says, "I have a couple of options."

He does? Here, I thought we were going down in flames together. "You do?"

He nods, but doesn't say anything else. He quickly changes the subject, leading me to think that he doesn't want to talk about it. Why do I get the feeling these options are the kind that are going to rip my heart out of my chest? Why else would he be so evasive?

A little while later, Mike is so drunk that he actually begins to get argumentative with the waiter, and almost picks a fight with a couple of fishermen at the bar. Who knew he was an angry drunk? We wind up pulling him from the bar, and Brooks offers to drive him home to his place in South Portland.

It's only two in the afternoon. It feels like the day is dragging. I've never had so much free time in all my life. Since I have nothing better to do, I go with them, making sure Mike doesn't puke in the back seat.

When we pull up at Mike's place, we say goodbye. As we watch Mike stumble into his house, I open my mouth to ask the question that's been rattling in my head for hours.

But Brooks says, "I don't know what the hell we're going to do with the Perry case. I guess I'll call her."

Funny, I hadn't even thought about my caseload. I'd been too focused on my own devastation. But this is going to be a big blow to Courtney. "Oh. Yes. She'll have to get a new attorney."

He nods. Then he drags his hands down his face. "What a mess."

"Well, not really..." I say, watching him. "Right? You said you had options."

He doesn't look at me. "None of them are good, though."

"What..." The cabin of the car is too fraught with tension. Whatever he's dragging out telling me, I know it's bad. So I decide to inject some humor. "You're not talking suicide, are you? Because that's not really an option."

He chokes out a laugh. "*No.* I have a professor. From Yale. He moved to Chicago and started his own firm there a few years ago, and he's been trying to recruit me, ever since."

I blink. He's never mentioned this before. Chicago? That might be halfway across the country, but it feels like another planet. "He has?"

"Yeah. He doesn't want to take no for an answer. Keeps sweetening the pot, every time he calls me. I bet I could hop on a plane tomorrow and have an amazing job out there. But..."

He trails off, staring at the steering wheel.

I know that "but." It's not me. It's not even Ellie. It's Jace.

But that sounds like one hell of a job. A dream job. Chicago? Most attorneys only wish they can practice big-time in a big-city firm. I know I'd be salivating for that kind of opportunity. The Foster & Foster partnership is small potatoes, compared to that.

And he'd had it in his back pocket, this whole time.

He was giving it up, for his nephew.

"You should be there," I say quietly.

He turns to look at me. "I can't."

"You can't, because of your family. But I can keep an eye on Ellie, and make sure that—"

"Ellie isn't your responsibility." He says it harshly, in a conversation-ending way. As if he doesn't want or need my vote in the matter. He starts the ignition and points the car toward Portland. When he speaks again, his voice is quieter. "Anyway, I don't need to make the decision tonight."

No, he does not. But we do have to make some potentially life-altering ones, soon.

At least, *he'll* be making one. I have no prospects right now. This blow has completely knocked me out from behind.

It strikes me at that moment that the only reason I was keeping it together was because I was going through it with Brooks.

Without him, what the hell am I going to do?

36

Brooks

"And that's the end."

I close the book and look over at Jace, who is snuggling under the covers in his Paw Patrol pajamas. His eyes are drooping. He's ready. "That was sooo good," he yawns.

"The best. I love those books." Pressing a kiss to the top of his head, I help him get comfortable and say, "Good night, Bud."

"'Night, Brooksy."

I turn on his star projector, go to the door, and as I'm about to flip the light switch, catch him looking at me.

"Brooksy?"

"Yeah, Bud?"

"Can we go watch the Sea Dogs this summer?"

I stare at him. I know he only asked about a baseball, game, but for some reason, my ears heard: *Can you never leave me? Ever?* "Sure. I've been meaning to get you to a game."

"Jayden said his parents have season tickets."

There's that Jayden, again. I don't know why, but he sounds like a little snot. "Good for him. Maybe we'll see him there."

He nods. "That would be cool."

"All right. I'll see you in the morning." I flip the lights and close the door halfway, to the Jace-approved limit.

Then I go to my bedroom and, thinking about what I discussed with Tenley, crack open my laptop. A moment later, I find an email dated two weeks ago, from my professor at Yale, Dr. Anderson. Well, he was Dr. Anderson, back when I was a law student. The day I graduated, he told me to call him Marc.

Hey, Kid, Just wanted to let you know, the partner offer is still open. We need a real shark on our team. $250k to start, full benefits and stock options. Call me.

—M

I'd responded that the offer was tempting, but I'd have to refuse.

Now, it feels like I can't refuse.

I'd softened it with Tenley, because I knew that if I told her all the details, she'd call me crazy for passing it up.

But yes, it's everything I want. If only it wasn't in damn Chicago.

I think of Jace's sleepy little face as he begged me to take him to a baseball game. How can I disappoint him?

Well, he might like the Sea Dogs, but he'd love the Chicago Cubs. That would be iconic. And...

Who am I kidding? Ellie would never move. She has her roots so deep in this place that the thought alone of even stepping beyond the state lines would probably kill her.

But still...

Marc kept sweetening the pot for me. If I sweetened it

for Ellie... if I told her how much better our lives would be, and I gave Jace the best schooling money could buy? She would hate it. She'd fight me. But eventually, she might realize it was the best decision for all of us.

I stare at the email until it all blurs together, and a realization hits me.

I'd need Tenley with me. I'm not about to lose her now. And she doesn't have anything tying her here, anymore, either, does she? She needs a new job, and all the ones around here are going to be a step down from the partnership at Foster and Foster.

Picking up the phone, I dial my professor. When he answers, I say, "Hey, there, Mark. How's it going? It's Brooks."

"Brooks! My man." He sounds ecstatic to even be getting a call from me. "I knew this day would come! The day you finally reconsider my offer."

I smile at the sound of his voice. "Hold on, hold on. I'm still considering."

"You serious? I knew I'd gotten your attention with my last email."

"Well, it turns out, Foster and Foster is closing its doors, so I'm out of a job," I explain.

"No kidding? That's crazy. When are they shuttering?"

"Actually. They already did. It's kind of sudden."

"Shit. Well, you get on the first plane out here, and you'll be employed by tomorrow morning. You're going to love it here."

I swallow. "I mean, yeah, it sounds great. But I have... other things..."

"I get it. Whatever we can do to make the relocation process easier for you, you let me know."

"Yeah..." There's one thing that would definitely make

it easier, on all of us. "You have any other open senior attorney positions there?"

A pause. "Oh, I get it. No... not at the moment, unfortunately. Things are always opening up, but I can't make any promises. Something could open up in a week, or a couple years. You never know."

Shit. That doesn't help. I'm sure there'd be lots of opportunities for Tenley if she moved with me to Chicago, but I want her *with* me. Not working for a rival firm. "Oh. Okay. Just thought I'd check."

"So when can I expect you here?"

I grit my teeth with indecision. "Hey. I don't know yet. Just putting out feelers. Trying to figure out the logistics."

"Okay, buddy, I get it. Well, just say the word whenever you know for sure, and I'll pull the trigger with HR. Sound good?"

"Yeah. Take care."

I end the call, feeling listless, trying to figure out how all this would work.

Tossing my phone on the bed, I'm about to get up and go downstairs when I see Jace, standing in the doorway.

"Who were you on the phone with?" he asks.

I shake my head. "No one. Why are you out of—"

"Are you moving to Chicago?"

"No. Of course not," I say instantly, taking him by the shoulders and leading him down the hall to his room.

But am I? The last thing I ever want to do is lie to this kid.

As I reach the end of the hallway, I notice Ellie, standing in front of the mirror in the bathroom, doing her hair. Looks like she's going out.

I help him back into his bed and put the covers back on. "Look at me. I'm never leaving you. Okay?"

He nods. "Okay."

Another kiss. "This time, go to sleep," I whisper, making a silly face and heading out the door as he giggles.

The smile disappears from my face the instant I close the door.

When I get downstairs, Ellie is piling her things into her purse. She's dressed for a night on the town. Things have been a lot better for us in the time since Jace was left home alone. Ted must like her, because he added an extra couple of shifts to her waitressing schedule, and either she feels guilty over leaving Jace or she's too tired to go out, most nights. So I can't complain as I walk past her, to the couch, and flip on the game.

She glances at me in the foyer mirror as she applies lipstick. "You should go, you know."

I flip off the television, sure she didn't say what I think she said. "What?"

"To Chicago. Did you get offered a job there?"

I nod. "Foster & Foster is shuttering."

"Really?" She doesn't seem all that fazed by it, likely because she'd had plenty of businesses she worked for shutter, in her long employment history. "That sucks. So what is this new job?"

"It's partner."

"Partner? Isn't that like a big deal?"

I nod.

"Wasn't that the position you were fighting Tenley for, here?"

I nod.

"It pays more?"

"Substantially."

"Dude. Why haven't you jumped on that? And don't

give me your excuses. I don't want to hear that bullshit about me dragging you down."

Now I really want her to go out; I don't want to get into this. "I never said—"

"You might not say it. But you'd think it." She caps the lipstick, tosses it in her bag, and spinning to fix me with an accusing stare, folds her arms in front of her. "You already think it."

I glance up the stairs and keep my voice low. "Don't. I've *never*—"

"Right."

Raising my voice so that it's not much of a whisper anymore, I continue. "I've *never* considered either of you to be dragging me down."

"Oh, yes you did. Me, at least." She pushes aside the curtain and looks out, probably for her ride. "And so I think you shouldn't worry about us. Just go."

I give her a doubtful look. As if I could do that.

She catches me and shrugs. "It's true. Ted loves me. I made over $200 in tips last night alone. I'm doing well."

For now, maybe. But it only takes one bump in the road to send her life into another tailspin. "What will you do without my free babysitting?"

"I have friends that will help me."

Her friends are the same ones who drag her out at two in the morning and spend most of their lives high. I don't consider them viable options for Jace. "What if you came with me?"

She gives me a horrified look. "Hell, no."

"Wait, now listen." I sit up on the edge of the couch and turn off the television. "Look. I'm going to be making really good money. They have great schools in Chicago. Jace could go anywhere. And—"

"And me?" Ellie's still looking at me like I'm insane. "What'll I do?"

"You can do anything! The city's a hundred times the size of Portland. You can do—"

"That's just the thing," she says, hugging herself. "It's too big. A city like that would swallow me."

I stare at her. *A city like that would swallow me.*

I know what she means. Ellie has been through a lot. I've seen her, swallowed and spit out, every time, a little weaker. I don't know if she can handle the trauma, if it happens much more.

I want Jace to have it all. And yes, I can give many things to him with that job. But one thing I can't give him? A mother who is well enough to take care of him. And he needs that, most of all.

She pulls open the door. "There's my ride." Stepping out, she looks back at me. "Don't make me."

And she slams the door shut.

I *could* make her. But I wouldn't. No job is worth what it might do to our family.

37

Tenley

I have plenty of time to stop and look around now.

Unemployment is the weirdest thing. For the first few hours of it, I wallowed in desperation. Then I looked around and realized how much I could get done, now that I didn't have to work. I unpacked all those boxes, cleaned every room in the house from top to bottom, and even alphabetized my entire bookshelf.

Now that all that is done, I'm back to desperation.

Not only is my bank account not going to last out the month and the unemployment website is giving me trouble, but I've been scrolling through online job boards for an hour and haven't seen so much as a single attorney job, in the entire state.

I need some cheering up. So I climb into bed, grab my phone, and dial my mom. "Hi, mom. How's life in East Bay?"

"Oh, it's great, honey. So relaxing."

My mom deserves that rest, after everything she's been through. I suppose it's her reward, living in semi-retirement, in an oceanside community where everybody knows everybody else. Every time I see her, now, she's practically glowing. There, she feels needed.

I can't say I would feel the same. That's where a person goes at the end of their career. Not when it's just beginning. "Good. How is everything?"

"Good. Are you coming to tell me you're taking time off to visit this summer?"

"Oh, I wish."

It's not that I don't like East Bay. She moved there when I was in law school because the town's only attorney was retiring and they needed someone local. Before she passed away, Ruth had recommended her for the job. East Bay is an island of just over 1,500 people, off the coast of Maine. It's pretty far north, close to Canada, so it might as well be in another universe. The drive is four hours but the ferry only goes that way randomly.

"You're not?" She sounds sad. "Work still busy?"

"Actually... work isn't busy at all. Foster & Foster shuttered."

She gasps. "What happened?"

"Some partners stole money from the firm, and it had to close," I explain quickly. "So I think I'm going to be spending the next few weeks, scouring for jobs."

"You can do that from here," she offers. "Or better yet, why don't you work with me?"

I laugh. She's got to be kidding. My mother is my best friend, but we're both ridiculously headstrong and always lock horns. I could just imagine the bickering, being heard all over that quiet seaside down. They'd probably force us out. "Mom, I don't think East Bay really needs two attorneys. They probably barely need the one."

She sighs. "I guess you're right about that. But of course you'll find another job down there."

Something else has been pressing on my heart lately. Maybe it's the abundance of free time. If anyone will understand it, it's my mother. "I was thinking..."

"Oh, dear. You sound worried. Do you need money, honey? Is that the problem?"

"No, I've been putting money in my retirement account like you showed me. So I have a little in there. And I was thinking, this might be crazy, but... what if I cashed that out and started my own women's center, here in Sapphire Shores?"

For the longest time, it was just my mom and me, so we're probably as close as two people could be. That's why, even before I she speaks, I know she isn't a fan of the idea. It's the long silence that prevails, before she says, "Honey, your retirement is your future. You don't sacrifice that for anything."

Yes, I understood that. The penalties of withdrawing from my 401k would be ugly, yes. But this felt more important than that. "I know, but... I really want to make a difference. I want to do something, give hope to people, the way Ruth--"

"Hope and good karma don't pay the bills, Tenley." Her voice softens when she adds, "Honey, your heart is always in the right place. But the truth is, if you don't have a way of sustaining it with regular employment, it doesn't matter how much heart you put into the women's center. Those places are hard to keep afloat, even when you do have adequate funding. Ruth was wealthy, and even she struggled."

I nod, my hopes deflating. But I can always count on my mom to give it to me straight. I'm glad to have her to stop me from jumping off the ledge.

"Okay, thanks, Mom. I've got to go," I say, and end the call quickly after that.

Then I burrow myself deeper under the covers of my bed. My mother might have been giving me solid advice, but it doesn't mean I can't sulk and feel bad about it.

So now what do I do?

I grab my phone and start looking for jobs again. This time, I broaden my search to New Hampshire and Massachusetts.

There's a junior attorney position in Boston that pays three times what I was making at Foster & Foster. Higher cost of living, though. And I bet I'll be the low woman on the totem pole, and have to claw my way up. Again.

The thought makes me exhausted. Not to mention, how long is the commute by train into Boston? Like two hours, each way?

Ugh. That's a recipe for total burnout.

On a whim, I enter Chicago into the location section, and press enter.

Dozens of jobs appear, for a number of different firms. I even find one that looks perfect—it's a fast-track to partner in three years. Plus, Chicago has always sounded exciting to me. Actually, I've always wanted to see the world beyond Maine. Hmm...

But then I remember that Brooks never told me he wanted me to go with him. The thought probably hasn't even crossed his mind. That would make this more than a boyfriend-girlfriend thing. Moving across the country together? That would make things serious.

And we've only been truly dating a few days. That's the textbook definition of *moving too fast.*

Besides, I know someone else who did that. She fell hard and fast in love and moved forward at lightning speed, giving up her own dreams in pursuit of a dream with her husband that never came true. She was left, alone and scared and pregnant, at the age of twenty-one, with no one, until an angel named Ruth helped her become who she was truly meant to be.

So, no. I X out of the search and decide to stick close to home.

My phone starts to ring, then, and my heart does a little dance when I see Brooks's name appear on my screen. What are the chances he's calling to invite me to Chicago with him? "Hey," I say, pressing the phone to my ear.

"Hey, you. I want to see you."

I smile at his directness. "I want to see you, too. We are people of leisure, though, so we should be able to fit it into our schedules. Unless you already bought your plane ticket to the Windy City?"

"I have not."

"Well, why not? You should. It's better than the garbage I've been looking at. There's nothing available in this whole state. How much does it pay again?"

He's never told me. I got the feeling he was keeping it from me, so I don't expect him to answer. But he does. "Two-fifty."

"Oh my god. For senior associate?"

He hesitates. "Partner, actually."

"Oh my god. Brooks!"

He's quiet for a moment. "Are you trying to get rid of me?"

"No... but I know a good opportunity when I see it."

"I can find a job in Boston. It's closer."

"Not a partnership. You'd have to start as a junior, making at most, one-hundred. And commuting two hours each way? It's not worth it, Brooks." I know what's holding him back, even if he won't say it. "Did you even talk to her about? I bet you she would tell you to go. The last thing she wants to be is a burden to you."

He doesn't say anything for a long time. Something tells me he already knows this, but it's not helping. Their relationship is tenuous, and just like Ellie said, he doesn't trust her.

"I don't want to talk about this anymore," he says, his voice tight. "I called to tell you I want to see you."

I know what he's waiting for. Since he can't have me over, he's waiting for my invitation. To tease him and break the ice, I decide to make him wait a little longer. "Please hold while I check my schedule."

He doesn't even laugh.

"All right. Looks like I'm free right now. Do you want to come over?"

He grunts a yes and ends the call.

I guess I found someone in this state who's in a worse mood than I am. And why should he be? He has the amazing, life-changing job offer.

And right now, I have nothing.

38

Brooks

When I arrive at her place, I'm so worked up into a bundle of nerves that I think I might lose it.

She's waiting at the door for me, like in my fantasies, except everything else is different. She's not naked underneath her apron; she's wearing a little red dress that skims her upper thigh. Maybe a nightgown—who can tell? Whatever it is, it's sexy. But I can tell she's just as tense by the way she's standing rigid, arms folded over her chest, gnawing on her lip.

The gnawing on the lip is sexy, too. Jesus, everything this woman does turns me on.

And that's why I know it is right, to be here. When I'm with her, I don't think about our problems.

She opens her mouth to say something, but I don't want to talk. It'll end in an argument. So I silence her with a finger to her lips.

Then I replace it with my mouth, devouring her.

She lets me. She might have wanted a discussion, but the second her lips touch mine, I feel her anxiety drain away, and she relaxes against me. She throws her arms around my neck and grinds up against me.

It's just what I need. But I want more.

Breathless, I break the kiss and say, "Your bedroom."

She nods and guides me upstairs.

Inside, I pull off my jacket and toss it on the dresser, then stand by the bed and hook my finger toward her. "Come here."

She moves toward me with purpose, like a puppet on a string.

I know that look in her eyes. I know exactly what she wants. I grab her neck forcefully, drawing her to me so that all the air leaves her lungs in a rush. Forcing her head back, I devour her neck, taking in her sweet smell as she responds by arching her back, pressing her breasts against my chest. She massages my cock through my pants and then digs her hands under the waistband, sliding them easily behind me, grabbing savagely at my ass.

I hoist her off the floor, wrap her legs around me and cradle her ass as she pushes us off the wall. "I want you to fuck me."

She unbuttons her way down my shirt, as I lay her down on her bed, quickly lifting up her layers of dress, sliding down her panties and diving between her legs.

She comes almost the instant my tongue touches her clit, bucking against me and smashing my face into her pussy as it hits her in wave after wave. After she thrashes around for a bit, she sits up on her elbows, pushes a stray hair off her face.

I pull my tie off and unbuttoning my shirt the rest of the way. That I can get her that excited? Fuck. "You clearly needed that."

"Yes. But I need more."

When I shrug the shirt off, she leans over so that I can untie the knot at the back of her neck, letting the top of her dress fall down to her hips. Ah, those beautiful, glorious, perfect breasts.

She starts to pull on my belt buckle.

"Come here," I say gruffly, urging her up and pushing away the fabric of the dress that is scrunched around her middle. I wrap my hands around her hips and she straddles me, then lifting my dick into position, sinks onto me. I pull my hips up, meeting her halfway, and we both let out a groan at once as I'm totally engulfed in her. Then she starts to slide up and down on me, her eyes closed in bliss, slowly at first, then getting faster and faster. I let her control the rhythm and guide my hands to her breasts, where she wants them to be.

It isn't long before she's screaming again. I start to moan, too, rocking my hips up into her. "Come with me," I say, and just like that, as easily as if we'd planned it, we both come together.

We both needed this.

She rolls over onto her side and props herself up on her elbow, still breathing hard. I stare up at her. She's beautiful this way, her cheeks red from the exertion, a light sheen of sweat on her sweet skin, her hair falling loose around her face.

"Come with me," I say as I come down.

She gives me a confused look. "I *did*."

"No... I mean, to Chicago."

Her eyes go wide. I've surprised her. "You want that?"

I nod. "Why not?"

"Well, we've only been dating a few weeks. I don't know, I— did your sister agree to come with you?"

At that moment, reality crashes in. I was living in a bubble. Me, here with her, where nothing else mattered. But there are things that matter, and I need to think about them, first. So I don't answer.

She sucks in a breath and lets it out. "I told you, you shouldn't pass up that job. I can be here to look after Ellie and Jace."

There's something she's not telling me. "Forget about them for a second. If I didn't have them to worry about, you still wouldn't come with me."

She looks down at the space of white sheet between us. "No. I wouldn't."

"Why?"

"Because I don't have a job there."

I scoff. "Did you forget? You don't have a job *here*, either."

"But I'd have nothing there, Brooks," she says, her fingers working over a seam in the sheet. "You know my mother was a single mom. She had it really tough. And part of the reason she did is because she put all of her trust in a man who let her down. She gave up her hopes of a career, education, everything, because she believed that man would take care of her for the rest of her life. I'm not my mother. I'm sorry, but I'm not moving to a place where I have nothing, just so you can have everything."

Shit. I wish I could say her argument makes no sense, but we both know that it does. Things do fall apart. We have seen it, first-hand. We have to be cautious. "What if you got a job there?"

She shakes her head, a small smile appearing on her

face. "I don't think so. I've been thinking a lot about it. I've always wanted to travel, but I don't want to leave Maine. I don't have much, but what I do have—my mom, my place, Sapphire Shores—I want to keep close. I don't want to give them up. If I'm going to make a difference in the world, I want to do it in a place that loves me back. Here."

I frown. "Okay, then that's it. I'm not going, either."

Tenley sits up straight, the sheet falling to her laps. "Are you listening to me? You're not doing that! You have your dream job, the thing you've been working your whole career for, waiting for you in Chicago. You need to go."

"No, I don't," I say, raising my voice. Why does she keep hammering me with that? It really does feel like she's casting me off. "There's got to be another solution. What if we start our own practice? We could bring in our clients from Foster & Foster and—"

"You need money for that, Brooks. I have nothing. That's why I wanted the promotion to begin with—so I could have that money and freedom. But right now, my hands are tied. I need a job, paying me, first, before I can even think about striking out on my own."

More reality trickles in. She's right. All these pie-in-the-sky ideas... and none of them can happen. They're all too risky. Someone's going to get hurt, no matter what we do.

"You want to end this." It's not a question.

I throw the sheet off and stand up as she reaches for my hand, but I snatch it away.

"No, Brooks. I don't. We can try long-distance. It's not ideal. But people make it work."

"In the short-term, maybe," I say, fishing for my clothes. "But it's not a real solution. You know that. It'll only delay the inevitable."

She stares at me sadly. She knows I'm right. I get dressed in silence, and when I leave, she doesn't try to stop me.

It's over.

39

Tenley

You want to end this.

Sitting at my computer, sipping tea, I'm trying to get some needed work done. But all I keep thinking about is Brooks.

No, the last thing I wanted to do was end things.

But he's right. There's no way it would work between us.

The though sends a spear of pain, right through my heart.

Again, I'm looking for jobs. I keep expanding the radius of my search, but so far, I've only managed to find a handful of options. I've applied to all of them, and have registered with a headhunter in Portland, but so far, I haven't gotten a single bite.

As I'm scrolling, I notice a job for a senior attorney in Portsmouth. That sounds promising. Scrolling through the job expectations, I decide it's a match. I personalize a cover letter, put it together with my email, and send it off.

Portsmouth would be good.

Even if it's without Brooks.

Oh, who am I kidding? I'm an idiot for forcing him away, when he wanted to stay. But that job was amazing. If he didn't take it, he'd have come to resent me. I'm sure of it. And that would've caused a rift in our relationship that would have only widened.

Maybe I'm just scared. Scared that in trusting any man, what happened to my mother could happen to me, and derail my entire life.

It doesn't matter. If he'd really wanted to be with me, he could've fought. Instead, he simply got up and left. It's been three days, and I haven't heard from him since. For all I know, he can already be on a plane to Chicago.

My heart lurches as I think of how adorable and hopeful he'd looked when he asked me to come with him.

How could I have turned him down?

It doesn't matter, Tenley. You did it. What's done is done.

He would have resented me. If I'd gone with him, I'd be dead weight. If I'd made him stay to be with me, I'd have held him back. I'd be what my father thought my mother was.

This was right. Definitely.

Even so, I find myself on the Chicago page, looking for jobs, there.

After a moment of scrolling, I shake my head and snap the laptop closed. It wouldn't have worked. Period. End of story.

I am a strong, independent woman, like my mother.

Looking around my condo, I wince. The walls of this place have brought me down, ever since I decided I probably can't afford the rent after the end of this month. I need to find a new, cheaper place to live, but I have no motivation to do so. It feels like failure.

I climb out of bed and go downstairs for something to eat. Unfortunately, I am a strong, independent woman who hasn't been to the grocery store in ages, because I don't even have Cheerios, this time.

I grab my phone to order via an app, but for some reason, it's down.

That's okay. This strong, independent woman has no problem, eating in a restaurant by herself.

I quickly get changed and head out, but the only place open in Sapphire Shores at this time of night is Ted's, home of the worst pizza on the planet. Finding a spot in the parking lot, I go inside.

From the back, a disembodied voice calls, "Seat your— oh hey!"

I locate the speaker behind the counter, among the take-out pizza boxes. It's Ellie. "Hey!"

I'd like to think it's fate, but something tells me my subconscious was leading me here, all along, because I wanted to get the inside scoop on what Brooks has been up to. She comes around the counter and grabs my arm, then leads me to a corner booth. "If you sit here, I'll wait on you."

"Okay, great." She hands me a menu, but I don't look at it. "I'll just have a root beer and a couple of slices."

"Coming right up!" She grins at me and heads off to wait on another table.

Meanwhile, I sit there, looking around at all the other patrons. There's one family, but the rest are in pairs, which makes me feel less like a strong, independent woman, and more... lonely.

I have an inner war, telling myself I shouldn't ask Ellie

about Brooks when she returns. It's over. Whatever he's up to doesn't matter, and an independent woman doesn't need to know.

But the second she sets my food down, I say, "So, how is everything?"

She looks at her tables and then sits across from me. "Good. I've been working more shifts at Ted's and am taking a free business class at the community college."

"Really? That's great!" I pick at the cheese of the pizza, trying to decide how to delicately work the conversation toward Brooks. "And Jace is good?"

"He's great. He's actually in a free after-school soccer program. Loves it!"

"That's fantastic." I lower my eyes to my plate and tear off a piece of cheese, stuffing it into my mouth before casually saying, "And—"

"How are you?"

I was going to ask about her brother, but Ellie's question saves me from going down that torturous route. "Oh. Fine."

"Did you get a new job?"

I shake my head. "But I'm still volunteering at the women's center, if you ever want to stop by there. We can help you with anything you need."

She smiles. "Sure."

There's a lull in the conversation, and the dreaded question finds its way to the tip of my tongue again.

But as I open my mouth, a voice says, "Excuse me, Miss?"

Ellie's attention swerves elsewhere, grabbed by another restaurant patron looking for a drink refill.

"Hold that thought!" She scoots up and rushes to grab the empty glass from the customer.

Saved. Really, Tenley. You don't need to know how

Brooks is. Ellie and Jace are doing much better, and that's all that matters.

Ellie reappears a minute later, with a drink for the customer, and another one for me, since I've somehow slogged down the whole thing without realizing it. She sits in front of me and says, "Whew. It was a busy one tonight."

Okay. We're not on the subject of Brooks. And we don't need to be. I should just ask her how she likes the job and what her classes are about.

But instead, the second my mouth opens, it slips out. "How is Brooks?"

Instantly, I hate myself for asking. I'm trying to be casual, to not look like I'm waiting with bated breath for the answer.

She sure takes her time. Then she shrugs. "No idea."

That's not the answer I was looking for. I blurt, "What do you mean?" desperate to sate my curiosity. Does she not know how he is because he's already in Chicago?

"Oh, you know Brooks. Tries to be the big strong man. Doesn't like anyone to see him sweat. Internalizes *everything.*"

"Is something wrong? I thought he was going to Chicago?"

She shakes her head. "I told him he should. But he refuses. He said he's looking for something here."

My heart does a little dance, knowing he's still nearby. As much as I wanted him to take that Chicago job, I'm glad he's still here. That's selfish of me. "I think he's going to regret that. It was a perfect job for him."

Ellie smiles. "No, it's not."

She gives me a meaningful look, which I don't understand. "What do you mean? It was a partnership. Did he tell you that? The pay was incredible, and--"

"Yes. But it wasn't near you," she says.

I stare, speechless.

She puts a hand on mine. "Girl, I know my brother better than anyone. And I've never seen him so smitten by a woman before."

"Oh," I say, my face heating. "No. I'm not the reason he's not going to Chicago. I can't be. You—"

"Okay. So maybe it a bunch of things. But you're the biggest. I told him he's a great guy, but you probably want someone a little more boring. More stable. Not his crazy ass. But I still think he's holding out that you'll change your mind and want to be with him. Show up at his door, tell him you'll go anywhere with him."

I imagine myself doing that. My entire body aches to do that. But it's not possible. "No. I can't do that. He needs to go to Chicago. That's his future."

"How do you know that? Do you have a crystal ball?"

"We're too different," I declare with a nod, though I don't sound nearly as sure of myself as I wanted to be. "It won't work."

She shakes her head. "I think that's the problem. There are so many relationships that have ended badly, that people are too quick to think that theirs will end up part of that statistic. But it doesn't have to. Sometimes, you just have to close your eyes, and jump." She leans in. "Do you love him?"

I don't even have to think. I nod.

Yes, I do. I love him. We may be totally different, but we complement each other in so many ways. All the ways that count.

"Then go get him," she says, checking her phone. "He's probably still awake right now, you know."

I imagine myself going there, telling him that I've made

a mistake and I'd go anywhere with him. But this isn't a romance movie. This is real life. And if we do that, if we selfishly ignore everything and everyone else, we're going to regret it.

"I can't." It comes out as soft as a breath.

She just stares at me. Then she says, "He said the same thing. You two are more alike than you know. Stubborn as hell."

She gets up and leaves to help another customer, and when I look down at my pizza, I no longer have an appetite.

40

Brooks

I haven't lost hope yet.

It might be noon, and I might be sitting at the kitchen table, eating a bowl of cereal while typing one-handed into my laptop in my pajama bottoms. I might not have shaved in a week.

But I am still not giving up hope that I can find a job in this state.

I told my professor in Chicago that I needed a month to think it over. I figured that would be enough time to see whether I'll sink or swim in this job market.

So far, it's been mostly sinking. But I'm still fighting.

As soon as I hit "send" on another resume, the front door opens, and I hear Jace's high-pitched voice.

"Brooksy! Brooksy! Brooksy!" he shouts, zooming into my arms. "Guess what?"

I notice he has blue-raspberry-colored lips, so I have a good idea. "You're on a sugar high."

Behind him, Ellie rolls her eyes and pulls her messenger bag over her head. "He begged me for a slushie."

"I'm sure he did." I grab him and tickle his belly.

He giggles as I toss him over my lap. "But that's not all! Guess what? Guess what?"

"You're secretly a monkey?"

He sits up, face red. "No! I'm going—" He stops and runs a critical eye over me. "Uncle Brooksy, why are you still in your PJs?"

I look down. "I just woke up."

He gasps and his eyes narrow. "Are you playing hooky?"

Wondering where he gets this stuff, I look over at Ellie, who just shrugs. "No." I rub his shoulder, and try to get him back on track. "What were you going to tell me?"

He squints, as if he can't remember. "Oh. I'm going to have my own bed! In my own room!"

At first I think it's just a joke. Or that he's playing make-believe again. But then I shoot a questioning look at my sister and realize she's holding a manila envelope in her hands and nodding, a look of unspoken pride bursting from her face.

"What's this all about?"

She sits down across from me and opens the folder. "There's a new low-income apartment complex that just opened up, across the street from Ted's. I went to the women's center and they helped me fill out my application, and I got it. We move in next week."

"Really?" Now I'm proud. Shit.

Jace nods excitedly, and then his face falls. "But wait. Mommy. Isn't Brooksy going to come with us?"

I laugh. "No, this is my house. But of course, I'm going to be over there, with you, whenever I can. It's practically right down the block."

He's all smiles again. He claps his hands. "Mom says I can paint my room any color I want."

"Cool. And what's the verdict?" When he looks at me in confusion, I add, "What color?"

"Electric blue!"

"Yeesh," I look up at Ellie, who rolls her eyes, though she's still smiling. "Good luck with that." I pause. "Okay, okay. I'll help."

I can't believe it. I look around the house, full of Legos and Pokémon and toy cars and trains, and can't imagine it going back to a real grown-up place. It's going to feel so empty.

"I was wondering if you could do a little more than that," she says quietly, as Jace zooms around the place, pretending to be a dragon, chasing his tail. When I raise an eyebrow, she takes a deep breath and says, "You know that business course I was taking on Mondays?"

I nod.

"It was the introductory course to their business management program. I want to enroll." She gives me an unsure look and then holds up three fingers, like a boy scout pledge. "For real, this time. I mean, it's a boring major, but I think it'll give me a lot of options, job-wise. And I actually didn't mind the class. It was fun."

My sister has a certain expression she uses—only rarely —when she's serious about something. Her eyes go big and there's a deep crease at the bridge of her nose. The last time I saw it, I think she was trying to convince my parents to let her buy an old Camaro that he boyfriend had fixed up. "And the cost?"

"It's nothing. Actually, the women's center's covering it."

The women's center. Tenley. It's on the tip of my tongue to ask if it's her.

"And... I'm not asking your permission. I already signed up. I just wanted to let you know. I'd love your help with Jace, but if not, I can probably ask Kelly to—"

"No. Hell no. I'll help. I'll always help," I say, standing up. "I'm... proud of you."

She stands, too, and I think there might be tears in her eyes. "You are?"

I nod. "Absolutely."

She's incredulous, and it strikes me at that moment that I've never said those words before. And yet, I've always admired her for standing by Jace, trying to be a good mom to him. We don't do it often, but this seems like the right time. I open my arms and she moves forward, so I fold her into a hug.

"I've always been proud of you," I say to the top of her head.

Not wanting to be left out, Jace joins us, trying to wiggle his way in between us. "Group hug!"

I laugh and pull away. "So, what changed to make you decide to do this?"

She shrugs. "I don't know. Tenley's story inspired me, I think. She told me about how her mom was in the same situation I was in and how one little act of kindness from a stranger had turned it all around. I kind of want to be able to pass that on, one day, to someone else. You know?"

I know. Tenley has a way of inspiring a lot of people.

Turning away, silent, I wish I didn't have to think about her. And yet, it's not Ellie's fault, for mentioning her name. Tenley's in my head, as surely as if she was etched there. I can't think of anything else. When I go out, every brunette I see, I do a double-take, thinking it's her. Whenever I'm scrolling through attorney jobs, I wonder if she's applying for the same ones, and we're unwittingly competing against each other again. She's in my bloodstream, and I doubt I'll ever get her out.

"She helped me, you know."

I break from my trance to see Ellie, smiling at me. "What?"

"Tenley. She's the one who helped me get the apartment. I saw her a week ago, at Ted's. She asked about you."

I don't know why, but that lifts my spirits. "She did?"

She leans in. "She loves you."

"What?"

"She told me that."

I don't believe it. After all this time, I thought she might call or text. I've looked at my phone a thousand times, hoping. "No, she didn't."

"Yes, she did," Ellie says more forcefully. "Do you love her?"

That's easy. "Yeah, but..." I know the song says that love is all you need, but... she can't love me. "She wouldn't go to Chicago with me."

Ellie fixes me with a look. "Dude. She has a life here. That doesn't mean she doesn't love you." Ellie rolls her eyes. "I told her she should find someone else. Someone boring, normal... not as thick in the head."

I shake my head, as if that will help it sink in. "But..."

"I'd tell you to go talk to her, but I know you. You're like her. Stubborn." She laughs. "Both of you are going to keep on being stubborn, alone and apart, when you know you'd be better, in love and together."

I look at her. "What should I do?"

It's the first time I'm asking her for advice, and I can tell by the way she smiles that she likes the turnaround. "What I know you won't."

I stare.

She gives me a look like it's obvious. "Go over there and talk to her."

Ellie might think she knows me better than anyone, but one of the things I've always lived for is the chance to prove her wrong. "We'll see about that."

I march for the door, looking for my keys in my pockets, when I realize I'm still in my pajamas. Yeah, I'll need to take care of that, first.

"You'd better get changed," Jace calls as I jog up the stairs to catch a shower. "You can't go anywhere looking like a slob!"

"Thanks, Bud," I call down to him.

I think my sister's right, for the first time in her life. Tenley and I are better together.

41

Tenley

I'm an idiot.

I fully realize that, as I look around my place while getting ready for my apartment-hunting mission.

All those boxes I've finally just unpacked and tossed away, after three years?

I'm going to be needing them again.

Truthfully, I don't mind leaving this place. I've never formed an attachment to it. It's nice, one of the swankiest in town, but it never became home. And now that I've scoured the online classifieds and found bigger places with much cheaper rent, I'm confident I'll find someplace better.

That's what I'm getting ready to do today. I have a couple of job interviews in downtown Portland later this week, nothing really great... but I have found a few studio apartments down by the Maine Mall that will suit my needs.

I finish brushing my hair and applying lip gloss, then straighten my dress, give myself a once-over, and head for the door. It's raining out, so I grab my umbrella. I'm backing out the door, about to pull it shut behind me while pushing the button on the umbrella to open it so I don't get wet, when I stumbled into a wall.

Not a wall, I realize, too late. Brooks is standing in the doorway, hand raised, knuckles out, as if poised to knock, but by the time I realize it's him, my trigger finger's already been activated, and the umbrella shoots open, between us.

"Oh my god!" I say as he stumbles back a couple of steps, taking the umbrella from my hands. "I didn't see you! Oh—"

"It's okay," he says, murmuring other comforting words, too, so I know which Brooks I'm getting. He's not here to argue, at least.

Well, with Brooks, arguments are par for the course.

"You were going out?" He asks.

Yes. I have an appointment in twenty minutes. I shouldn't be late. The words are on the tip of my tongue. But now, I can't get them out.

Instead, I close the umbrella and stare, thinking about everything we've been through, back when he was my insufferable partner and I was charmed by an online stranger. Before, I'd known so much about those two people—or at least, I thought I did.

Now I know so much more. I know the way his face looks in the near darkness, what the faint brush of his stubble feels like against my stomach as he kisses down my body.

I know there's a scar near his ear from shaving and that that impeccable white dress shirt hides the most perfect abs and that his smile lights up his face like the early Maine sun does the sky.

My fingers are numb. So's my tongue. Actually, I'm having an out of body experience, because although he's standing right in front of me, I don't have a thing to say.

Not a single thing.

"T," he says with the smile I've only ever seen him use on me. Not the practiced one he gives to clients and service people and even Ellie and Jace—it's a warm, sweet smile that touches his eyes and crinkles the corners of them.

In that moment, I know, without a shadow of a doubt, that I am in love with him. I am in love with Brooks Gentry.

And, yet, I still don't know what to say to him. I can't find the words.

He meets my gaze and there's so much warmth there, just for me, that my chest squeezes. The rain is falling hard on his face, pasting his dark, unruly hair to his forehead, making him squint, but I can't let him in. I do that, and it's all over. I will succumb to his strong arms, his intoxicating smell, his *everything*... and that will be bad.

Won't it?

Now, I'm not so sure.

"Brooks," I finally manage, looking around. "I know you are not about to apologize for the way things ended."

He folds his arms defensively before dropping them again. "I don't think I need to."

"You don't? Because you're always right?" I start to push past him. "I do have to go. I'm looking at apartments, and I'm late."

I start to brush past him.

"Wait." He grabs my wrist. "I'll admit I was wrong. But you were wrong, too."

I gasp in indignation. "How... ?" I start, as a door to my neighbor's place opens. I don't want to do this here, where my neighbors can hear us get into this. "I don't want to get into this here."

"We *have* to get into it."

So of course, it is an argument. And it's a war he'll ensure I lose, with that silver tongue of his.

"Fine. Okay," I say, grabbing him and pulling him inside, then looking up at him. He's soaked, a drowned rat. But it somehow makes him look hotter than ever, with his shirt pasted to his body, his skin glistening. "I'm here. You've got me. What do you want to say?"

"It's been a week." He laughs, looking like he hardly knows what to say, though knowing Brooks, he's had this whole thing planned out. "I've spent a lot of time thinking."

"That can't be good," I say before I can help myself.

"Right. But in this case I think it was a good thing. I've never had this much time off by myself just to think before."

Part of me wants to be mad he had all that time to think and never once reached out to me, but that wouldn't be fair. He needed this time to think. I did, too, even if I didn't want to accept it at the time.

I brush my hair back with both hands. "And?"

"I was insulted."

I raise an eyebrow. I knew this wasn't going to be an apology, but is he asking me for one? Because it isn't happening. I fist my hands at my hips. "By me?"

Rivulets of water drip from his hair, down his temples. He scrapes his hair back with one hand. "You were all too eager to ship me off. To get rid of me. After—"

"I wasn't getting rid of you. I said that we could—"

"A long-distance relationship is the kiss of death. Your

way of putting distance between yourself and the hard stuff. Which is admitting that you could be happy, if you just took the risk."

"The risk..." I repeat.

He nods. "You don't think I'm scared, too? I come from just as broken a home as you do. I know that things fall apart. But they don't have to. If we're both committed to making it work—it will work. And I am. I never want to lose you, T. Ever. So me being where you are not is not an option. Do you understand that?"

The tears spring to my eyes so easily, I can't blink them back fast enough.

His warmth surrounds me, his eyes, full of earnestness, strike my heartstrings in just the same way he's able to hold juries rapt. And just like that, I'm crying. He advances on me, folding me into his arms. He's wet, and yet his body heat is all I feel; I've never felt anything more wonderful.

This is all I'd dreamed of him doing. All week, I'd imagined him coming back and comforting me, because he's the only one who really understands. He knows what I've been through, the fear that has plagued me, every time I even thought about having a relationship with the opposite sex. I trust him.

But if I let myself fall too deeply into his embrace, I'll never climb back out again.

"I know how hard we were both going for that partnership," I tell him, my voice too thick.

"The partnership doesn't matter to—"

"Let me finish." He's not the only one who's been practicing lines, although mine were all hypothetical. I never thought I'd get a chance to say them to his face. "I've thought about it a lot, too. You don't spend your life fighting through years of education and law school, just to give your career up."

His arms tighten defensively around me, but he doesn't say a word.

"All these years, nothing else has ever mattered to me." This is the hardest part to get out, and my throat closes. I squeeze my eyes shut and pretend I'm not telling him these things at all. "And when I met you, I hated you so much I wanted it even more."

"You are the most stubborn person I've ever met," he murmurs against my ear, that same hand tracing the shell in movements that send tickling delight through me.

I lean back so I can see his face. "But now I don't even care. I've finally found something I want more."

He wipes under my eyes and I resolve not to tell him this week has involved a lot of crying. "Is that right?"

I'm not sure what it means. "My being right doesn't mean you are wrong."

He shrugs. "Does that mean we actually agree on something?"

I nod, easing back out of his arms so I can look at him properly. "Don't let it go to your head."

He laughs and spreads his hands. "If we put as much work into us as we did into getting that partnership, I don't see how we can fail."

This is probably the point I should say something, but I'm just opening and closing my mouth like a fish sucking air.

"I want to be with you. Always. Forever," he tells me, more of that warmness in his eyes, voice, spilling out until it drowns me, and I willingly drown in it. "I didn't realize how much until I almost lost you."

I swallow. "Forever?"

"I promise. And I don't go back on my promises."

This is a dream. It has to be a dream. "What about Chicago?" I manage.

"The city's been there awhile. I think it will survive just fine without me."

"And the job...?"

He shrugs. "It's great. There's no doubt about it. But I turned it down. It's not you."

I have to be dreaming. I need to pinch myself.

"I love you," he says, and his face has lost its smile. He's deadly serious as he looks at me. "I know I do. And I don't care where we are. If it's in a tent by the beach, that's fine with me. As long as we're together."

"I'm going to cry again," I warn him, fighting my trembling lips. He pulls me into him for a second time and I let him.

He chuckles, the sound reverberating through his chest.

"You're such an ass," I tell him, my eyes brimming again. But this time—and it feels insane it can be in so short a time—it's from happiness. Brooks has my heart, and though I know that the future is uncertain, I trust him with it. I trust him to take care of it as if it were his own. "But I love you, too. You stubborn, idiotic—"

He kisses me. I taste my tears, the salt mingling with the mint of his toothpaste. His lips are gentle. His fingers linger on my chin, tilting my face up to his, tightening his arms around my waist, holding me to him so close that I lose track of where I end and he begins.

Maybe this is what love is supposed to feel like.

"You know, I can help you. With the contracts for your new place? I *am* an attorney, after all," he murmurs against my mouth.

"Tempting. But unnecessary. Did you forget I'm one, too?" I tease back.

"Hmm. You may be... but I don't think it's yet been proven, which of us is the better one... ?"

Oh not that again. I tug his face back down to mine, unable to help smiling against his lips. "Just shut up and kiss me."

42

Brooks

"We'll definitely be in touch," the hiring manager at Milton and Ray says to me as I shake her hand.

"It was a pleasure," I tell her, giving her a firm handshake and making eye contact, before spinning to head out the doors.

I've been on enough interviews to know when a job is in the bag. Actually, I'm a great interviewer. I've never not gotten a position I've interviewed for. There's just something that clicks, and I have to say, this one with the panel of partners was stellar, probably my best performance yet. We'd laughed, bantered, and I'd already felt like one of the team.

Swinging my briefcase as I walk, I head down to Commercial Street, and a little café on the wharf with outdoor seating. I spot Tenley at once, sitting at a table in the corner, wearing dark sunglasses, her warm brown hair waving in the breeze. A smile lights up her face as I approach and slip into the plastic chair next to her.

"That was fast! How did it go?"

"It's a definite," I say surely, taking a gulp from my water goblet.

She gives me an incredulous look. "How can you say that?" Then she laughs. "Forget it. I know. Everyone just loves you."

I smirk and take her hand. "What's not to love?"

"*Maybe* that you're not so sure of yourself? You really need to have more self-confidence."

"You're right. I'm working on that."

The day is perfect, mid-eighties, light breeze coming off the mirror-flat ocean. And yet it's barely eleven, so the place is empty. It's just me and Tenley, exactly how I like it.

In the past week, we've gotten even closer. She helped us move Ellie out of my place and into her new apartment, and even helped her decorate so it would feel more like home. It's only half a mile away from my condo, and on a cul de sac, so I'm planning to get Jace a new bike, so I can teach him how to ride.

It feels like everything is working out. We just had to take that first step.

"I have news," she says to me with a small, sly smile, her eyes dancing.

"Do you?" I can't wait, because I can already tell it's something good.

"I was just at the women's center before I came here," she says, tucking a loose strand of hair behind her ear.

Of course she was. She's there all the time, now, between job interviews. "There's a shocker."

"I know, right? Well, it turns out that Melanie—she's the manager of the center—is moving to San Diego at the end of the month. They need someone to serve, at least on an interim basis. So they asked me."

I chuckle. "Not a shocker, either, considering you are the best volunteer they have."

"Yes, well, this is the best part. It comes with a small stipend, so I can set up a law clinic there, to help women with their legal needs. It's going to be every Saturday, and staffed by volunteer lawyers, which I'll obviously have to recruit. Isn't that amazing? It's like, everything I dreamed about, I'll get to do."

I lift her hand and kiss her knuckles. "Abs—"

My phone rings. I lift it to silence it, but recognize the number, hold up a finger, and take the call. As I'd thought, it's Mr. Ray, from the Law Offices of Milton and Ray, where I'd just finished interviewing, not twenty minutes before. "Hello, sir."

I listen as he outlines the details of the job they're offering me. Not partner salary, no, but a good bump up from my pay at Foster and Foster. Three-day workweek, handling wills and estates and boring stuff like that, but hey. It'll leave plenty of room for other things. I ask for twenty-four hours to think it over, thank him profusely, and then end the call.

When I look at her, Tenley's staring at me in shock. "I guess they do love you. I have never, *ever* gotten a job that easily."

I laugh. "You thought that was easy?"

"So are you going to take it?"

"I'll consider it," I tease, even though I know that I'll be calling Mr. Ray tonight with my acceptance. "As long as you make sure I'm the first attorney you hire to work pro bono at the women's center."

"I think we have a deal," she says, offering me her hand to shake.

I take it, shake it, then turn it over, kissing her knuckles. "Good."

But it's more than good. It's absolutely amazing, the way things work out.

43

Tenley

It isn't much, but it's getting there.

The walls are white and still studded with pinpoint holes from the posters the last director had put up. There is no expansive, sweeping view of the Portland harbor. The desk is scuffed, and the task chair behind it is bleeding stuffing.

But I don't care. What I'll get to do here is so much better than anything I could've done as partner in Foster and Foster.

I rearrange the vase with cheery, fake daffodils at the corner of the desk, then fill the plastic holder with my brand-new business cards.

Portland Women's Center
Tenley Bayliss, Director

"Tenley?" Francine's voice comes through the intercom. "Your three o'clock is here."

"Oh, please how her in."

The woman who steps through the door isn't much different from Ellie had been, when she first arrived. Shoulders slumped, eyes full of worry and doubt. I imagine my mother looked the same way, once upon a time. This woman is named Ann. She's eighteen, and visibly pregnant with her third child. According to her intake form, her boyfriend left two months ago, and she hasn't seen him since. No family, no friends, no money to speak of, she's at the end of her rope.

"Hi!" I say to her, coming around the desk and shaking her hands. "Ann, right? It's so good to meet you. Sorry, my office needs some décor. It's pretty bland right now. Sit down. Can I get you anything? Coffee? Water?"

She shakes her head and perches on the edge of the chair. I slip onto my desk, letting my feet dangle.

"I'm so glad you found us," I tell her. "You came to the right place. We're here to help. So, tell me about these kids of yours."

I always ask about the kids first, because inevitably, a mother's eyes will light up, and I've found it tends to be the best way to get someone to open up.

"Matthew ... and Grace ..." She takes out her phone and starts to show me picture after picture of the two kids, telling me little stories about them until I actually see her laugh.

"And now, you're having another. Do you know if it's a boy or a girl? Have you been to the doctor recently?"

She shakes her head. "I don't have insurance, and I'm about to be evicted from my place. My boyfriend..."

I know that story. *My boyfriend left.* It's not an

uncommon scenario, but I know the devastation it can bring. That's something both Brooks and I understand, which is why he loves this cause almost as much as I do. He's come in to help me almost every day this week after work.

A lot of the women don't want help from men, after being scarred so badly by them ... but Brooks has an uncanny way of putting everyone at ease. He's gentle, understanding, and personable, and sometimes I have a hard time believing he's the same guy who once fought me so mercilessly for a promotion.

"We'll take care of that. We have an OB/GYN we work with at the Maine Medical Center who's one of the best in the state," I say, looking through the desk for the right prenatal care pamphlets. "One second. I'll get you a packet of things you can take with you, and then we can discuss your immediate needs."

I go out to the wall of pamphlets in the lobby, grabbing the right brochures. Francine is talking with a young former addict who looks *loads* better than she had a few months ago, when she was pale, withdrawn, and sickly. I give her a wave and ask how things are.

"Fine, Ms. Bayliss," she says, and when she smiles, it radiates.

In the break room, a couple of law students I hired to intern with me are putting together care packages for expectant mothers. Brimming with toys and necessities, they look fantastic. "Great job, guys!" I say, tucking one under my arm and heading back to my office with the goodies.

I get Ann all settled, arrange for another meeting to ensure she has someplace to stay. As I'm seeing her out the door, Ellie appears, holding Jace's hand.

"Hey there," I say, excited. I haven't seen her in weeks, not since I helped her move in. "What are you doing here?"

"Just in the neighborhood. I heard you're the head honcho here now?"

"Interim head honcho, but yes. How are things going with you?"

"Great. I'm actually just coming back from a job interview. They gave me the job!"

I gape at her. Like, brother, like sister, I guess. They both know how to ace the interview. "Ellie, that's so great! So happy for you."

"It's working in records, at the Maine Medical Center," she says, beaming. "It pays so much more than Ted's, too. Plus, it starts in September and the hours are flexible, for when Jace is in school. And they're going to pay for me to get my business degree. Can you believe it?"

"It sounds perfect," I say, tears coming to my eyes. I couldn't be more thrilled; it's like having it happen to my own family. "But I absolutely believe it. I always knew you had it in you."

She hugs me. "I couldn't have done it without you."

That, right there, is why I'm here. It only makes me want to do more, to help others. So what if I never get another job as an attorney? This is where I feel most at home. Where I belong.

When she pulls away, she's giving me a grin. "Are you two going out for his birthday?"

"Yep. His favorite place."

I'm glad she doesn't ask where, because it's a secret only Brooks and I know. I have a picnic all ready, and we're going to have dinner on the cliff outside of Sapphire Shores, overlooking the ocean, just like he did for me, a couple of months ago.

It's not just his favorite place, either. It's *ours*. In fact, the more layers I peel away from him, the more I realize we actually have so much in common. We just happened to hide it under a lot of scar tissue.

She waves goodbye, and I give Jace a kiss on the head and send them off.

By then, it's closing time, and I have to go home to prepare the picnic for tomorrow. But before I do, I stop at the jewelry store on the corner, to pick up my gift for him. I make it in just as it's about to close. "Hello," I say as I breeze in. "I made it!

The old jeweler recognizes me, probably because of my odd request. "Hello, there, Tenley. I have your order ready."

He reaches under the counter and pulls out a velvet jewelry box, which he opens for me to reveal two silver cufflinks embedded with ebony stones. Not terribly expensive, but I know he'll love them. "Oh, they're beautiful."

The jeweler carefully takes them out to show me the words engraved on them. One says Stranger88, the other Stranger7721.

I smile. "Perfect."

"Are you going to tell me now what that means?" the jeweler asks, eyebrow arched as he slips them back into the jewelry box and rings up the sale.

I shake my head and give him a sly grin. "It is a secret between me and the man I am desperately in love with."

He hands me the bag. "It's a nice gift. I hope he gives you something just as nice."

Yes. He's already given me the most perfect thing I could've ever imagined.

Epilogue

Tenley

I'm late. Oh no, I'm late.

I have a reason to be, though. These days, I'm not moving as quickly as I used to.

When I reach the bedroom, Brooks is standing in front of his dresser, shirtless, trying to pick out a new shirt to wear. I'm so jealous of his abs, right now, I want to scream.

He lifts a white one out of the stack and looks at me. "You got it under control?"

I check my phone and shake my head as I rush for the shower, ripping my t-shirt over my head. "No, we should be there already. Remind me about the casserole?"

"Yep."

Great. He's not going to remember. As I undo my bra, still caught in the tangles of my shirt, I realize I need to write out the card. Damn. "I've got to—"

I stop as he clamps his hand over my wrist. "No, stop—"

"Tenley." His voice is calm, but there's a warning in it.

And he's right. My heartbeat's going a million beats and hour.

Still caught in the confines of my shirt, I go boneless in defeat and let him pull me toward him.

He sits down on the bed, pushing the t-shirt down over my head so he can look me in the eye. "Hey. Look at me."

"I've got to—" I wriggle, but he holds me firm.

"It's a party. No one will care if we're a half hour late. Calm yourself."

I'm so worked up, my body's shaking, the tension spiraling off of me in hot waves. "But—"

"Deep breath."

I swallow a gulp of air. Let it out, slowly. He's right. It does make me feel a little better. I stand there, between his open legs, as he looks up at me, hands clamped firmly onto both of my arms.

"Now what?" I ask.

"Take another one."

I roll my eyes. "I don't have time for this."

He gives me that silently commanding look.

I take another one. Okay, even better.

He reaches up and gently lifts the shirt over my head, pulling it through my hair. Slips the undone bra straps from my shoulders, and off my arms. Gazing at me with hunger, he slowly wraps a hand around my swollen breast and brings the nipple to his mouth. He licks at it, and I'm instantly wet.

It feels so good. "Okay. Let's be a *lot* late."

Placing both hands on my growing stomach, he kisses his way up my breastbone, up my throat, and to my chin. "Stop tempting me. You know you look too sexy, like this, and if we start, I'm going to want to keep you home all night."

Personally, I think I look like a whale, but he's turned on by the way my pregnant belly looks. He, however, has managed to keep those washboard abs, which have always turned me on. But he's right. We have to go. It's Jace's twelfth birthday, and we can't miss that. "Okay. Tonight?"

He kisses my stomach. "Yes. Tonight."

He swats my ass as I rush into the shower and turn it on. After hosing off, I run outside and dry my hair in front of the mirror, while mentally going through my wardrobe to find the outfit that makes me look least Orca-like. Hair still wet, I throw it up in a ponytail and put on some quick mascara.

When I throw on a dress and turn around, Brooks is watching me. He reaches for me, his fingers walking their way under the dress, caressing my ass. "Not sure I want to share you, looking that good."

I swat him away, but only half-heartedly, because I love the feeling on his hands on me. I wish I could enjoy it. I wish I didn't have this party to attend. I wish...

He wraps his hands around my bottom, squeezes, and stares up at me. Then he lets go. "All right. I'm ready when you are."

I look at him. Yes, he looks good, the way I like him. His white button-down shirt and khakis are very country club, but that unshaven jaw, his hair a little too long, giving the hint of the man underneath. The man few people in his law office ever get to see.

The one I am lucky to have found.

It occurs to me at that moment, that if I hadn't sent a message to Stranger88, who was just looking to get laid, we'd never be here today.

And yet, now, we've been married two years, and are expecting our first child, a girl.

I check my phone. Only twenty minutes late. Not too bad.

Going to the door, I look expectantly at him.

"Can you get the casserole from the fridge for me?" I ask as he opens the door for me.

"Shit. I forgot that."

I grin and kiss his cheek. "I know. But at least you remember the important things."

Twenty minutes later, we pull up at Ellie's house. The lot is already choked with cars. The house she and her husband Brad have has a high fence up around the back-yard, but I can hear the chatter of people, along with some quiet music, wafting up over the barrier.

I look at Brooks, and he reaches over and takes my hand. I entwine my fingers with his as he says, "We'll be fine."

When he looks at me like that, with that endearing, warm expression, it's impossible to believe I spent months in an office, hating him as much as I did.

"Do you think we should knock?"

He shrugs, slips off his sunglasses, and tucked them in the pocket of his shirt. I walk toward the front door and start to reach for the doorbell when the door opens. Ellie stands there, smiling at us. "You're here!"

I smile and offer up the foil-wrapped dish. "Sorry we're late. I brought mac and cheese."

"Great!" She takes it and steps aside, because the two of us can't fit our pregnant bellies in the same doorway together. She's been married to Brad for a year, and is expecting a girl, too, a month after me. She hugs her brother. "Well, come on in! Everyone's waiting."

But it's so quiet inside. Too quiet for a kid's party. And there are no kids to be seen. I walk into the foyer, in a daze, not sure what the hell was going on. "Where is everyone?"

"Outside," Ellie tells me, motioning me to the sliding doors. "Go on out."

I give Brooks a look and shrug. He shrugs back, silently communicating, *Who knows what the hell is going on?*

The second I step out onto the patio, the cheer rises up from the crowd. "Congratulations!"

I look around, stunned, at all the pink "It's a Girl" banners and balloons. What the hell...?

Oh, my gosh, and my hands find my belly. Is this... all for me?

For *her*?

I scan the crowd. It's everyone. From family to friends, co-workers from Foster & Foster, fellow volunteers from the women's center, and my old friends from USM. My jaw drops as I see my mother and my stepfather. "Mom!"

She smiles. "Hi, darling."

This was a party for Brooks and me. A baby shower. And from the way Brooks is grinning at me slyly, he'd known about it all along.

"You're a sneaky thing," I whisper to him between smiles.

Still dazed, I walk around and greet them all. Hugs and congratulations go up all around. Jace giggles at me and says, "Just so you know, I turned twelve two months ago. You gave me a card with money in it."

I did, didn't I? I thump my head. Baby-brain. It's a thing.

The party is amazing. Ellie has gone all out, and I've never seen her happier. She's a marketing manager at the medical center, but she still finds time to volunteer at the women's center with me. Turned out, it wound up being a permanent job move for me, and I couldn't be happier. Together, we get to help the way we were once helped, which I think is what life is all about. Not just holding onto the blessings you receive, but sharing them.

And today is a dream come true, being here with everyone I love. And with Brooks, who I'm sure I couldn't possibly love any more. In the past five years, he's proven to me that love doesn't have to hurt. In fact, it can heal. Every day we're together, we grow farther and farther away from the scars of the past. Now, they hardly shade my life anymore. Now, Brooks and I can concentrate on giving our daughter the best future, free of worry or fear.

I can't wait for this little girl to meet her daddy. Because she's going to love him.

"Thank you," I whisper to Brooks when we finally have a minute alone.

He touches my stomach. "Anything for my girls."

"That's right," I say, entwining my fingers with his as I rest my head on his shoulder. "We're your girls, forever and always."

SAMPLE - You or Someone Like You

CHAPTER ONE

SLOANE

"Can I just say . . . you make one hell of a me." My twin, Margaux, eyes my reflection from across the room before flinging her lavender velvet comforter off her legs. "Ugh."

Dashing to the hall bathroom, my sister's bare feet skitter and slide against the slick hardwood floors of our Midtown apartment. The clank of the toilet seat hitting the ceramic tank behind it sounds next, followed by god-awful retching that sends a flash of sympathy nausea to my middle. In the midst of everything, my stomach rumbles as if to remind me I haven't eaten since breakfast—not the wisest move when I'm about to go on a blind date with a total stranger on Margaux's behalf.

Dating—in and of itself—is hard enough.

Serving as someone's dating avatar? It's a whole new level of insanity that's going to require a substantial amount of liquid courage.

"I'm never eating leftover sushi again," Margaux says when she returns. Climbing beneath her blankets again, she rests her arm across her forehead like a sickly Victorian woman on a fainting couch. She's always been a glutton for sympathy, though. Anytime she has so much as a sniffle, you'd think she were dying of the Black Plague. Pointing across the room in my direction, she adds, "And I mean it this time."

"Sure you do." I wink and fix my attention on the pearl buttons on the cardigan I'm borrowing from her closet before running my palm along my fresh honey-blonde highlights.

"You should curl your hair," Margaux says. Food poisoning aside, she can't help but micromanage me. Despite being a mere two minutes older than me, she takes her big-sister role seriously, often wearing it like a badge of honor. At least that's what I tell myself. It very well could be that Margaux is just a control freak who lives to call the shots.

"What? No." I wrinkle my nose and fasten the last button on my sweater. Despite it being June and an agreeable eighty degrees out, she insisted that this is what she had planned to wear.

"I literally curl mine every single day," she says. "You can't play the part without dressing the part, and that includes how I do my hair."

"But if he's never met you, how would he know you curl your hair every day?"

I was twelve the first time I attempted to wield a curling iron. It was an utter and complete failure of an ordeal, and I walked away smelling like singed hair and sporting a burnt spot the size of a postage stamp in the middle of my forehead. I've been curling iron celibate ever since, and I've vowed to embrace my stick-straight hair until my dying day.

My sister can pry my flat iron from my cold, dead fingers.

"It's not about that," she says. "It's about authenticity. You're standing there in my heels, my skirt, and my cardigan. You're wearing my bracelet and my perfume and my lipstick. Your modern bob just looks low-key jarring with everything else going on."

She's not wrong about that last part. The lace and pearls on the sweater juxtaposed with the dainty gold tennis bracelet, hip-hugging wool pencil skirt, and classic red lip would be better served with loose, cascading waves, something romantic and feminine.

But there's no time.

And even if there were, I'd still give her a hard and resounding no.

"I thought you weren't trying to impress this guy? I thought you were just going on a date to appease your boss? I don't see how any of this matters." I bite my tongue to keep from pointing out that control-freak Margaux has entered the building, and she needs to take a back seat because she's knee deep in a bad case of food poisoning and I'm five minutes from climbing into an Uber, walking into a restaurant, and meeting some stranger as her.

She's not exactly in a position to be running the show.

"I just got my hair done this morning," I add, "which means I won't be curling a single strand."

The last time I pretended to be Margaux, I was twenty-one, and we were college seniors back in Ohio. She'd hit the frat parties a little too hard during finals week and all but promised me her firstborn child if I'd take her art history exam as her. Seeing how art history was (and still is) my favorite subject in the entire world, it was an easy yes. Hell, I'd have done it for fun because that's the kind of nose-in-a-book, head-in-the-clouds girl I was back then. I lived and breathed art in all its forms. Contemporary. Renaissance. Neoclassical. Cinematic. Literary. Undiscovered. Controversial. If it had a creative pulse, I couldn't get enough.

Meanwhile, Margaux lived and breathed boys, boss-girl besties, and being seen.

We may share facial features and a shoe size, but that's where our similarities end. Our personalities are night and day. If we didn't look undeniably identical, I might question our genetic relation.

"Fine, whatever," she says with a relenting sigh.

"Relax." I make my way to the side of her bed, adjust her blankets, and give her a reassuring smile before handing her the TV remote and her cell phone. "I've got this. Just rest, watch a funny movie, scroll TikTok, and try to refrain from puking your guts out again, okay?"

Sinking against her pillows, she nods. "I'll try."

"I'm going to grab you a ginger ale and some buttered saltines, and then I'm out." My watch vibrates on my wrist, letting me know my Uber driver is almost here. My stomach somersaults. Even though this isn't my blind date, it's nerve racking all the same.

A first date is a first date is a first date.

I head to the kitchen and return with her drink and crackers and collect my phone, keys, and purse off her dresser where I'd left them earlier. She'd cornered me the second I got home from work—a mere fifty-two minutes ago —and begged me to go on her date tonight. Apparently she's gunning for a promotion, and her boss keeps dropping hints about setting her up with her single nephew. Coming from personal experience, I know what it feels like to not have the job you want, the job you've worked your entire life to have. I'd hate that for her.

"Sloane?" Margaux calls out before I leave for the night.

"Yeah?" I turn back, leaning against the doorjamb.

"Don't try too hard, okay?"

"What do you mean?"

"I don't want him to like you . . . I mean me," she says. "I don't exactly have the best track record with relationships."

It's true. All Margaux's romantic endeavors tend to go down in flames. The splits are rarely mutual and always accompanied by some dramatic fanfare. I love my sister, but I'd pity any man who attempts a relationship with her. There aren't a lot of men who can handle her larger-than-life persona and her boss-girl energy. She's not some diminutive wallflower with stay-at-home-wife ambitions. She has a personality, and she likes to call the shots. Most men tend to be more intimidated by her than anything. She's yet to find her equal, even in a city of millions.

"If I dated this guy . . . and if for some reason it didn't end well . . . Theodora could have me blacklisted from the industry." Sitting up, she adds, "Be nice. Be pleasant. But maybe don't flirt with him. Maybe . . . maybe just be boring."

Of all the things my sister has asked of me in our twenty-seven years on this planet, this one takes the cake.

"Can you do that?" Her round baby blues are filled with hope. "Can you be boring?"

"According to you, I already am, so it shouldn't be that hard," I say with a little more sarcasm lacing my voice than I intended. It's not easy being the introvert of our duo, to be made to feel like some kind of social pariah for not having twenty best friends on speed dial, for preferring a quiet Friday night in to an expensive blacked-out blur of a night out.

"Stop." Margaux rolls her eyes, her expression softening. "You're not boring. You're just . . ." I hold my breath, waiting for her to replace the word boring with some adjacent term that'll only serve as a backhanded compliment. Something like quiet, reserved, or introverted. "You know what I'm trying to say. Anyway, thank you for doing this. Truly. Thank you."

My watch vibrates, letting me know my ride is here.

"What's this guy's name?" I adjust my purse strap over my shoulder before tugging at the itchy lace sticking out from my collar. "I don't think you've told me yet."

"Roman Bellisario," she says. "Theodora showed me a picture of him once. Dark hair, dark eyes, razor-sharp jawline, tall . . ."

Margaux's voice grows distant as she continues to describe him, and the world around me fades away by the second.

I don't need to hear another word.

I know exactly who he is.

"My ride's downstairs." I swallow a hard lump that has suddenly formed in my throat. "Guess I'll . . . see you in a few."

Before I shut the door, my sister calls out a quick good luck—which is ironic because that's exactly what I'm going to need to get through tonight.

CHAPTER TWO

ROMAN

I trace a fingertip against the side of a perspiring crystal tumbler, focusing on the indentation on my left ring finger where my platinum wedding band has resided for the past ten years—three years too long, if you ask my aunt Theodora.

If it weren't for the mindless chatter of bar patrons around me, I could almost hear her voice gently scolding me for still wearing it, not mincing a single word as she reminds me I'll never find another woman with that thing on my finger, all but referring to it as deadweight.

But that's kind of the point.

I don't want another woman.

I want the one I had before she was heartlessly ripped from this world without warning by some spineless coward who hit her with their car and fled the scene before they could answer for what they did. The fact that the bastard is still out there, living life like nothing ever happened while our lives were permanently altered, is something I've yet to get over.

I don't know that I ever will.

Not even sure that I can.

"Another one, sir?" The young, overly friendly bartender points to my empty drink. He can't be much older than twenty-two or twenty-three, if I had to guess. Judging by the stars in his eyes, life hasn't screwed with him yet.

But it will.

Sooner or later, it always does.

I check the time on my phone—my blind date should be here any minute.

"Might as well." I slide the glass his way, and he uncaps a bottle of top-shelf Macallan, pouring two fingers' worth and then some, like he senses I'm on the cusp of something . . . unnatural. I've never been one to let nerves show, but I imagine I'm giving off the kind of vibe that tells everyone within a ten-foot radius that this is the last place I want to be tonight. "That's good. Thank you."

I take a sip and scan the restaurant portion of the bar in search of the poor woman my aunt sent to "save me from myself."

Her words, of course.

For the past few months, she hasn't stopped telling me about one of her employees at Lucerne Product Development, some blue-eyed, blonde-haired, bubbly "fun-time girl" who would "pull me out of my shell" and "usher me back into the world of the living."

I didn't waste my breath telling her blondes have never been my type.

And I love my shell—it's impenetrable.

It's Teflon and Kevlar and Fort Knox.

It's where my daughters are.

It's my entire world . . . what remains of it, anyway.

While I've no doubt been existing with one foot in the grave and the other one in the land of the living, there's no time stamp on grief. It takes however long it takes. I'm not going to hurry it up so my meddling-but-well-intentioned aunt has one less thing to worry about.

That's the thing about death—it's inconvenient as hell, and there's not a damn thing anyone can do about it.

Nevertheless, Theodora is the most persistent person on the face of the earth. She refuses to take no for an answer—which is how I ended up here . . . at the bar of some hotel restaurant in Gramercy Park, waiting for some poor stranger who's likely only doing this as a favor to her insistent boss.

Sliding my phone from my pocket, I pull up the Lucerne Product Development site, tap on the employee directory, and type in the name my aunt gave me: Margo.

Zero results.

Exhaling, I change the spelling, this time searching up Margaux.

The first result, Margaux Abbott, looks old enough to be

my grandmother—white hair, chained glasses, librarian frown and all.

The second listing, Margaux Sheridan, matches Aunt Theodora's description of blonde and blue eyed. A blinding white smile that takes up the entire lower half of her face alludes to the bubbly part. I zoom in, examining her as if I'm looking for clues to some mystery—or a sign that tonight's not going to be an awkward, uncomfortable, complete waste of time.

Pale-pink earrings in the shape of large-petaled flowers hang from Margaux's ears in her company directory photo, and her lashes are much too long, dark, and thick to be natural. A triple-layer pearl necklace is fastened around her neck, and a diamond cameo brooch adorns her lapel. I can't be sure if she's going for a coastal grandma look or if this is some kind of a joke.

Darkening my screen, I return my phone to my pocket and my attention to my scotch.

"Mr. Bellisario?" A petite hostess dressed fittingly in head-to-toe black places a palm on my shoulder. "Your table is ready."

Drink in hand, I follow her to a corner booth with a single flickering candle, a pristine white tablecloth, and a small vase of three red roses in full bloom.

It's so romantically cliché it's almost laughable.

Once seated, I take a deep breath, get my shit together, and steal a glance around the room. All around me, silverware clinks against china and stemware. Voices drone on, conversations layered one on top of the other. The smell of expensive perfume and aftershave dances through the air, mixed with the savory scents of a five-star dining experience.

Everywhere I look are couples, their faces painted in

soft candlelight as they gaze across the table at one another with stars for eyes. This restaurant gives a whole new meaning to the phrase "Love is in the air."

Theodora chose this place on purpose, I have no doubt.

I haven't been on a first date since Emma, and the day I married her, I promised she'd be my last date.

My forever date.

Death has a way of changing things, though, of making agreements null and void whether you like it or not.

I check the time, resisting the urge to roll my eyes at the fact that the allegedly effervescent Ms. Margaux Sheridan is eight minutes late. I'll give her seven more, and then I'm leaving. If there's anything I've learned in the past three years, it's that life is too short for the things that don't matter —like blind dates people agree to under duress.

For a moment, I visualize my life as sand falling through the center of an hourglass, each granule representing a second I'll never get back. When you lose something—or in my case someone—it forever alters your perspective on things.

All a person has, truly, is their time.

Everything else is inconsequential.

"I'm so sorry I'm late." A breathy voice pulls me from my muddling thoughts. Glancing up, I'm met with frosty Alaskan-blue eyes, a fringe of dark lashes, and hair the color of glazed honey and summer sunshine. "Traffic was terrible getting over here, and the Uber driver refused to take a different route and—never mind. I'm here. That's all that matters, right?" Her full lips pull into a nervous smile before she extends her hand like she's about to interview for a job. "Margaux. Margaux Sheridan. It's nice to meet you."

She's no Emma, but at least she has basic manners.

That and she's not the worst thing in the world to look

at. Far from it. I'd have to be blind not to notice the subtle, radiant beauty emanating off her, quietly commanding my attention. Not that I have any intention of doing anything with said attention, but maybe tonight won't be the worst thing I've experienced in a while.

Could absolutely be worse.

"Roman." Rising, I meet her buttery-soft hand with mine and give it a firm shake better suited for a business meeting than a date, and then I wait like a proper gentleman as she takes the seat across from me.

Studying her in the quivering candlelight that filters the space between us, a strange twinge of familiarity hits me—like I've seen her somewhere before. I've never set foot in my aunt's building downtown, so it wouldn't be that.

"I'm sorry . . . Have we met before?" I ask.

She squints as if she's studying me. "Um, no? I don't believe so?"

"You look familiar." My gaze narrows as I try to place her, but my concentration is interrupted by our server.

"I get that a lot." She orders a cucumber gin and tonic before turning her attention to the food menu.

Sniffing, I say, "I took you as more of a rosé kind of girl."

"I would never." A flicker of a grin crosses her full lips before fading completely, like it was never there to begin with. Nerves, perhaps. I won't hold it against her. "There are rosé girls, then there are cucumber-gin-and-tonic girls. I can see how you might mix us up, but trust me, we're night and day."

Witty without being flirty.

I can respect that.

"Fascinating," I say with a gracious smile to compensate for my sarcasm. "So, Margaux, tell me about yourself."

I hate this.

I hate every damn second of this.

It's not who I am. It's not who I want to be. It's not where I want to be.

My muscles are riddled with tension, perhaps in an attempt to keep me from crawling out of my skin.

"Oh," she says, eyes sparking as if she's surprised by my question. That or she's nervous. I tend to have that effect on people—but tonight I'm doing my best to not come off like a giant prick allergic to happiness. It's the least I can do since she got dressed up and came all this way. "Um, what all has Theodora told you about me?"

"Very little, actually." I don't want to offend her with the fact that my aunt sold her as a good-time girl. To Theodora's generation, that sort of label has other connotations. I also don't want to offend her by confessing that I asked zero questions because I have zero interest in pursuing anything beyond this insufferable evening. "What has she told you about me?"

"Not a whole lot." She looks around the restaurant, though whether she's searching for our server and her drink or taking in the scenery is beyond me. It's all the same, I suppose. Tucking a strand of glossy hair behind one ear, she returns her serene gaze to mine.

"Okay, so on that note," I say as if I'm conducting a work interview, "let's start with you."

This is excruciating.

And it's clear I'm going to be doing the conversational heavy lifting tonight.

"What do you want to know?" She blinks at me with those baby doll eyes of hers, and I'm not sure if there's a single thought behind them.

My jaw tightens, and a dull ache floods the sides of my face as a tension headache forms in real time.

Margaux toys with her pearl necklace, tugging on it as if it's almost choking her. In the process, the top button of her cardigan has come undone, revealing a hint of creamy skin, but the rest of her is conservatively covered despite the early-summer heat wave we're having. When she's finished fussing with her necklace, she pulls at the itchy-looking lace collar of her sweater.

Nothing about her looks comfortable.

Nothing about her looks like she wants to be here either.

Perhaps we have something in common already.

CHAPTER THREE

SLOANE

This is painful.

Physically painful—all the way to the marrow of my bones.

I'm baking in this sweater and filtering every word that comes out of my mouth in an attempt to ensure that I'm dreadfully boring per Margaux's orders. My back hurts from sitting straight and proper and my face hurts from smiling and my head hurts from nodding.

It's taking everything I have not to wince and cringe my way through this clunky, flavorless conversation.

I take a generous swill of my gin and tonic, which isn't kicking in fast enough.

If Margaux were here—like she was meant to be—she'd breeze through all this small talk with a smile on her face and a witticism on the tip of her tongue. That woman has the art of conversation down to a science. She can talk to anyone, anywhere, about anything, and make it look like child's play. She can walk into a room full of strangers and walk out with five new best friends and an invitation to be in some stranger's wedding.

Me, on the other hand? I'd rather stick a rusty needle in my eye than talk about the weather, mayoral candidates, whatever new restaurant opened up in the East Village last week, or my favorite Hamptons hot spots. Superficial topics have never appealed to me.

At least I'm killing it in the uninteresting department, though I can't tell whether Roman's eyes are glazed over because of his half-empty glass of liquor or because I'm quite literally boring the man to tears.

"Food's taking a while, isn't it?" he asks only a few minutes after we order.

I get the sense he wants the evening to hurry along just as much as I do.

"Places like this aren't exactly known for their speed," I say in the most monotone voice I can muster in accordance with Margaux's rules. "Plus, I think it's only been five minutes."

Who knew three hundred seconds could feel like three hundred years?

He takes a substantial sip from his glass. I swear each drink that passes his lips is bigger than the one before it. The next time our server stops by, he'll be due for a refill, and the night is exhaustingly young.

I steal a look around the restaurant—it's all I can do to distract myself from the fact that I'm sitting across from Roman Bellisario . . . a notoriously elusive and demanding New York art collector whose reputation I'm far too familiar with, given my line of work. As the director of the Westfeldt International Art Gallery in SoHo, I've conversed and negotiated with his personal curator more times than I care to count, though this is the first time I've ever been face to face with the jerk himself.

Only so far, he's yet to be a jerk.

Bland, maybe.

But not an asshole.

Certainly not the arrogant dumpster fire of a man I was anticipating.

I imagine he's on his best behavior, given that this is a first date. Fortunately for him, he won't need to maintain the illusion that he's actually some kind of decent person because this first date will be our last date too.

Our paths first crossed three years ago, and in one of the worst ways.

"So did you grow up in the city or . . . ?" His voice tapers into nothing, like he doesn't have the energy to finish his sentence. The lack of excitement in his tone tells me this small talk is just as painful for him as it is for me. There's no twinkle in his eye that hints he's enjoying a single second of our evening so far.

"Ohio," I say. "A small town about forty miles north of Columbus. You?"

I keep the details to a minimum to avoid the risk of diving into any kind of conversation with meaning. This needs to be bare bones, dry, stilted, and forgettable.

"Born and raised here," he says. I can't be sure, but I swear he's stifling a yawn. He dips his head down and checks his phone.

I do the same.

"Sorry—it's my sitter," he says a moment later. "If you'll excuse me, I'll be right back."

With that, he leaves me alone at the table, disappearing into some hallway behind the hostess stand. Pressing my lips together, I wrap my head around the fact that Roman Bellisario is a dad.

There isn't a fatherly thing about this man.

He's a ruthless negotiator, a nepotism trust-fund type—

the last kind of person I can picture tucking in a child at night or reading bedtime stories or doing the whole tooth fairy, Easter bunny, Santa Claus thing.

Though I imagine he has paid help who do that for him.

Most people like him leave the child-rearing to the salaried, résuméd professionals.

They outsource.

I nurse my drink as I wait for his return, and I take the opportunity to check a few work emails.

Our food arrives in his absence, and for a moment I contemplate whether he made the phone call up so he could bail. You never know with people, and to be completely honest, it would be a bold but fair move.

No one should have to suffer through this a minute longer than necessary.

From the corner of my eye, I watch the couple to my right. His hand brushes hers from across the table. She reaches to catch a drip of red wine from the corner of his mouth. In the midst of it all, he can't seem to take his eyes off her for a single second. They're connected, entranced, infatuated with one another.

It's been years since I've had that, and 99 percent of the time I don't think twice about it. Dating . . . sex . . . relationships . . . it's all taken a back seat these days while I focus on my career. The art-collector world is intricate, strategic, and all about who you know. Any spare time I have is spent on fostering my professional connections. I'm on an elevator to the top, and I have no plans to disembark anytime soon.

"Apologies," Roman says when he (shockingly) returns. "It's the first time in years that I've left the girls alone for more . . . they wanted to tell me good night before they went to bed."

Nearly choking on my drink, I clear my throat. "Girls? You have daughters?"

Being a father is one thing.

But being a girl dad? Completely different ball game.

"Two," he says. His dark eyes illuminate for the first time tonight. "Adeline's five and Marabel's four."

I've never been one to fawn over children and babies—to be honest, sometimes they scare me. They seem so delicate, so unpredictable, so fueled with unbridled emotion. But the idea of this tall, dark, and grumpy megawatt millionaire melting over his two little girls is . . . kind of sweet.

Immediately I picture two little darlings with velvet ribbons in their hair, patent leather Mary Janes, and dimpled grins. Like two little Eloises living at the Plaza.

And their names . . . I could melt.

Straightening my shoulders and clearing my throat, I remind myself I'm on a very simple mission. No need to complicate it or get off track. Besides, he could be the best dad in the entire world to them, but it doesn't change the way he treats other people—especially in my industry.

There's no excuse for being a grade-A asshole.

Ever.

Biting my tongue, I swallow my curiosity away to keep from asking about his ex. Even if this were a real date, the question would be completely out of pocket.

"So what brought you all the way here from Ohio?" he asks.

"A—" I stop myself before I blurt out the word art. "All the things the city has to offer."

I give myself an invisible pat on the back for that save.

"Right, but why Manhattan? Why not Chicago? Los Angeles? London? What brought you here?" he asks.

Bless his heart—he's making an effort now.

Though there's still a lack of enthusiasm in his dark-brown eyes or a hint of genuine interest in his monotone Bruce Wayne voice.

Roman slices into his filet mignon, forks it, and lifts it to his full lips. Two dimples flank his mouth as he chews, and his jaw muscles divot. There's no denying the man is attractive. Some might even argue he's hotter than sin. Broad shoulders, a permanent poker face, and Big Dick Energy tend to do that to a man.

Fortunately I'm not the shallow sort—and even more fortunately, I'm not here for myself.

"Came here in high school for a school trip." I leave out the part about the trip being an Alice Calhoun High Art Club trip. "Fell in love and instantly knew it's where I wanted to live after college."

"Where'd you go to school?" he asks. "And what'd you study?"

Again, there's very little interest being conveyed beyond his actual words, but since he asked, I'll answer. Each question, each bite only brings us closer to the inevitable end of the evening.

"The Ohio State University," I say, which is the truth. But I give him Margaux's major. "I studied marketing with a minor in communications."

"That's how you ended up in product development, I take it?" He forks another bite of his steak, and I deduce he'd much rather be putting a fork in this date.

It's funny—as much as Theodora was pushing for Margaux to go out with her nephew, I'd have assumed he at least wanted to take her out. Now I get the sense that he's merely doing her a favor.

"Exactly." The fewer words I utter tonight, the better. No need to wax poetic about the brand deals Margaux brokers—specifically the ones with social media influencers wanting to start a skin-care line or branch into athleisure or whatever "merch" is trending at the moment. I don't pretend to know half of what she does on a daily basis. All I know is she's really good at it. One of the best. "You?"

"Beg your pardon?" he asks, though I'm quite certain he heard me clear as a bell.

"You?" I repeat.

"What about me?" His eyes glint, as if he's keen to the fact that I'm using as few words as possible, as if he finds amusement in making me ask a proper, fully formed question.

"Where did you go to school and what did you study?" I ask. While I'm well aware of this man's reputation in the art-collecting underworld of the city, I don't know much about him otherwise.

There's no Wikipedia page on Roman Bellisario.

No website.

No red carpet charity gala photos.

Nothing.

At least there wasn't anything when I googled him years ago after he had me fired from my dream job over an honest mix-up.

I'd seen him at my old gallery a handful of times, walking around like he owned the place. Negotiating prices on nonnegotiable pieces. Demanding private showings before or after hours. No one ever told him no. He was one of their biggest clients.

"NYU," he says, washing down his answer with a sip of amber-colored liquor. "I studied art history. Had every intention of advancing my degree and pursuing a career in higher education. Teaching, to be specific." He pauses, his attention flicking down for a beat. "Still think I'd have made one hell of an art history professor, but I guess things don't always work out the way we plan them."

"What stopped you?" I can't help myself.

I also can't help myself from imagining him commanding an auditorium full of young minds, his broad shoulders and generous biceps straining inside a tweed jacket, his messy hair and tortoise-framed glasses giving him that dark-academia edge that's all the rage right now. The front row would be filled with girls, all taking notes, all raising their hands for a chance to be in his hot seat, if only long enough to ask a single question.

As much as I hate it, the man is speaking my language. My skin is on fire, sparked with the electric urge to wax poetic on favorite painters, periods, and Picasso pieces. No doubt he's a man who knows his stuff, and I'm sure he could teach me a thing or two.

But Margaux wouldn't know a Picasso if it hit her in the face.

Margaux would talk about a Taylor Swift or Bruno Mars concert she attended at Madison Square Garden last month or some trendy, hard-to-find candle she hunted down in a boutique on Bleecker.

Still, I'm pleasantly surprised by the fact that he's not just some old-moneyed jerk trying to pad his portfolio with priceless works of art he can use for tax-evasion purposes down the road (it's a thing).

"My father." A hint of a wince colors his handsome face, and a divot forms along his jaw. "It wasn't the Bellisario way, or something along those lines. Feels like a lifetime ago. I try not to think about it too much."

"What's stopping you now?" I ask. If I had to guess, he looks to be somewhere in his midthirties . . . surely he's not still living under his father's thumb? If he's got enough cash to drop millions on Stefan DuMonde paintings and Ophelia Finnegan sculptures, he's got enough cash to pursue his PhD.

"Between running my father's company and raising my daughters, my spare time is limited these days."

"Do you have help?" I ask before clarifying. "Raising them?"

I shouldn't be engaging in this conversation, taking it to deeper levels and veering off the small-talk beaten path, but surely a question or two won't hurt.

"I have hired help, if that's what you're asking," he says.

His lips press flat like he wants to say more but changes his mind.

"I'm sorry. That must be difficult," I say.

"It's not the way we planned it, but it is what it is."

I would love to know what exactly "it" is.

Did they divorce?

Did she suddenly decide motherhood and marriage weren't for her and fly the coop?

Did she somehow tragically pass away?

What was her name?

What was she like?

And most importantly, what kind of woman can turn Roman Bellisario from a bona fide heartless bastard into a doting girl dad?

A hundred other questions flood my mind, but I wash them down, one after another, with my cucumber gin and tonic.

"Anyway." He tosses back the remainder of his drink before placing his fork and knife at the bottom of his plate.

He's done with dinner.

Probably done with this conversation too.

I don't say another word. I simply work on finishing my duck à l'orange and cauliflower mash.

"I'm sorry." I point at my still-full plate between bites. I've always been a slow eater, but tonight it seems especially that way.

"Take your time," he says, though I can't tell if he means it, if he's being sarcastic or gracious or all of that or none of that. All his mixed signals make him impossible to read.

Roman checks his phone . . . again.

Taking one more bite, I place my napkin over my plate to signal that I, too, am done. I'm still hungry. Famished, actually, given that I accidentally skipped lunch today. But no need to drag this date on longer than necessary. I'll hoover a bowl of Reese's Puffs over the sink like a heathen the second I get home if it means cutting out of this early.

Roman drags in a long, slow breath, pinches the bridge of his nose, and turns his attention back to me. I brace myself, preparing for some uncomfortable speech or phony excuse that'll put us both out of our miseries.

"I'm sorry," he says. "I haven't done this in a long time . . . the dating thing . . ." He begins to say something again, only to stop and pause. "Look, you seem nice and all, and I know my aunt meant well when she set this up, but I'm just not—"

His speech is cut short by the server, who presents a leather folder with tonight's bill. Lifting his finger, he motions for the man to wait, and then he retrieves three crisp hundred-dollar bills.

"Keep the change," he tells the guy, who walks off with raised eyebrows and a subdued smile on his face. Turning back to me, he continues, "My wife died, Margaux. Three years ago. To say it's been difficult would be the understatement of the century. I'm not really looking to move on. Not anytime soon, anyway. I'm focusing on my business and my daughters, and I don't really know how someone new would fit into any of that."

"You don't have to explain yourself." I stop him before he can continue since it isn't necessary.

Exhaling, he leans back, as if he's relieved, as if all the pressure has been released from the room.

"I'm pretty career focused myself," I say. "I'm flattered Theodora thought of me in this way, but I think we can both agree we're not a match."

Roman tosses back the final few drops of his drink before giving a nod, and he even flashes some semblance of a smile. While he doesn't seem like a happy man, there's no denying he's happy about this.

"I'm sorry about your wife," I say. And I mean it. He might be a colossal asshole who had me fired, but he's still a human being sporting a gaping hole where his heart should be. "Your daughters are lucky to have a dad who puts them first."

I would know.

Our father always put us first, even after my mother left him. We were his everything, his reason for existing. He made that crystal clear. He was hurting, but he still kept room in his heart for us. He never did get over my mother, but it wasn't for a lack of trying. She was it for him. Everyone else paled in comparison.

Roman returns his wallet to his pocket, an official signal that this date is over.

Reaching for my purse, I rise from the table. "Thank you for dinner."

"My pleasure," he says, though he doesn't mean it, I'm sure. It's just one of those things you say without thinking.

We leave the dining room together, head past the hostess, and weave through pockets of waiting patrons before hitting the sidewalk.

Stopping next to a newspaper rack, we give each other one final awkward smile and nod. No goodbye, good luck, or words of formality necessary. A moment later, he checks his phone for the millionth time tonight. If we were on a real date, it'd be a red flag, and I'd take it personally.

"Hm," he says, though he doesn't elaborate.

His mouth turns down at the sides.

I don't ask.

It's not my business, and it doesn't matter.

"All right then . . . ," I say to myself before turning to leave. Starting my walk home, I feel almost weightless as the stress of the evening evaporates into the city air. I Ubered here out of necessity earlier, given that time was of the essence, but nothing beats a Friday-night walk in an emptied-out Manhattan. The smells. The sights. The sounds. The people-watching. It's like being a fly on the wall of the most interesting place in existence. It's one of my favorite little pastimes, if one can call it that. Margaux always teases that I absorb my surroundings as if by osmosis. "See you around, I guess."

He lifts his phone to his ear, his dark brows knit. I don't think he heard me, nor is he aware that I'm walking away.

As he said earlier, it is what it is.

It's an expression I've always found banal yet somehow applicable to every situation in existence. Growing up, my father always taught us that we can't always change a situation, but we can always change our attitude toward that situation. Sometimes the best attitude a person can have is simply acceptance.

Chuckling to myself as I leave, I accept that this was the strangest date I've ever had in my life.

I'm four blocks into my journey when I bump into Roman at a crosswalk. Had I noticed him any sooner, I'd have kept my eyes down, only now it's too late. We're staring at each other, separated by four people and a restless standard poodle with a Louis Vuitton collar.

"Hi . . . ," I say, though it comes out as more of a question than a greeting.

"My driver had a family emergency," he says with a slight air of annoyance.

"You didn't want to Uber or . . . ?" I ask. There's always the subway. Or a yellow cab. Buses, of course. He has options. Trekking home in those expensive-looking leather loafers seems like it should be the last of them.

A brunette woman between us looks at him, then me, then rolls her eyes, as if our conversation inconveniences her. She pops a white earbud into her ear and steps aside, leaving a gap where she once stood.

"You headed uptown?" he asks, ignoring my question.

"Midtown," I say. The crosswalk light changes, indicating it's safe to walk. "You?"

"Upper East Side," he says.

Somehow in the process of making our way across the street, we wind up behind the four people and the poodle, the two of us walking side by side.

A block later and we're still walking . . . together.

It's strange, even stranger than the date we just ended, but I'm not going to be rude and suddenly veer off onto some side street only to risk bumping into him again.

My goal tonight was to be boring, not weird.

Huge difference.

Soon, though, that one block becomes two, which then becomes three, then four, and before I know it, we're approaching my street, and we still haven't breathed a single additional word to one another.

The second my building comes into view, I nonchalantly dig my keys out of my purse, jangling them as if to wordlessly let him know I've reached my destination. I'd thank him for walking me home, but I don't know if that's what he did? We simply happened to be going in the same direction on the same route at the same time.

"This is your place?" He breaks the silence.

I point toward the front door of my building. "This is me."

He stops in his tracks. His Italian shoes look out of place on this humble stretch of Midtown street.

"This building," he says, scratching at his temple. He points at the brown structure with matching front steps and the black iron railings and a sign that says The Mayberry—Established 1912. "This one right here?"

My gaze narrows as I attempt to wrap my head around what he's getting at. Does he want me to invite him up for a nightcap? Or god forbid, a one-night stand? I don't care how disarmingly attractive this man is, I could never let him into my home or my pants.

He stands frozen beside me, contemplative, lost in thought, staring at the steps like he's seen a ghost. Snapping out of it, his gaze lowers. He runs his hands through his dark hair before blowing a hard breath between his full lips.

"I'm, um, going to head up now . . ." I jingle my keys once again. He looks straight at them as he rakes his hand along his jaw. "Have a good rest of your night."

His eyes drift toward my hand before settling on a cracked section of sidewalk.

"Jesus Christ," he mutters under his breath.

He's visibly upset about something.

Meanwhile, I've never been more confused about anything in my entire life.

"Everything okay?" I can't, in good conscience, leave him like this.

Is he diabetic? Is he having an episode?

His lips press together as our eyes meet. The streetlight above paints harsh shadows on his chiseled face, so I'm unable to accurately gauge his expression.

"Where did you get that key chain?" he asks.

I lift my keys, isolating the canary-yellow enameled H with the red leather lover's knot—a limited edition Halcyon key chain I happened to get during my tenure at the very gallery he got me fired from.

Years ago, we were attempting to broker a deal with an up-and-coming artist who went by the pseudonym Halcyon. Much like Banksy, Halcyon preferred to be faceless and nameless. An enigma known only for what they created and not what (or who) they were. Only Halcyon hasn't reached near the notoriety that Banksy has over the years. The average person wouldn't have the faintest clue who Halcyon is.

And to this day, no one knows.

They only worked through a third-party representative who kept their identity anonymous, and they haven't produced anything in years.

A cold flush of panic sears through me, and heat creeps along the back of my neck. It was a mix-up over a Halcyon piece three years ago that cost me my job. I'd sold a piece entitled You or Someone like You to a local collector for a sizable sum—the biggest sale my gallery had made that entire year—only to learn Roman had reserved it with another staff member. It was an honest communication mix-up. We didn't find out until it was too late.

It was a whole thing that I'd sooner wipe from my memory if I could.

"This one?" I ask.

"Yes." His reply is impatient, pressing. "Where did you get that?"

The yellow key chains with the lover's knots were made in a limited batch for promotional purposes, and I managed to nab one of only ten in existence. Being that it's a collector's item, it's slightly frivolous of me to use it as an everyday item, but its sunny yellow color makes me happy every time I see it, and it'd be a shame to let it sit in some box in some drawer collecting dust. Besides, it's a symbol of resilience to me. Mix-up or not, the sale of that piece was (and still is) my biggest to date.

To me, this key chain represents strength and perseverance.

I didn't let that firing get the best of me. If anything, it only made me tougher and more determined than ever to make it in my industry. I know how it feels to love your career more than anything in the entire world. As different as Margaux and I are, we're both dedicated, loyal, hardworking professionals. If being on this date tonight helps my sister get that much closer to her promotion, it's a small price to pay.

"Someone gave it to me a few years back," I say, feigning a foggy memory in hopes he won't pry any further. Then again, Halcyon is a popular topic among those in the art-world know. That said, Halcyon hasn't produced any work in years. Word on the street is that it was some PR stunt or get-rich-quick scheme, and that Halcyon (whoever they are) went back to their day job. I don't want to believe that, seeing how the paintings Halcyon made were visually stunning and original masterpieces. Guess we'll have no way of knowing until the faceless, nameless person behind the paintbrush steps forward.

If they ever do . . .

"You like Halcyon?" I ask. It's a stupid question, I'm sure. Every art collector loves Halcyon. Even if they don't like their work, they like how much their work is worth. Art that has only appreciated in value sevenfold since Halcyon quit painting.

I stop myself before asking if he owns any Halcyon pieces.

He never revealed during dinner that he collects art—only that he wanted to teach art history once upon a time—and it's a tidbit I only know because of my profession.

Margaux wouldn't know any of this.

"How do you know who Halcyon is?" he asks. But before I can answer, he adds, "I told you I was an art history major at NYU, that I wanted to be a professor, and you didn't mention you were a fan of one of the most obscure artists in the city? Someone only those in the know would . . ."

He stops talking.

I wrinkle my nose. I'm not sure what he's getting at.

"I'm sorry—I'm terrible at small talk," I say, hoping that's an acceptable answer. "I guess I should've worked that into the conversation, huh?"

His piercing stare burns into me. I shudder, worried he's somehow piecing everything together. I should have said my sister is an art dealer and gave me the key chain as a gift. Maybe that would've sufficed? Maybe he wouldn't have thought anything of it and let it go instead of pinning me into place with the weight of his scrutinizing glower.

I'm seconds from accepting the fact that the jig is up when his expression softens, and he waves his hand.

"I'm sorry," Roman says. "Forget I said anything. Just . . . forget all of this."

Before I get the chance to reply, he's making his way up the block.

And to think, I was worried about being the weird one tonight.

Halcyon key chain in hand, I traipse up the steps and head to my apartment, grateful that this night is over and that I'll never have to deal with Roman Bellisario ever again.

Read FREE with Kindle Unlimited!

About the Author

Winter Renshaw is a Wall Street Journal and #1 Amazon bestselling author of contemporary romance novels that have sold nearly 5 million copies all over the world. An Iowa native and a graduate of Iowa State University, Winter still calls Iowa home, where she resides with her husband, three children, and their extremely spoiled dogs.

Winter also writes psychological suspense under her Minka Kent pseudonym. Her debut, THE MEMORY WATCHER, hit #9 in the Kindle store and is currently being screen-adapted in South Korea. Her follow-up, THE THINNEST AIR, hit #1 in the Kindle store and spent five weeks as a Washington Post bestseller. Over the years, her suspense work has been nominated for International Thriller Writer awards, mentioned by The New York Post and People Magazine, as well as optioned for film and television.

She is represented by Jill Marsal at Marsal Lyon Literary Agency.

Connect at www.facebook.com/authorwinterrenshaw, winterrenshaw.com, or follow her @winterrenshaw on Instagram!

Visit www.winterrenshaw.com for free content or to apply for the ARC Reviewer Team.

Never miss a new release! Sign up for Winter's MAILING LIST!